PRAISE FOR ANTHONY HARY

"If you like amazing -and sometimes hilarious- characters locked in supernatural action and nail-biting suspense that will keep you on the edge of your seat until the very end then this is the book for you!"

— **KB CARLISLE** - IMADJINN AWARD WINNING
AUTHOR OF *THE BOOK OF ROSE*

"This book has as much masculine energy as Hemingway. It is a very enjoyable read. I recommend it!"

— **T. KING** - READER REVIEW OF *DECEMBER REIGN*

"The whole story was amazing and beautiful. Anthony created a world I felt like I had visited, and I would love to go back."

— **DUSTIN MORGAN** - READER REVIEW OF
DECEMBER REIGN

THINGS ONCE LOST

DEDICATED ETHEREAL RESPONSE TEAM BOOK 1

A LORE OF MAN NOVEL

ANTHONY HARY

Cover Illustration by: Anthony Hary

Cover Digitally Painted by: Freddy Lopez Jr. - FreddyLopezjr.com

Internal Illustrations by: Anthony Hary

Editorial by: 9Ravens LLC - Editorial

Book Design by: 9Ravens LLC - Design

ISBN: 978-1-7333972-4-7

For my Family - There simply is none of this without your love and support. Thank you for believing in me, and supporting this adventure.

Special THANK YOU to the brilliant minds that helped develop the characters in this book: Will Voorhees, Aaron Irvine, Justin Will, Aaron Holmgren, Justin Siegert, and James Roggenbuck. Together we created something special, and this is jut the beginning. Thank you my friends!

Also for the readers. As a writer I have to get these stories out, and initially the story is written for me. Yet, when we get here the story is for you. I hope you enjoy the journey with Charlie and the DERT team. Thank you for reading this and I hope you come back for more.

Thank you.

CHAPTER I

MISSOURI MISERY

By all accounts, them being in the same place for ten days, and nothing having blown up, caught fire, or died, things were going well. There were reasons one didn't readily return to Florida, or wherever it may be that things went sideways for them. Still, it had been ten days, and it was almost time to head out.

Grey, and Nikolai, walked back from the motel's complimentary continental breakfast of stale donuts, and too thick coffee. Grey was pleased. They had powdered sugar donuts, and almost any coffee was better than barracks coffee. He had enjoyed his fill for the both of them. Nikolai came along more for the company than for food itself. The motel offerings didn't speak to Nikolai's dietary preferences. With breakfast done they headed back to wake Charlie, and get moving.

"The last time I woke him up he threatened my scrotum with a staple gun." Grey said.

"That may be, but he likes you more."

"I'm not doing it, man." Grey said. "You're the immortal. You wake him up."

Nikolai paused, taking in Grey's logic. His eyes rested upon the normally exuberant man. Grey was a kind soul, and someone Nikolai knew he could trust. In that moment, it was clear Grey was sincerely concerned. "Together."

"Huh?"

"We'll wake him together." Nikolai said. "I believe he is suffering. He may need us both."

"He should have never made that deal," Grey offered, as Nikolai nodded in agreement. "He could have come to us, Nic. Ya know?" Grey said. "I wish he would have."

They walked in silence together, taking the stairs of the motel complex to the second floor. Nikolai reached the door to room 320 first. "Why is this room 320 in a complex only two stories high?"

Grey scoffed. "I don't know, man! I don't run motels, I just stay at them. Typically, less tech used in these than in hotels, ya know?" Grey looked to Nikolai to catch his often silent reply through subtle body language. It amused Grey, almost like it was a game. He chalked it up to Nikolai being alive so long that he has mastered the art of conserving his energy by talking, and moving as little as possible. Or maybe he was extremely introverted. Grey saw the nod of acknowledgement and continued. "Can never be too careful, you know. Someone is always watching."

"Who?"

"Them." Grey said in a hard whisper. "You know what I'm talking about. THEM!" There was no response from Nikolai this time. Instead, Nikolai's face remained stoic. "Stop messing with me, man." Grey said, giving a jovial push to Nikolai's shoulder.

Nikolai gave way to a full, wide, toothy smile. His smooth, white front teeth evolved into sharp, dangerous points at the canines. He said nothing. Instead, he placed a hand on Grey's shoulder, giving it a firm, approving squeeze with a soft single shake.

"You have an odd sense of humor, man." Grey said. "Let's wake him up. But, ah..." Grey looked at Nikolai. "You go first?" He asked more than said, a petitioning look in his eyes.

Nikolai turned the door handle and checked the door. It was

unlocked. Charlie never locked his motel rooms when he slept alone. Instead, Charlie figured if they were brave enough to come for him, let them come. A locked door wasn't going to do anyone any favors. Leading the way, Nikolai opened the door wide, and the two men stepped inside. They entered a simple room, in relatively fair shape. Nothing appeared broken or askew, though the TV was on some news channel. Empty beer cans littered the top of the dresser, and the floor around the clearly missed waste basket. There was the lingering smell of pizza in the air. The bed was in shambles. And there was no sign of Charlie.

Grey checked the bathroom, while Nikolai powered down the TV, and checked the area around the bed. Coming out from the bathroom, Grey shook his head from side to side, and went to the phone. He picked up the receiver, and hit redial. The line connected to the local pizza place, its name matching the name displayed on the discarded pizza boxes atop the nightstand. Grey hung up on the youthful sounding voice that answered without saying a word. Aside from the pizza and beer being the variety Grey and Nikolai knew Charlie enjoyed, there was no sign of the big man. Charlie always traveled light. Maybe three changes of clothes at most, often no changes at all. He kept all his toiletries in his duster, along with his flask. Charlie was always ready to go when the time came, and from what they could see, Charlie was gone.

Behind the motel was a thick grove of trees and foliage. Into the trees, far enough for the canopy to obfuscate the failing light of the setting sun, laid a large man on a bed of dry leaves. Charlie wore his dark, knee length duster, dark gray shirt, black jeans, and black leather motorcycle boots. Around him were two circles of salt. Inside the larger outer circle were symbols marked with spray paint following the circumference of the circle. Inside the smaller inner circle, just at the edge of the salt line, were five white candles. Each had been lit, and now lay extinguished. Charlie appeared to have fallen backwards into the leaves. His arm broke the inner circle of salt, and had pushed one of the candles into the outer circle. He laid there unconscious, shaking, as he fought the experience in his mind.

"Help! I need help." Charlie called out within his mind. It felt like a void, and a crowded space all at once. An ominous, dark chuckle echoed within the recesses of his subconscious. Charlie growled, "Please. I don't know how this works. Praying ain't my thing." His body convulsed. "Hell! I need to grasp my abilities. Need to know why this is happening to me." Charlie's back arched in the physical world, the leaves crunched beneath him, as pain pierced his body. He gritted his teeth as a growl and spit passed through his lips. Once more, he called out within his mind. "Whoever can hear me, help! Don't let me die like this. Send me someone, something, a sign on how I can get outta this mess." Everything was going red. Charlie screamed in his mind. "I ain't being no one's puppet!"

The pain surged, and Charlie's eyes opened. To his dilated eyes, the waning world shone like flood lamps before him. Charlie shot to his feet, rubbing at his eyes, and worked to reorient himself. He patted at his duster, taking inventory of his belongings. Flask? Check. Wallet and keys? Check. His gun? Double check. He even had his spare underwear. A comforting fact, all things considered. Charlie made a mental note to check as soon as he was able, and determine if he should switch out his current pair for the clean pair. The world came more into focus, and he looked upon the remaining elements of his work.

"Such a fucking mess." Charlie muttered to himself. He worked his way around the summoning circles, collected the candles, and broke up the remaining salt and leaves. Last thing he wanted was for any unsavory types to see his work, and discern what he tried to do. That done, Charlie headed back to the motel.

"Charlie!" Grey exclaimed as he saw Charlie step around the building into the parking lot. "Charlie, man! Where were you?"

Charlie didn't yell back. He didn't feel like yelling. He never felt like yelling. Calmly, he walked the distance between them, amused by the excited, impatient posturing of Grey. Nikolai stood behind

Grey. He leaned against the railing of the stairs that led to the second level. Charlie could see amusement in his eyes. This brought a smirk to Charlie's face. No doubt Nikolai could have sought him out easily, considering his abilities. Instead, he likely went along with Grey's lead, knowing Charlie needed space.

"Where were you, man?" Grey asked again, now that Charlie was near.

"In the woods." Charlie said, making a gesture toward the general area of the trees. "I had something to do."

"Have you developed a prejudice against bathrooms?" Grey jabbed. Seeing a sideways look on Charlie's face, he continued. "I mean, I understand. Bathrooms are a hotbed for planting bugs, and cameras." Grey said conspiratorially.

"Funny, Grey." Charlie said. "I didn't go out there to take a shit," he said, thinking again that he needed to check his underwear. Charlie looked Grey eye to eye. "I had to... make a call."

Grey's eyes widened, registering Charlie's words. They'd been working together for some time to help Charlie better manage his skill with his magic, and abilities. They had enjoyed progress, but both knew they were reaching the extent of Grey's own abilities, and nowhere near the fulfillment of Charlie's needs.

"Are you having the dreams again?" Nikolai asked.

"Yes." Charlie said.

"Why have you.." Nikolai started.

"Why didn't you tell us?" Grey interrupted.

"They've been manageable." Charlie said.

"Manageable?" Grey repeated back.

"Manageable, Grey. As in, I didn't think there was anything you two could do." Charlie said. "I need to learn to manage it. Last night I tried."

"How do you think it went?" Nikolai asked.

Charlie gave him a sidelong look. "I am not sure."

"Are you hurt?"

"No."

"Well, that is something," Nikolai said.

"What did you do, exactly?" Grey asked.

"I asked for help. Not sure anyone heard me."

"You prayed?" Nikolai asked, snickering the words.

"No." Charlie said dismissively. "I did what I thought was necessary, what I thought would help. I woke up on my ass in a bed of leaves."

"The liquor?" Nikolai proposed to Grey.

"The liquor." Grey confirmed. Recalling an ongoing struggle with Charlie to help him understand that inebriation will do no service in helping him connect with his abilities. He looked at Charlie. He was going to ask Charlie how much he had had to drink that night, but Charlie must have seen the logic forming.

"I wasn't drunk." Charlie interjected.

"Ok!" Grey said, putting his hands up in surrender. "We'll worry about your dreams later. How about that?"

"Sounds fine." Charlie said. He turned to walk away.

"Where are you going?" Grey asked.

"I need caffeine." Charlie called back. "You insist on staying in places that do not offer breakfast. I'm hoping their office at least has coffee." He said as he continued to walk.

"They have a continental breakfast here!" Grey yelled.

"Stale donuts are not breakfast!" Charlie yelled back.

Moments later, Charlie returned, a small foam cup in his hands. He had both of his large hands around the cup, as if he was using all of his will to pull the liquid's warmth into his body. Nikolai and Grey stood and looked at him. Each having an expectant feel to their posture. Charlie took a sip of his coffee, and gestured at the other men as if to say, "What?"

"We got a call this morning." Grey said. "My people say they need us in Iowa."

"I got no need to be in Iowa." Charlie said between sips. The coffee was oddly thick, but hellishly hot. Charlie liked it. The pain reminded him he was alive.

"That may be, but we need to go," Grey said. "Grant is asking for us."

This got Charlie's attention. "Grant? As in, Grant Bowman?" he asked.

"The same." Nikolai confirmed.

Charlie took another drink from his coffee, trying to drag out the beverage for as long as possible. Why would Grant need them? He hadn't seen his half-brother in quite a span of time. There was no ill blood. Just the last time they saw each other was when their daddy had died. Grant remained convinced it was a cardiac episode. While Charlie knew the succubus killed their father. Charlie finished his coffee.

"We gotta go, man." Grey said.

"We do." Nikolai confirmed. "While we awaited your return, we cleared our bill, and loaded everything into the car."

Charlie nodded, tossed his empty cup towards the nearby trash bin. He missed, much like each can of beer in the room upstairs. Grey picked up the rebound, and Charlie gave him a nod of thanks. "Well, let's go." he said. The three men climbed into Charlie's 1989 Chevy Caprice. Turning the key, Charlie smiled. He appreciated the low rumble as his big black beauty came to life. He moved the gears into reverse, backing out, then shifted to drive, and slowly moved them towards the exit to the motel lot.

A blinding light filled the air. The Caprice rocked as it came to an abrupt, forced stop. Charlie rubbed his eyes again, concerned he was being struck by a waking dream. His concerns were relieved only slightly as he registered Grey's panicked sounds coming from the back seat. At that same time he felt Nikolai's familiar powerful grip upon his arm, softly shaking him to attention. He patted Nikolai's hand, nodded, and indicated he was ok.

Opening his eyes, recovering as the world dimmed and returned to focus, he could make out that there was an object at the center of his car's front end. Had he driven them into an electrical pole? Was that another vehicle? Charlie looked harder, and could see it was no such thing. At the front of his car was a figure. A woman. Panic flushed Charlie as he became concerned that he had hurt someone. That panic flowed into its own level of uneasy concern as the figure moved. Her hands were flat to the hood, and her body bent slightly forward as if she were leaning upon the vehicle. Charlie noted severe damage to the front of his vehicle. Steam and smoke flowed freely from within the hood, and from under where the woman was resting her hands. This was terrible. His car was ruined. It was all he had remaining from his time in Florida. It was all he had. Fury stirred within him. He reached for his gun as his eyes made out the face of the woman.

She was beautiful. She was powerful. He couldn't believe it. This tall, Amazonian-like figure that stood at the front of his car. Her hips curved as if they demanded attention. Her breasts, the perfect fullness for her frame. Fire-like hair flowed down over her shoulders, and in front of her breasts. She was naked, gloriously full, powerful, shapely, and so very naked. Charlie couldn't move. He'd not seen such beauty in all his life. Her beauty ran any thought of anger, vengeance, or concern from his mind. It no longer mattered that she ruined his precious Caprice. All he could think of was her. As she bent forward, her eyes met his own. They shined of amber, and fire. He tried to speak. Wanted to ask her name. To know if she was alright, or hurt in any way. He couldn't form the words, and instead he looked at her. Their eyes lay upon each other, and her lips parted. She spoke.

"I am Ifotia." She said with a voice that was like the audio equivalent of a warm blanket on a cool day. "Might you help me? I'm looking for Charlie Blackwater."

CHAPTER 2

LOTS AND LIGHTS

The swirl of blue, and red lights filled the scene as firefighters tended to the remaining flames, and local police interviewed witnesses. Witness's stories varied regarding what happened. This made it difficult to pin down what exactly happened. A clear assessment proved impossible for the authorities. It was a lightning strike, a gas leak, and one guy in a gray suit, with vertical hair, claimed he wasn't saying it was aliens, but it was aliens.

As far as the police were concerned there was no sign of foul play, and no casualties. Except for Charlie's Caprice, of course. A fact he emphasized so fully that the police had determined they had no more to learn from him. Instead they left him with a form to file a report with their office, and police went their way. This suited Charlie fine. The loss of a car was a small price to get out of having to talk to the police. Damn, he loved that car though.

"Did you get a hold of him?" Charlie asked Grey, who was working even harder than Charlie had to avoid the police.

"Yeah. Yeah, I did. He's sending Bob."

"Bob? Why would he send Bob?"

"I guess he was in the area. Bob's a bit boring, but good people."

Grey said. Bob was like getting ice water at a diner, he didn't offend anyone. Grey couldn't think of why Charlie would be "Did you guys have a falling out?"

"No." Charlie said sharply. "Nothin' like that." he noticed Nikolai had joined them. "Grant is sending Bob to pick us up."

"Good. Good. I like Bob." Nikolai said.

"Of course you like Bob. Poor fool is enamored with you." Charlie quipped, then saw the look in Nikolai's eyes. "Speaking of. How'd your lil' chat go with Officer Diez?" Charlie watched a subtle smirk pass across Nikolai's face. "That good? Great. We need to move." he said, and stood from leaning on the rear fender of his seared Caprice. Charlie looked sorrowful at his beloved car. "When is Bob supposed to arrive, Grey?"

"Grant said he should only be about an hour…"

"What?" Charlie asked, seeing the look on Grey's face.

"Well. I mean. We all know how Bob drives. Ya know?" Grey said.

"Means we have time." Charlie said, a sly, conspiratorial expression took hold upon his rugged features. "Where's the fire lady?"

Nikolai pointed to an open backed ambulance parked a short ways off. An emergency medical technician was minding the mystery woman. What did she say her name was? Ifotia. That was it. Charlie was sure. She sat there, mild, and unassuming. Her once naked form, now draped with loose fitting clothing, struggled for decency against her full contours. The cops had talked to her, and taken her story. The only part of which Charlie knew was that she claimed to be with him.

"Suppose we need to go talk to her?" Charlie asked.

"We should." Nikolai said.

"I mean, yeah, but I think I'll stay here." Grey said, and got a sidelong glance from Charlie. "Radios, man. Too many people could be listening over there. Ya know?"

"Yeah." Charlie said, patting Grey's shoulder. "Get our gear from the car, ok. Nic, and I will go talk to Miss Ifotia."

"Will do, Charlie. Will do."

Ifotia pulled a blanket around her shoulders as the two men approached. Seemed an odd thing for someone of her disposition to do, and even she looked perplexed by her actions. She saw Charlie, and Nikolai draw near. She abandoned her blanket, and moved to meet them halfway.

"Oh my." Nikolai said.

"Keep it in your centuries old pants, buddy." Charlie said.

"No. I know her, Charlie."

"You what?"

Ifotia reached them at that moment, and any sound that Nikolai may have thought to make was lost in the momentum of her arrival. Charlie hadn't noticed that Nikolai had stopped moving, and now stood strides behind him.

"We need to talk, lady." Charlie said.

"Hello, Charlie Blackwater." she said sweetly. "I do apologize for whatever damage I may have caused to your transportation, your... car, I think they called it."

"About that..." Charlie started to say. Flames seemed to wave behind her eyes, and Charlie took an involuntary step back. "Who, or what are you?" he asked.

"I am Ifotia." she proclaimed. "I am of the Archon, the embodiment of fire, the divine." she paused, and looked directly into the startled eyes of Charlie Blackwater. "I am here to see the prophecy fulfilled. To defend Cahya, and to keep Bob pure. Above all else, I am here because you called me, Charlie. I am here to help you."

The flood of information rushed like a torrent within Charlie's mind. What was that last thing she said? He called her? She was here to help him? And she was of the divine, a goddess? Charlie grasped for words.

"Hey. Excuse me." Grey said. "Did she say Cahya?" To which Nikolai nodded in confirmation. "Uh, Charlie." Grey continued.

"Yeah, Grey."

"Cahya is with Grant."

"What was that?" Charlie asked, his senses returning to him.

"It is just that, when I talked to Grant earlier. Well, he told me that Cahya was already with him."

"And I know you." Ifotia interjected. "I know you both." she said, stepped forward, past Charlie, to Nikolai. Her hand softly grazed his skin, and brought a flush to it that Charlie knew was rarely seen. "I've not seen you for centuries."

"Hello, divine one." Nikolai said in acknowledgment.

"I never did get those mushrooms, you know." she said with a forgiving smile, and stepped towards Grey.

Nikolai and Charlie met eyes. Charlie clearly wanted an explanation. "Long story." Nikolai said, dismissing the conversation.

"Um. Um. Hi, ah... Miss... We haven't met...Yet. Hello." Grey's words stumbled out as Ifotia approached him. His hands instinctively patted the many pockets of his second hand army surplus gear, looking for anything to provide him security.

"Calm yourself." Ifotia said, and took his hands in her own. "You do not know me, not yet. I do know you. I come from a realm where time is more fluid than linear, and I've known you for years." She pulled his hands together with her own, and held them near to her bosom. "You save my life."

"I do?" Grey exclaims. "I mean. Yeah. You're welcome. Sure." the words flowed out of him like a spilled glass of water.

"Now hold on." Charlie said. "I've got more questions, some things aren't connecting. Least of which is the bit about me calling you."

"You did, Charlie. I heard you in the woods." she said. "Your words were a bit messy, but I heard you nonetheless, and here I am."

"Messy?" Grey asked.

"He was drunk." Nikolai explained.

Charlie scoffed. "Did you finish grabbing our gear?" he asked Grey as he turned toward the car. The parking lot had gone empty. All remnants of the police, and firefighter presence were gone. Speckled areas of ash, and burnt remains were present on the ground, and buildings near the Caprice. Had he gotten so distracted by Ifotia that he forgot to notice when everyone left? Charlie picked up the large duffle bag, and placed the strap over his shoulder. He turned to say something to the group when he heard an all too chipper trumpet of a horn. Headlights bounced into the lot. It was time to go.

The purple Ford Windstar emerged from the street in all its last century glory. It moved at a speed that the geriatric populous could easily avoid the minivan. It pulled into an open spot near the group, parked with precision, and care. The driver checked their mirrors, turned off the vehicle fully, only then did they release their safety belt. Bob stepped out of the purple Ford Windstar, and closed the door behind him using both hands to securely, but gently, press the door closed.

"Hey Charlie!" Bob called out.

Charlie waved a still raised hand to Bob in acknowledgement. As he walked past the group he said in a low grumble. "Let's go. Grab the gear."

Nikolai shook his head, knowing all too well the moods that Charlie was prone to. He grabbed his portion of the gear Grey had pulled from the Caprice. As he stood he saw the lights of the tow truck as it backed in to retrieve the car. The beeping warning of the truck's approach pierced the air as Grey stood next to him. "I liked that car." Nikolai said.

"Yeahhh…"

"It went with my aesthetic." Nikolai added.

"Yeah. Like a spooky sleek."

"Hmm. Spooky sleek." Nikolai repeated, like he was tasting the words. "I like that. Though, I believe Charlie is the spooky one."

"Ha! Yeah, he is." Grey agreed.

Together they turned to the purple minivan, and carried the last of their gear. Bob, and Ifotia waited for them.

"Oh my." Bob said as he connected that he was now looking at Charlie's totaled car. "That isn't something that'll be fixed easily. I mean, I could probably fix it. I'd need a couple special parts. And it'd be best if we were at my shop I had in Florida."

"We're not going back to Florida!" Charlie yelled from the van.

Nikolai, Grey, and Bob all looked at each other in acknowledgement. Bob said. "I had forgotten about that. Florida is likely not a good idea."

"Hey, Bob." Grey said in greeting.

"Hi, Grey! How have you been?"

"I'm good, Bob. Fine. Fine. Look, is your fan... clean?" Grey asked.

"Clean? I wash it every couple days." Bob said proudly.

"No, not that kind of clean." Grey corrected. "I mean does it have any devices or bugs in it?"

"Oh dear, no. There are no bugs. The only device I have is my cassette player, with my best of the 70's and 80's collections. Is that okay?" Bob said.

Grey took a moment, evaluating Bob's answers. "We're good. It's good. Thanks man." he said, and walked to the van.

Bob turned to Nikolai. "Please forgive my rudeness. I didn't introduce myself. I'm Bob." he said, and extended his hand to Nikolai, who was loaded down with gear, and had no hands available. "Oh my, I'm sorry. Hello, Nikolai. It is nice to see you again."

"It is good to see you, Bob." Nikolai said, with an understanding smile. "Do I put these in your van?"

"Yes. Just in the back would be fine." Bob said, and watched the impressive specimen that is Nikolai Vigor walk to the van. Suddenly uncomfortable with the appeal he had been feeling towards Nikolai, Bob shook himself to his senses.

"Good to meet you, Bob." The soft voice flowed out, and over Bob. The voice held power, grace, and promise.

Bob stiffened. He didn't possess a point of reference for what he was feeling, but he knew it was not normal. Certainly not the kind of thing a person experiences every day. Slowly he looked at Ifotia, and Bob could have sworn she was glowing. "Hello there, miss."

"My name is Ifotia, and you are a good, and righteous person,

Bob Doe." she said with a warm smile. "I'm going to be joining you on your journey."

"I'm just here to get Charlie to Iowa for Mr. Grant." Bob said.

"No, I am afraid there is much more in store for you, my dear Bob. There is a prophecy unfolding, and I'm going to keep you safe." she said.

"Well that sounds good to me." Bob said in his jovial way.

The two of them joined the others in the van. Bob went through his pre-drive checklist. He noted his gauges, tested his lights, and signals. No warning lights showing, and they had plenty of fuel in the tank. Satisfied, Bob put the van in gear, and started them on their way towards Iowa.

The Windstar offered three rows of seating. Ifotia sat in front with Bob. Grey and Nikolai occupied the center seats. While Charlie lounged in the rear. General conversation fell upon the group as they hit the interstate. Charlie listened as they danced around the elephant in the van, and the tension of it was like ants crawling on Charlie's skin.

"She is a goddess, Bob. You're sittin' next to a proper divine being there, son." Charlie called out from the back of the van.

"Oh." Bob said, looking at Ifotia. "That sounds swell."

Charlie pulled his flask out, and tipped back a mouthful. The whiskey felt warm and welcoming. Just what Charlie needed. "Grey, did my brother give us any idea why he wants to pull us all the way to Iowa, of all places."

"Said it was for pest control, Charlie." Grey replied.

"Hell kind of pests are so bad they need us in corn country?"

Grey looked around the van, unsure how much to share out loud. Grey pulled his cell phone from his pocket and began typing.

"Grey! I know you heard me."

Without a word, Grey turned in his seat, handed his cell phone to Charlie. Charlie took it, set his flask against his leg and read the single word message Grey had typed.

"Werewolves."

CHAPTER 3
THE NOWHERE DINER

The mid-day sun shone sharply across the open scene. Like the old westerns they watched with their daddy as children, the lightly grassed area rolled in, sparse trees, or foliage was seen, and if not for the two lane paved road you'd expect a tumbleweed to roll through at any moment. Fact was, Hangerford, Iowa was not on anyone's list of travel destinations, yet here he was. Seemed to have become a habit for him, ending up in out of the way, hole-in-the-wall, places like this.

Country music played over the sound system of the small diner. The place looked like the love child of a semi trailer, and a double wide mobile home. A long counter bar ran down the length of the middle of the dining room. Small booth tables flanked the outer rim of the dining room. Chrome accents adorned the edges of the tables, the backs of chairs, and the long counter bar. Because it couldn't be a proper diner without chrome. Though a smoking ban had been in place for years, the stale smell of cigarettes lingered in the air, and some tables still had aluminum ashtray-napkin holder combos. The nostalgic charm of the diner was complete with a jukebox, and a waitstaff decked out in matching aprons, and aqua blue tops.

"Would you like me to top you off, mister?" asked the waitress.

"Yes. That would be nice. Thank you." he replied, then added. "And it's Grant."

"Oh, no. We can accept credit cards though." the waitress said. "We don't accept checks any longer, is all."

"I apologize." he said with a chuckle. "I mean my name is Grant. Figured that would be better than you calling me 'mister' for however long I have to be here."

"Ah. Nice to meet you, Grant. I'm Shelly." she offered, instinctively pointing to the name badge on her chest. "Do you know how long you will be here? Not that you need to leave." Shelly said, looking at the less than half full diner. "We're not terribly busy, and we're open until midnight."

"I shouldn't be long. My companions should arrive within the next hour."

"Alright." she said. "Well, you flag me down if you need anything, okay?"

"I will do just that." Grant said.

No sooner had Shelly walked away when Grant heard the brass bell of the entry door chime, and chime, and chime again. The chimes were followed by low speaking voices, and the all too recognizable sound of Grey's ever-stressed vocal tones. Grant could swear that man didn't know how to speak as if he wasn't telling you a secret. An audible, easy to hear, enthusiastic secret, that you weren't supposed to repeat, even under the threat of death.

"There he is!" Grey said. "Hey Grant. Sorry we're late."

"Just glad you made it, Grey." Grant said. His eyes moved past Grey, to his brother. He raised his hand in their common greeting, Charlie reciprocated. As he was lowering his hand, Grant saw the man that walked behind Charlie, next to a tall, impressive woman. Instinct pressed heavily upon him, and Grant's lowering hand proceeded past its original place on the table, towards his gun, at his belt. Grant began to rise to his feet, his hand now on the weapon. Before he could pull the gun, Charlie was in front of him. One of

Charlie's hands gripped Grant's left bicep, and the other pressed upon the wrist of his right hand. The gun remained holstered.

"Now, brother." Charlie said in a low, hard tone, as he pressed Grant toward the corner beyond the booth table where he had been seated. "I know you ain't happy to see 'im, but we don't need to be making choices we won't like later."

Grant's eyes burned towards the vile creature beyond Charlie's shoulder. He spoke, not removing his eyes from his prey. "There's nothing about this I'm going to regret."

"No?"

"No. Charlie." Grant said. "Now let me go."

"You ain't doin' anything against Nikolai while I'm here." Charlie growled. "You hear me? Nothin'."

"You know what he is, don't you?" Grant asked, and looked at Charlie through the side of his eyes.

"I do."

"And you are with him?"

"It is a long road, brother." Charlie said. "He is misunderstood, but he has been a good friend to me." he paused, as he hoped the words would settle in Grant's mind. "He is with me, Grant. You don't need to trust him, but you need to trust me." he squeezed Grant with a firm single shake. "Trust me."

Grant took a breath. He willed his body to calm, his heart to slow, and took deep, controlled breaths. Grant turned, and made eye contact with his brother. He waited for that sensation of when you know the person you are looking at is really seeing you before speaking. "Alright, Charlie. You can let me go. Just know, if he steps out of line, I will end him. Permanently, this time."

"I know." Charlie acknowledged, and released Grant from his grip. He stood a noticeable difference above his younger half-brother. A fact he held on a bit too strongly to, he knew, as he always envied Grant for being the handsome one. "Let's sit, and you tell us why the hell you had Grey drag me to Iowa."

Grant nodded, patted his brother on the back, as they returned to the table. He looked at Nikolai, who had taken a seat, and watched them return. Their eyes met, and Grant nodded to the creature. Nikolai nodded in return. Both men understood the deal without any more words needed. Grant took his seat, and moved to address his brother, when he realized the impressively statured woman that had walked in with them, didn't simply enter at the same time. Instead she was seated right next to Charlie.

The woman's clothes were a terrible fit for her, yet something about her made her stand out like a candle in a dark room. She was radiant, powerful, and her eyes seemed to burn with a flame behind them, as she looked at Grant. "Who is this?" Grant asked.

"I am Ifotia." the woman said before Charlie could reply. "I am of the Archon, the living embodiment of fire."

"She is a pain in the ass, is what she is." Charlie interrupted. "She ruined the Caprice."

"No, not the Caprice." Grant said.

"Yeah." Grey said. "She came out of nowhere, and burned out the entire front end, along with part of the registration office at the motel. Wild stuff, man."

Grant didn't want to encourage Grey, and remained quiet. Turning back to Charlie he said "You know I don't believe in things like this. There's no science behind this. Now you have a lady claiming to be a goddess?"

"I am a goddess."

"She is a goddess." Charlie confirmed.

"Then let's hope she proves beneficial for our mission."

"I'm here to stop the apocalypse." Ifotia said plainly. "The old ones are bringing the end of times, and I'm here to stop them."

"Of course you are." Grant said.

"I'm also here because Charlie called for my help."

"Did he?" Grant said, and looked to Charlie for a response.

"I wasn't praying." Charlie tried to say, but he was interrupted by the arrival of Shelly.

"Hello all, welcome to Big Will's Dine and Shine. Where we can feed ya, clean ya, and set you right. Is there anything I can get you to start you off? Would you like coffee, like Grant is having, or perhaps a soda?"

Nikolai looked up from the menu he had retrieved from the table. "I see here you have blood pudding? Could I please have three pounds of blood pudding?"

"Goodness." Grant mumbled to himself.

Shelly looked perplexed. "Three... three pounds?" she asked, giving Nikolai an 'are you serious' look. "Excuse me, while I check." she said, and walked away from the table.

"Nice work." Grey said.

"What?"

"I think you grossed her out." Grey explained. "We may need to learn from these people, and a waitress is a hard resource to lose."

"Hate to admit it, but he's right." Grant said, and suddenly noticed something was missing. "Where is Bob?"

"He's around. Said something about looking for a Dr. Pepper." Charlie said.

"Right, well let's get to it." Grant said. "Cahya should join us soon. He's briefed, and doesn't likely need a repeat."

"Just order the eggs when she comes back." Grey whispered to Nikolai who nodded in agreement, while he stayed focused on Grant.

Grant shook his head, and dismissed the interruption. "My team has received credible information that there are curious happenings happening in this area. Cows mutilated. Strong movements in the electromagnetic fields in the area. Specifically around the Hanger-ford Museum of Weird."

"You say 'electromagnetic fields', huh?" Grey asked.

"Calm down, Grey." Grant said. "Point is, I've been tasked with figuring out what is really going on. We're short staffed in the office, and I needed a team I could trust." he paused looking at the table. "Guess I'm a lucky guy to get so much more than I hoped for." Grant said, taking a drink of his coffee.

The empty chair to Charlie's left pulled out, and a good sized man took a seat in it. "Charlie, this is Cahya." Grant said between sips. Cahya nodded in acknowledgment to the table.

"Hello. Hello, dear friends. It is good to make your acquaintance." Cahya said.

A smile filled Charlie's rough, bearded face. "Hey Fu. Good to see you again buddy."

"Hello Charlie. It is wonderful to see you as well." he said. "What are you drinking today? They don't have any good beer here. I checked."

"Can always count on you to do the important research, Fu." Charlie said.

"You are Cahya?" Asked Ifotia.

"Yes. That I am." he confirmed. "Who may you be?"

"I am Ifotia, and I am sworn to protect you."

"What will you be protecting me from?"

There was a stillness to the room, as if the diner was only them alone, at that one table, then Ifotia spoke. "I do not yet know."

"Fascinating." Grant said. "Really. I'm so intrigued. Unfortunately, other, more pressing matters need minding first." he looked to his brother. "We really shouldn't waste time, Charlie."

"I'm reading you loud and clear, brother." he said. "Me, and the boys, been on the road since you called. Let them take a moment to eat before we go. Fair?"

"Yeah. I'm going to find Bob." Grant said. He set money under his coffee cup, and left the diner.

Shelly returned, a renewed expression of unimpressed disinterest upon her face. Grey, and Nikolai, both made efforts to speak with her about the area, and the happenings therein, but she was having none of it. They placed their orders for food. Nikolai went with the steak, and eggs, with an extra rare steak. Grey had oatmeal, with berries. Charlie had six over-easy eggs, two sausage patties, and six slices of bacon. Cahya finished whatever he had already ordered prior to their arrival, and Ifotia watched.

"You ain't getting anything, divine one?" Charlie asked Ifotia.

"Do I need to?"

"I s'pose not," he conceded. "Do you feel hungry?"

"I do not believe so, though... those strips of meat you have consumed smell of heaven."

Charlie laughed. "That's because bacon is from god himself."

"Is it really?" Ifotia asked, a sure sound of wonder in her voice. "He rarely responds to requests these days, it seems. How do you get his attention?"

"No." Charlie said, as he shook his head. Why does everything keep leading back to the idea of him praying? "Not literally, from god. I was speaking exaggeratedly. It is good." he said. "Would you like to try some?" Charlie said, and offered a piece to Ifotia.

Tentatively, she took it. Ifotia watched as Charlie took his last piece, and ate it. She followed his example, placed the strip of meat between her teeth, bit down, and chewed. It was amazing. She chewed, and chewed, savoring each drop of flavor. She must have chewed for a noticeable span of time, because Charlie reminded her she was allowed to swallow the bacon. She did. Her body immediately craved more.

"Good, ain't it?" Charlie asked.

"It certainly is." she agreed, a playful tone filling her voice. "Charlie. May I confess something?"

"Sure thing, Ifotia. What is it?"

"I know much, much more than most. Yet, I am very uninformed with the way of men, and of this world."

"Figured as much, seein' as how you've responded so far to things."

"Would you help me understand better?" she asked.

"It'd be only fair, divine one. Seein' as I need your help with better mastering my abilities." Charlie said. "What would you like to know?"

"I would like to know more about this, bacon."

Charlie smiled, knowing no better place in life to start. They paid their check, and also ordered a package of three pounds of bacon to go. It was given to them, uncooked. Charlie didn't notice until they were outside. Much to his dismay, Grant had no cooler in his van.

"Give it to me." Ifotia said.

"No, you don't understand. It needs to be kept cool, or it will spoil before you can cook it." Charlie said.

"Give it to me, Charlie. It will be safe." Ifotia said.

Unsure why he trusted her, he found himself handing over the three pounds of wrapped bacon. Then, in the blink of an eye it was gone. "Where did it go?" Charlie asked.

"I put it in my otherworldly pouch."

"Your what?" Charlie asked.

"My otherworldly pouch." Ifotia said.

"I'm afraid to ask." Grey commented.

"That makes two of us." Charlie said.

"You see, it is a place I can..." Ifotia began.

"Explain that later." Charlie interrupted.

"As you wish, Charlie."

Nikolai retrieved his water bottle from the purple Windstar. The minivan was empty. Bob must have sought out a bathroom, Nikolai reasoned. That suited him fine. He wanted a moment alone. Needed one after what almost happened in the diner. Nikolai knew it wasn't going to be an easy time with Grant, but he didn't see it almost going that way. Thank the dark goddess that Charlie interceded on his behalf. A shiver ran down Nikolai's back, and he took a drink from his water bottle. As he reached to slide the door closed, he froze, feeling that age old sensation of being watched.

"Why are you alive?" came a hush growl of a voice from behind him.

"Hello, Grant Bowman." Nikolai said as he calmly turned around. "I am no threat to you." he said as he caught Grant's eyes. "I never was."

"I killed you." Grant said.

"I believe I deserved that."

"You tried to eat me." Grant said, a tinge of disgust in his voice.

"Not eat you. I don't eat people, specifically." Nikolai said calmly. "Nonetheless, I do apologize. It was nothing personal. I... lost control."

"Do you think that changes things?" Grant asked.

"No." Nikolai said. "Though I do not specifically seek to change anything. What happened, happened, Grant. What I need you to know is that I am on your side in this." he said, and paused for a drink of his water. "Whatever this turns out to be."

"Time will tell. Don't think for a second that I'm not watching you." Grant said. "I will finish what we started. Do you understand? I will end you." Grant didn't wait for a response. He walked past Nikolai towards his van, and away from that moment.

Grant's van was a large black, fully armored, Ford 350 cargo van. It was customized just enough to both blend in, and stand out all at once. The matte black finish doubled as a protection from certain scanners, and radars. On the top of the van were six solar panels, a satellite connection, and a sniper rack for, ya know, moments. Grey was sitting in the perch, with Charlie, Cahya, and the woman, Ifotia standing nearby as they talked amongst themselves.

"Hey Grant!" Grey called down from atop the van. "Sweet ride, man! Have you seen Bob?"

"No, I thought he was out here." Grant said.

"We should find him, and decide what we are going to do." Charlie said.

"Agreed." Grant said, stepping toward Charlie. "It is good to see you, brother."

"Ah, don't get sappy. You'll make me cry." Charlie said, giving Grant a brief hug. "Good to see you."

"I'm sorry about..."

"No. Grant. No." Charlie asserted. "It all worked out, and you never apologize to me for being you. Nikolai takes some getting used to, but he'll be fine. You'll see."

"Yeah."

"Hey guys!" called a warm voice from the diner entrance. Bob exited the building, two bottles of Dr. Pepper in his hands. "Sorry for the delay, guys. It took me a moment to get these sodas. The machine tried to eat my money, but I had my handy multitool, and was able to come to an understanding with the machine."

"That's great, Bob." Charlie offered.

"Oh... Hey Mr. Grant. Hope we didn't keep you waiting too long. I drove as fast as I could."

"You drove the speed limit, Bob." Charlie said.

"That was as fast as we could go, Charlie." Bob confirmed. "It is the speed limit for a reason."

Grant rolled his eyes, and looked at the group. "Come here for a moment." Charlie and Cahya walked around, while Grey slid along the top of the roof following Grant. He led them to the back of his van, opened one of the vertical doors, and moved down a panel giving him access to a computer display. Grant pressed a light blue light in the lower right corner, and the display came to life.

"Whoa." Grey said. "That is slick." as he hung out from the roof of the van.

Grant didn't acknowledge the comment, instead he continued to load up a map of the area they were in. "We're here." he said, as he pointed to a pulsing green circle on the screen. "My intel says the civilian population has experienced events of severe trauma at these locations." he pressed at three locations on the map. "I've been tasked to look into the events, evaluate, and resolve if possible. There is something that doesn't seem right, and that is why I called for your help. Well, your help, Charlie."

"Of course something doesn't seem right." Ifotia said. "The Old Ones are striving to bring about the end of the world as you know it."

"Charlie?" Grant asked, looking to his brother for help.

"That is a cat best dug up later." Charlie said. "Where are we starting?"

"The Offerman farm, and the Lowe farm have both suffered attacks to their livestock." Grant explained. "I was thinking we could start there."

"Excuse me, Mr. Grant, but I do not think that is our best starting point." Bob said, standing to the side of the group.

"Where would you recommend we start, Bob?" Grant asked. His tone disinterested.

"Well, you see, I was talking with Shelly inside."

"You got Shelly to talk to you?" Grey asked, and looked at Nikolai, and Charlie, confusion clear upon his face.

"Yes, she was quite a kind soul." Bob said, recognized Grant's gesture as one of encouragement to continue. "Ah, yes. Sorry. Well, Shelly mentioned we may want to visit the Hangerford Museum of Weird."

"Why would we go there?" Charlie asked.

"Seemed like a logical place to start. Shelly said the curator, umm, Bodegard Oldman, I think she said his name was. He has stuffed monsters on display."

"Stuffed monsters?" Grant asked.

"What is that word?" Bob asked.

"Taxidermy." Grey said from atop the van. "... and electromagnetic fields!" he mumbled to himself.

"Yes, thank you. Taxidermied Monsters. That's what he has." Bob said excitedly.

"That has to be a gag, right?" Grant said.

"No sir, Mr. Grant." Bob said. "Shelly said he's got all sorts. Chupacabra's, Jackalopes, and umm..."

"I've hunted those." Cahya said.

"Jackalopes?"

"No, chupacabra. Nasty things." Cahya clarified.

"Those aren't the kinds of monsters that would do this kind of damage, Bob." Grant said.

"Oh, I know, Mr. Grant." Bob said. "That's why I thought you'd like to know he had a werewolf statue too."

CHAPTER 4
BATHROOM MAGIC

"I know he meant to kill him." she said as she enjoyed another bite of bacon.

"Kill who?" Grey asked.

"Grant."

"Who meant to kill Grant?"

"Grant meant to kill Nikolai." Ifotia clarified.

"Where the hell did you get cooked bacon?" Charlie asked.

Ifotia said nothing, instead she presented a perfectly cooked strip of bacon to Charlie. She smiled at him. "I assume you asked because you would like one." she said, shaking the strip at him temptingly.

"Well, yeah I want ..." Charlie paused. "Did you pull that from your?"

"My pouch? Yes."

"And you cooked it?" Grey asked, an astonished sound to his voice.

"Um, it may not be safe to cook bacon in the van, guys." Bob suggested from the driver's seat.

"Everything is fine, Bob." Charlie said.

"Oh, okay. Good." Bob said. "Thank you, Charlie."

Charlie turned to Ifotia, and said in hushed tones. "How did you do that?"

"I'm the embodiment of fire, Charlie." she replied with a giggle. "I am literally a fire goddess."

"Probably best not to do any fire magic inside the van." Charlie said.

"I understand." she said. "Did you want this bacon?"

Charlie snapped it from her fingers, and devoured the strip of bacon. It was perfect. Absolutely perfect. So blissful that for a brief moment Charlie forgot all about their current situation, or his own circumstance. It was then, from the dark recesses of his mind that he heard the words. "Our time is coming, Charlie." The statement, the inclusion of his name, rocked him back to reality.

"Whoa, Charlie. Are you alright, buddy?" Grey asked.

"Yeah. I'm good, Grey. I'm good."

"What plagues him?" Ifotia asked.

"Charlie can commune with spirits." Grey said plainly. He saw the uncomfortable reaction that filled Charlie's face. "She said she is here to help you, man. She can't do that if she doesn't know." Grey said. Seeing Charlie's brief nod of agreement, Grey continued. "A few year's back, Charlie made a deal with a demon."

"A demon? Why?" Ifotia asked.

"Hadn't met you yet." Charlie quirked.

"No one remembers why." Grey said matter of factly. "At least, Charlie claims he doesn't."

"I don't." Charlie asserted.

"Hey. I believe you man." Grey said to Charlie. "I'm just saying, with all that we've done to help you learn your powers, we've never pieced that part together."

"What do you remember?" Ifotia asked Charlie.

"I know I made a deal. I know I can't get out of it." Charlie paused. "I also know that at some point he's going to come a callin' for his payment." he said. "Near as I figure, I have until then to get a handle on what I can do, and be ready for him. Or get settled on paying that debt."

"He went left, Bob." came Nikolai's deep baritone from the shotgun seat of the Windstar. He, Charlie, Grey, and Ifotia rode with Bob in the Windstar. While Cahya joined Grant in his van. Because of this, and Bob's habitual need to stick to traffic laws, he'd been spending most of this drive keeping track of Grant's van so they didn't lose him.

"Are we close?" Grey asked.

"Yes. I believe we are." Nikolai said.

"About time." Charlie said. "Better get ready. We don't know what we're walking into."

Grey nodded. Retrieved his, and Charlie's bags, passed Charlie's back to him. "I'm definitely checking these electromagnetic fields. You know what that means, don't ya, Charlie?" he asked excitedly.

"I know what it means, Grey."

"I do not know what it means." Ifotia said.

"Don't." Charlie said, knowing he was too late. "Shit." he said, and slapped his hand down on his bag.

Words burst forth from Grey with an enthusiasm reserved for candy stores, and those early nights as a kid when your parents let you stay up later than normal. "Electromagnetic fields, or EMF's, go askew whenever the temporal plane is affected. That's where we are now. As in this reality. There are others. So many others. But, wait. This one, see, EMF's go crazy here. It also relates to time. But I don't think this has to do with time travel." Grey looked at Charlie. "No? No. Excellent." he turned back to Ifotia. "I wish I'd have had my EMF meter out when you were about to arrive. We may not have avoided you ruining the Caprice, sorry Charlie, but I bet the meter would have went next level. Broke the needle and all that." Grey could see in Ifotia's face that she wasn't following. "But, hey, where we are going, I'm going to be prepared. You'll thank me too. If the EMF goes crazy, then we're dealing with more than just stories here. We're dealing with ghosts, ghouls, monsters, and all that goes bump in the night."

Grey could have continued all night, and into the next. Going on, and on, about every conspiracy theory there was, and how it is good that the average citizen considers them theories. Should all he knows to be real become common knowledge, the world would never be the same. Before he could get too carried away, the van came to a smooth, decisive stop.

"We're here." Nikolai said.

They piled out of the purple Windstar. Bob had parked precisely spaced from Grant's van, allowing just enough room for everyone to get out smoothly, and comfortably. Charlie saw this, and shook his head. Bob was peculiar, but he was "good people". Once upon a time he, and Charlie were close. This all changed around the time Charlie's powers began initially manifesting. Charlie had to make a tough choice, and Bob witnessed it. After this, Charlie backed away, and their relationship hadn't been the same since. Bob seemed to be fine with everything, and if Charlie was being honest, it was good to have Bob around. Peculiar as he is.

They were going into what could only be considered a public establishment. No need to be conspicuous about this. Charlie checked the clip on his 9mm handgun. Satisfied with its condition, he slipped into his holster that he kept on his belt at the small of his back. He also retrieved a couple pieces of chalk, some salt, and his flask. Satisfied with his choices, Charlie closed the bag, and set it in Grant's van. Grant saw him do it. He gave Charlie an inquisitive look. "I'm riding with you when we leave." Charlie said pointedly, and addressed the group. "How are we doing this?"

"Suppose we need to go in, and talk to him."

"Spose we do." Charlie agreed. He looked around the group. "Where are Grey, and Ifotia?"

Grey's EMF meter beeped steadily as he, and Ifotia walked the perimeter of the museum. Nothing out of the ordinary had registered, yet. Grey was sure they would find something. By the look of the building it was easily built in the mid to late 1800's. The brick, and stone structure stood at a confident one and a half, or two stories tall. Grey imagined it once served as an official meeting place for town, or state officials. They were in the upper middle of Iowa after all. Des Moines was not too far off. The EMF meter continued its steady, rhythmic beeping.

"Is that beeping good?" Ifotia asked.

"Nah... I mean, it isn't bad either." Grey said. "Beeping like this, combined with this." he pointed at the needle on the meter that only shifted slightly to the left or right as they moved. "This all means things are normal." he said. "Which is great for normal folk. Not so great for us, since we're looking for something."

"What are we looking for?"

Grey paused, as if he was surprised she hadn't discerned this from their conversation in the van. Then his face seemed to reset, and he looked at Ifotia. "I do not know. HA! But we'll know when we find it." he chirped, turning back to his work. "That is all part of the fun. The chase!"

"The beeping is annoying." Ifotia said, garnering no reply from Grey who was lost in his renewed focus upon their search.

The meter screeched a sudden, short beep, and then returned to normal. Grey jumped noticeably. He almost lost hold of his machine. "Oh boy!" he exclaimed in a hushed tone.

"What was it?" Ifotia asked. "Did we find what we are looking for?"

"Not quite." Grey said as he moved the EMF around him, to the left out toward the open grass, and to the right towards the outer wall of the Museum of Weird. The EMF didn't screech again, but the needle did move. Bobbing in and out of the red zone the closer Grey moved towards the building.

"What is it, Grey?"

"I'm not sure," he said. "Whatever it is, it's inside the building with the rest of our team." Grey's eyes met Ifotia, excitement, fear, and adrenaline surged behind them. "Come on!" he hissed out.

They raced to the front entrance to the museum, unsure if the team had entered yet. Their only focus was on getting to the team, and Grey's need to warn Charlie. Grey had seen readings like this before. Once before. Knowing this, it wouldn't have surprised Grey in the least to have known that two sets of glowing red eyes watched from the shadows of a nearby bush as they hurried to the front of the building. Reaching the front of the museum, and seeing no one remained outside, they entered.

Inside the group was chatting with the museum's caretaker, Bodegard Oldman. He lived up to his name, sometimes he appeared as old as the building itself. Still he was a simple man, somewhat shy, and clearly not good under pressure. Speaking with him had been like pulling teeth from a squirming, oiled up piglet.

Sure as advertised, he had taxidermic 'monsters', if one would call them that. For the most part they looked like well tended high school science fair projects. Except the werewolf. That looked legitimate, only the placard affixed to the piece claimed they were sensitive to gold. This rubbed the wrong way, because even a non-believer like Grant Bowman knew that werewolves are allergic to silver, not gold. Grant said as much to Charlie when he suggested the caretaker may be the werewolf himself.

They were clearly running out of time with the man. Either from his nerves, or limited patience, Charlie could tell they were close to the end of this conversation with Mr. Oldman. Don't ask Charlie how he knows such things. His skill in speaking with others, persuading them, is a dumpster fire at best. Yet he can always tell when an effort is reaching its end. Knowing this, he knew he wanted to utilize his other options before they were invited to leave. "Excuse me." he said, interrupting Grant's efforts to garner more information. "Do you have a restroom I could use?"

"Yes, certainly." Mr. Oldman said. "Just down the hall there, second door on the right." he said, and pointed in the general direction.

Charlie headed that way. He listened to the continued questioning as he went. Sounded like Nikolai was going to give the questions a shot. Kudos to Grant for allowing him the opportunity.

Charlie could only think that he hoped Nikolai didn't traumatize the caretaker in the process. Nikolai has a way about him. He can really get into a person's head, you might say. No time to worry about that, Charlie had something to do.

Inside the bathroom he was pleased to see it was a relatively open space, one urinal, and two stalls. A good ratio in Charlie's estimate. The room also looked clean, or at least clean enough. Charlie knelt down, pulled the chalk from his duster pocket, and drew a circle around him. With an application of his will he activated the circle, and began focussing his skill.

This wasn't a deep working of magic. Subtle enough for Charlie that the lights shouldn't even flicker in the next room. There was no need for blood, or other elements. Charlie had learned since his deal with the demon that he could commune with the spirits. Often all he needed to do was focus, and he could connect. In this effort though he was seeking to see. To know, or discern, what awaited them. Charlie said the words.

Grey, and Ifotia, entered the main room of the museum, finding the rest of the group. Grey went to Grant, as Nikolai was clearly occupied trying to talk to the old guy behind the counter.

"Where were you?" Grant asked.

"Hey, Grant." Grey said. "Look, where is Charlie?"

"He is using the bathroom. Why? What's up?"

"Oh, nothing. You know. Just chasing those chemtrails." Grey said. "So. Um, where is the bathroom?"

Grant shook his head. He clearly wasn't getting straight answers right now. "Down that hallway." he said, and directed Grey toward the way Charlie had gone.

"Hey, thanks, man!" Grey said, and headed that way. He saw Ifotia take a position near Nikolai, and found himself feeling pleased at how quickly she acclimated to their world. He had so many questions for her. Distracted as he was, he almost walked directly into a pole. Only it wasn't a pole.

"Well, pardon me, friend." the man said.

"Ah, sorry. Sorry. I didn't see you." Grey fluttered. He hadn't expected anyone else in the building. No other vehicles had been in the lot.

"Josh Rahtlu, is my name, and it's no problem." the man said. "You take care."

"Thank you." Grey said. He passed the man by, and moved towards the restroom. Grey turned to reciprocate the man's sentiments, but he was gone. Seemed odd. The man wasn't moving very fast as far as he could tell, and there was a fair bit of hallway there. Grey shrugged it off, and headed into the mens room.

Clouds passed between the earth, and sun, causing shadow pockets to dance upon the ground. The wind was sweet, and cool upon the skin. A gentle contrast to the warmth of the day. Charlie knew he was in the vision. It was a chilly day presently. What he was seeing had to be in the future. That was when he heard it. Charlie focused on the vision.

A young girl, strawberry blond hair pulled up into pigtails, sat playing in the sandbox with no care for the pretty robin egg blue dress she had on. Charlie heard it again. She giggled. He watched her play, and savored her moment. The sunlight played through the leaves of a nearby tree, and fell upon her. Caught up in her glee she never saw the tall grass of the field behind her move. Never heard the rustling as it came through the wheat directly towards her.

Charlie tried to call out to her, to warn her. His efforts were futile. He knew it. This was for him to see, so that hopefully he might change events to come. That knowledge did little to quell the pain as he watched the small, black, dog sized creature burst forth into the yard. It came up swiftly behind the young girl, sunk its teeth into her, around the neck and shoulder, effectively smothering her screams before then could come. Then, as quickly as it appeared, it was gone. It took the girl with it into the tall wheat field.

Shadows melted in, consuming the field, the yard, the sandbox. The shadows moved closer and closer, they converged on Charlie. In an instant Charlie was surrounded by black.

"You cannot stop what is coming."

Charlie froze. That wasn't his voice, yet he felt a familiarity to it that one only has for their own voice, or those of the caretakers of their youth. He knew it. "Who is this?"

"I'm happy you are here Charlie Blackwater."

Ice felt like it was creeping up Charlie's spine. He needed to get out of this. "What took that girl?" he asked. He tried to grasp something from this.

"One of my pets. I have many. Now that you're here we can begin."

"Is all of this because of you? Who are you?" Charlie asked.

"I'll see you soon, Charlie."

The words, 'I'll see you soon', echoed within his mind as the bathroom came back into focus. He heard a sound like tinkling bells. Charlie struggled to get his eyes to convert the swatches of color around him into defined shapes. The bells stopped, and a darker collection of shapes directly in front of him moved. There was the sound of a zipper, as Grey turned to him.

"Hey Charlie! Man, I'm glad you're ok. I didn't want to risk anything by interrupting your spell." Grey said.

"Did you just take a piss while waiting for me?" Charlie asked.

"Well... Yeah man. I had to go." Grey said. "It is a bathroom after all."

"You would." Charlie said, seeing Grey motioning as if to help him up. "Wash your hands," he instructed.

"Yeah. Sorry, Charlie." Grey said, moving to the adjacent sink. "You ok?"

"I'm ok. Did one of those premonition spells."

"Did it work?"

"I got more than I bargained for." Charlie said. "There is definitely something going on here."

"Yeah there is." Grey agreed.

"What do you know, Grey?" Charlie asked.

"Got some reading's outside." he started, thinking quickly of the layout of the building, of where he was when the EMF meter screeched. "I got the readings just outside of where we are now."

"And?" Charlie said. "You know I don't understand how that damned gadget of yours works." he said, raising his hand. "And, no, I do not need a lesson. Tell me what you found."

"It spiked, Charlie." Grey said, Charlie looked at him now with concern in his eyes. "Spiked, Charlie. Like it did in Florida."

"You think it's him?" Charlie asked, feeling the ice still melt from his spine.

"Maybe. Could be someone else. There is one thing that I am confident about." Grey took a breath. "We're dealing with a demon."

CHAPTER 5
ROOF WITH A VIEW

To call it a thud sound feels like a severe understatement. Mr. Oldman's body fell back, collided with the floor with such unrestricted momentum that the impact was heard by Grey, and Charlie, from their place in the bathroom.

"Oh my. That was unexpected." Ifotia said.

Bob moved toward the unconscious Mr. Oldman. Bob checked his pulse, and if he was breathing. He was.

"What the hell was that?" Charlie asked as he, and Grey, rounded the hallway corner. His eyes saw Ifotia. Took in the full beauty of her body, and noted the wisps of smoke and ash floating away from her. "Where are your clothes?" he said.

"She thought it would be helpful in getting poor Mr. Oldman here to understand the sincerity of our questions if she 'showed herself' to him." Grant said, his frustration evident. "Clearly, that worked out great."

"Showed herself?"

"Yes, Charlie." Ifotia said. "It was reasonable to think that if he knew he was talking to a divine being, he may have been more comfortable discussing our questions with us." she asserted. "How was I to know he would respond that way?"

Charlie looked at her. Just looked at her. She was so sure, so sincere. She clearly had no idea the effect burning her clothes away would have on the mind of an older, no doubt, lonely man. Hell, she likely had no idea the effect her nude form was currently having on the majority of them in the room. Bob seemed unaffected by Charlie's estimate. Whereas Nikolai, well, Nikolai looked hungry. In the most primal way one can be. For his own part, Charlie wasn't sure if this made all the trouble worth it. She was magnificent.

"What do we do?" Bob asked as he stood near Mr. Oldman.

"Did we learn anything?" Charlie asked.

"A couple leads, all in line with the information the company sent me." Grant said.

"What do we do with Mr. Oldman?" Bob clarified.

"Right." Charlie acknowledged. "Is there a phone on that desk?"

"Yeah. Right here." Bob said, holding up the receiver.

"Excellent. I have an idea. Before that, we need to find Ifotia some clothes." Charlie said. "Are there any souvenir t-shirts or anything for sale?"

"Why do I need... clothing?" Ifotia asked. Her tone indicated that she was not completely familiar with the term, clothing.

"To cover you up." Grey offered.

"Do you mean to hide me?" she asked.

"No. No." Grey assured, while trying to think of the best words to use.

"You're naked." Charlie said plainly. "Nice as that may be, it ain't appropriate by most people's standards, and we're unfortunately burdened by those standards. We need to clothe you." he turned to the group. "Someone tell me; she didn't burn anything else in the museum."

"What is wrong with my form?" she asked. "Am I too small? Too big? Did I not get these correct?" she asked, her hands moved over her breast, and hips. For the first time a sound of vulnerability crept into Ifotia's voice.

Nikolai stepped up next to her. "You are beautiful." his condition getting the best of him.

"Yeah." Grant agreed. "You look fine."

"You are like the flowers that grow behind my parents home." Cahya added. "They grow big and strong from all the manure that is spread over the land."

"So I didn't make myself too… full?" Ifotia asked. "I tried to emulate the commonalities I perceived among human women."

"You did well."

"Wait." Charlie interrupted. "You made yourself look this way?"

"Of course, Charlie. I could not enter this realm without a physical body." she said.

"So you chose to make yourself impressive?"

"It seemed a praised presentation of this form; is it not?" she asked. "I am a goddess. Am I not deserving of some praise? It seemed only logical."

"Well, praise to you, your divineness." Charlie said. "You did good, becoming all perky and wonderful. Ok. Praise. Praise. Praise." he added, his voice strained for breath. "Now I need you to choose to have clothing on, ok? Can you do that?"

Ifotia gave Charlie an appraising look. Then she became resolved, and nodded her head. She stepped one long step away from the group, closed her eyes, and as she did the air churned in the space. Her smooth, full skin rippled. Light flashed here and there, leaving lines upon her legs and waist. The room seemed to dim, a card rack fell over, and Bob gasped from where he stood. When the scene settled, Ifotia still stood before them. She wore a black v-neck shirt, tucked into black denim pants, with a black belt, and the legs of her pants were tucked into a pair of calf high leather boots, also black.

"I like your style." Charlie said with an approving chuckle.

"I will blend in, yes?"

"Yes, you certainly fit right in." Charlie agreed, paused a moment. "Ifotia. I need you to know there was nothing wrong with how you looked."

"I know, Charlie. I needed to cover up, is all."

"Right." he agreed. "You said you are still learning about our world, and I do not want to perpetuate bad habits."

"What do you mean?" she asked.

"Some people judge us on how our bodies look. Women get the worst of it." Charlie said. "Fact is, it's bullshit. You could come in, looking however you like. Big on top, small on bottom. Small on top, big on bottom. Hell, big or small all over, and it wouldn't have mattered. The asshats still judge. How you look is a small factor in your value as a person."

"Thank you, Charlie."

"For what?"

"Thank you for referring to me as a person." she said.

"Alright, divine one. I figure if you're learning bad habits from me, you'll learn the good ones." Charlie met her eyes with a smile, and he could see her sincerity. He gave Ifotia a tight, assuring nod, then turned to the rest of the group. "We gotta go. Grab what we need, take photos of anything else, and get outside. I'll be right behind you."

The team went into action. Grey, and Cahya wiped everything down. Nikolai snapped some photos with his smart phone of a map, and directory information on the wall. Meanwhile Bob, and Grant, went outside and moved the two vans out to the street. Charlie watched as they finished up, and headed out, before he picked up the phone.

"County sheriff's office, this is Jan, how may I help you?" said the chipper voice of the county office clerk.

"Hello. I'm at the Hangerford Museum of Weird, and the care-taker, Mr. Oldman, seems to have passed out, and is unresponsive. Please send help." he said, setting the phone down. He knew Jan at the county would have more questions, but he didn't have time. Charlie tossed some cash on Mr. Oldman's desk for any items they took, exited the building, using his sleeve to open the doors as he made his way outside.

Stepping outside he saw that Grey, and Cahya, had already removed any sign of the van tracks in the driveway, and the vans were waiting on the street. Charlie jumped from the stairs to the lawn, avoiding any contact with the gravel lot. He walked across the grass, and climbed into Grant's awaiting van. "Let's boogie."

"Hope Mr. Oldman is ok." Grey said.

"He'll be fine. I called the sheriff's office. They should be by soon, to check on him."

"Ah, wise." Grey said. "Maybe that other guy will find him."

"What other guy?"

"The other guy who was enjoying the museum." Grey asserted. "You had to see him, Charlie. I ran into him in the hallway to the bathroom."

"There wasn't anyone else there." Grant said.

"I didn't see anyone in the bathroom when I entered." Charlie said. "Are you sure, Grey?"

"Yeah, guys. I swear. I literally ran into him. He was there..." Grey trailed off, remembering the hallway. "Until he wasn't." he finished.

"What does that mean?" Grant asked.

"I don't remember his name, but he was really nice. Introduced himself, and wasn't mad at all that I bulled right into him. Only when I turned to wish him well, he was gone. Figured he just walked faster than me and had left the hallway."

"Grey." Grant said. "Are you sure?"

"Yeah, Grant. I'm sure."

"No one else came out of the hallway." Grant said plainly.

Grey, and Charlie, looked at each other. Grey's eyes were wide, and Charlie gave him a nod as if to assure him it was ok, and that it was time to drop it.

Charlie turned forward in his chair. "Do we have a place to stay?" he asked Grant.

"We do." Grant said confidently. "Got a room for me, and a room for you."

"Nice. Did you get rooms for the rest of the team?" Charlie asked.

"That was the, you, I mentioned." Grant clarified. "I got a room for me, and one for you, as in, all of you together."

Charlie shook his head, and suppressed a laugh as he heard Grey's reaction in the back. They reached the motel in short order. Grant was true to his word. He had a room, and adjacent to his room was a larger room for the rest of the team. It was furnished with two queen sized beds, a couch, and a pull out sleeping mattress. A door connected the two rooms, and as Nikolai, Cahya, Bob, and Grey settled in, Ifotia watched on in interest, and Charlie went next door to talk to his brother.

"That could have gone worse."

"Could'a gone a lot worse. Mighty glad it didn't."

"She is a liability, Charlie."

"I am a liability, Grant, and you have me here with you. Calm down." Charlie said. "I have a feeling she is supposed to be here."

"Supposed to?" Grant said scoffingly. "I haven't had enough to drink to indulge you in your metaphysical philosophy discussions."

"I know you don't buy into all this crap." Charlie said. "Don't much blame you, to be honest."

"What I believe in is facts, data, science. I know monsters exist. We have one in the other room."

"Hey now."

"Point is, it ain't a matter of buying in. What I need is better explanations, and proof, rather than magic, and the boogieman." Grant finished.

"I think we're dealing with a demon."

"Can I at least finish my drink?" Grant asked.

"I'm serious, little brother." Charlie said. "Not just any demon either. I think we're dealing with my demon."

"Yours?" Grant asked. "Then tell it to stop." he said jokingly.

"Not mine, per say. But the one I made a deal with."

"You've mentioned that before, but you have yet to fill me in on the details."

"Cuz I don't remember them. Not fully." Charlie admitted. "Made the deal a few years back. I know I did it, and it came with a price. What I don't recall is why I did it or when I'll have to pay up."

"That's a shitty deal, brother."

"That it is." Charlie agreed, making a toasting motion with his own drink, before tipping back a mouthful of the whiskey. "I'm just tellin' you what I know. What did you guys get from Mr. Oldman?"

"A lot of it is confirmation of what Grey, Cahya, and I got from our respective organizations." Grant said, and poured himself more whiskey. He held the bottle out to Charlie, who extended his glass to accept more. "There is weird shit happening here, Charlie. Cows are being mutilated every full moon, a couple people have seemed to disappear, and there are rumors about some creature in Lake Violet."

"That's just what we need. A water monster." Charlie said. "You do recall, I don't swim."

"You don't like to swim." Grant corrected. '

"Right. I don't swim."

"In the morning I want to talk to the sheriff, see if he can be of any help." Grant continued, bypassing Charlie's attempt to deviate into discussions over whether or not to swim.

"Is that wise?" Charlie asked. "Wouldn't it be better to keep ourselves as inconspicuous as possible?"

"Have you looked at us?" Grant said, almost full on laughing. "We have a vampire, a full tilt conspiracy junky who always wears army surplus survival gear, a fire goddess who at her most normal still looks like a teenage boy's amazonian wet dream."

"She is lovely." Charlie interjected.

"Then we have you."

"What about me?"

"You look like what we'd get if we mixed Lost Boys, with Sons of

Anarchy, and based it in the south." Grant said. "Seriously, even people at Hot Topic get uncomfortable when you're around."

"It's my look." Charlie said defensively.

"It is. And it is fine. I'm no better. You can tell I'm a federal agent from miles away." Grant said. "My point is we talk to the sheriff, and use that to our advantage."

"And when he asks for credentials?"

"I have 'em."

"You do, this time?" Charlie sounded surprised. "This isn't going to be like Tallahassee?"

"Why does everything go back to Florida for you, Charlie?"

"Everything changed in Florida. Ya know? That, and because I can never go back."

"It's not going to be like Tallahassee." Grant assured him.

"Good." Charlie said, throwing back the last of his whiskey. "You're an ass for getting your own room. You know this."

"Cahya, and Grey... they have an aroma to them. And I'm not sleeping in the same room with that creature." Grant said.

"Ifotia?" Charlie asked, a visible smirk on his face.

"Nikolai. Smart ass." Grant snipped back. "You're welcome to share this room with me." he offered, knowing full well Charlie would decline.

"No. Thank you, little brother." Charlie said. "I'm going to sleep on the roof."

"The roof?"

"I need some air." he said, an acknowledging smile on his face. "Let the boys know, will you. I'll meet you all downstairs for breakfast in the morning."

They bid each other good night, Grant agreed to do as Charlie asked. Charlie exited out of Grant's room door, and headed down to the van. He retrieved his bag, which contained his remaining supplies, toiletries, and some candles, and brought it with him to the roof.

Once on the roof, Charlie cleared away an open space. The roof was a hard, cement like material, which pleased Charlie. On the far end were the air conditioning units, and ventilation ports for airflow within the building. It was also where water seemed to collect. He would stay away from there. In the area he had cleared, the roof was dry, and a safe distance from the edge. The tops of the trees waved welcomingly at him in the wind, and he could hear the soft sounds of the night call out to him over the low hum of passing traffic.

Charlie pulled out a stick of chalk, and drew a circle large enough for him to lay in. He drew a second circle around that one, and wrote out runic symbols between the circles where the points of a five pointed star would be. Atop each rune he placed a candle, and lit them in a counter clockwise order. Candles lit, and himself with his belongings within the circle, Charlie applied his will to the outermost circle. Saying the words, he felt the circle engage, and create a barrier between him, and the energies of the world. Similarly he applied the same effort toward the inner circle, it too engaged, and Charlie watched the candle flames change from a warm yellow-orange hue, to a bright aqua-white.

Settled with his work he removed his jacket, folded it, and positioned it as his pillow as he lay upon the hard surface. He knew this was only the beginning. That inside the rooms below him were strangers, families, and his closest friends. Charlie wasn't burdened by sleeping upon the hard roof. He felt burdened by the possible danger his choices were bringing upon his friends. His brother. This was lessened by the circles of power around him, and the containment spells he cast. The circles should keep him from the eyes of those who may seek him, and also keep his thoughts to himself. Not knowing what was coming, Charlie hoped at the very least he would be able to secure a good night's sleep. A cool breeze crawled over him in that moment, like a comforting assurance.

In the parking lot below, the cool breeze carried in with it the evening mists. Light tendrils of fog moved between the vehicles, and around the buildings. Laughter could be heard from the rooms of the motel, along with the muddled sounds of televisions, disagreements, and romance. Charlie's cohorts were all turned in. Each having found a place to rest. They sought to slumber. None of them heard the beeping of Grey's EMF meter within Grant's van. Or how it steadily increased in intensity. Nor did anyone notice the collection of glowing red eyes that lined the edge of the roof, and how they watched Charlie as he slept.

CHAPTER 6
STEAMY SITUATIONS

"This place looks like a bad remake of the Andy Griffith show." Grey commented as they entered what could most closely be considered downtown Hangerford. He wasn't too far off. The buildings on Main Street looked like the buildings updated in the 50's from an old wild west town that had a love child with the effort to grasp the technology boom of the mid 80's. The automobiles of the town were a wide stretch of older and newer models. Everything seemed to have a golden brown hue in the mid-morning sun.

They parked Grant's van out front of the sheriff's office. It was a single story, brick building, that looked to at one time be a bank, or market front. The unassuming building had two police SUV squads parked out front, a parking lot in back, and a simple brass text sign on the front of the building that read "Adams County Sheriff's Office & Jail".

"Guess this is the place." Grey said.

"Let me do the talking." Grant said.

"Yeah, sure thing."

"You think it was good to leave the others back at the motel?" Charlie asked.

"They probably need the rest." Grey offered.

"That's a fair point." Charlie conceded. "I worry about Ifotia."

"Should be more worried about that creature you have with you." Grant quipped.

"He has a name, Grant, and Nikolai is no danger to anyone." Charlie said.

"You've mentioned that." Grant said. "Still, I don't think we are at a loss without him here."

"Why do you worry about Ifotia, Charlie?" Grey asked as they exited the vehicle. "She's a divine being, right? I'm sure she'll be alright."

"She cooked bacon in a moving van, Grey."

"Yeah, but..."

"She pulled bacon from her tinderbox, or whatever she calls it, and cooked it."

"I think she called it..."

"She cooked it, Grey." Charlie emphasized again. "Cooked it while in a van. Do you follow me?" he asked, looking intently at his friend. "She could burn that whole motel down, and have snacks to enjoy after she'd done it."

"Well, that wouldn't be good at all." Grey said. Though he wanted to point out that should she want to burn the place down, it wouldn't matter if they were there, or not, he stayed quiet.

"Here we go, boys." Grant said as they entered the building. "Stick to the plan." There was a mutual nod of agreement from all three men. Grant led them to the front desk, and face to face with the oldest woman he had ever seen.

The sun had crept through the motel room window, traversed the floor, over discarded clothing, shambled blankets, up the pullout mattress, and found its way to Bob's eyes. The light pulled at his consciousness, beckoned his attention, and it felt really warm.

"I do not believe you are yet sleeping."

"Good morning." Bob said with his all to common kindly tone.

"What, ah... What are we doing?" he asked the figure perched, and hung over him from the bed above.

Ifotia looked radiant, as she always did. Her clothes were the same. The garments being of her own making, they never needed changing, or washing. She looked at Bob, and had been looking at him for the better part of an hour since Charlie left. Well, since Charlie, Grant, and Grey left. There was something about Bob. A wonder, a curiosity, that pulled her attention in a kind of academic way. He reminded her of something she had seen before, but she couldn't fully articulate what it was. So pure.

"Hi, guys." called Cahya from the other end of the large room. "I brought up some pastries, and fruit, from the breakfast room. You are most welcome to partake if you like."

"Yes!" Bob said. "I love fruit. What kind were you able to get?" he asked as he pulled himself up, and situated his clothing. Bob's modesty wouldn't allow him to sleep as comfortably as someone like Cahya had, in his loose boxers, and nothing else. "Banana's would be good. I would definitely benefit from the potassium." Before he could finish, Cahya had already extended a ripe banana to him. "Ah! Thank you so much. This looks magnificent."

It baffles the mind how one man could retrieve, and bring up all the food that Cahya did, but it was safe to assume that he was not an ordinary man. Bob knew that Cahya was like Grant, and Grey, in that he belonged to an organization, secretive as any, and he was not new to this life. Cahya was a career monster hunter. A warrior. A traveler. And he had great taste in food and beverages.

Ifotia joined Bob in partaking of Cahya's smorgasbord of tastes and smells. So many were new to her. So many were delicious. She especially liked the little red, heart shaped circle fruits that had small cream colored seeds on them. She didn't care much for the things they called pastries. She found them too dry for her liking. "What are these called?" she asked, and held up one of the heart shaped fruits.

"Those are called Strawberries." Cahya said. "They aren't in season here, yet, but still a fine example of the fruit."

"Example? Is it not the actual fruit?" Ifotia asked. She took another bite. Her face took on an inquisitive, and questioning expression.

"It is. It is." Cahya assured her. "Fruit doesn't always grow the same. Especially from place to place, depending upon climate. Each fruit has a range of presentation. These are from Mexico, and I believe they are near perfect."

"From Mexico?"

"You can taste it in the soil residue."

Bob stopped eating. "Soil residue?" he repeated. "You can taste that?"

"Most certainly." Cahya said with a sure and proud voice.

"Excuse me." Bob said. He stood, and took his plate to the sink to wash his fruit, again.

"They are delicious." Ifotia said, then looked around the room. "Where is Nikolai?"

"He is utilizing the gym facilities here at the motel." Cahya said. "He expressed a need to expend energy."

"I would like to see a gym."

"That sounds nice." Bob agreed. "I could get a walk in on the treadmill."

After a bit more snacking the three of them went down to the gym, and found Nikolai doing resistance training alone. Cahya moved to join him. Bob went to the treadmills, reading book in hand, and began a gentle paced walk while enjoying his novel. Ifotia was left to her own devices, and found herself unsure of what to do. Now in the gym she could see it for what it was. Physical training, and honing one's body were not new concepts to her. Humans had been doing this for eons in an effort to protect themselves, or attach to each other. She watched Nikolai, and Cahya, and though she appreciated the aim of their efforts, she was quite certain no weight there would provide her a value adding workout. She looked at Bob, and as appealingly pure his company may be, his workout was far too vanilla for her.

A family passed through the gym. As they maneuvered around a contemplative Ifotia she felt it. Heat. Sharp, clean heat coming off of the adult male of the party. "Where did you find warmth?" she asked almost as if to no one.

"Huh?' the man replied, visibly caught off guard by Ifotia's sudden engagement. "Warmth?" he repeated. "Ah, right, the hot tubs. Cute, lady." he replied sarcastically. "They are just through there." The adult male pointed in the direction they came, at a glass door. He walked away awkwardly, keeping his eyes on Ifotia as he worked to catch up with his waiting family.

Ifotia turned the direction he pointed, and with him away she could feel the trail left in his wake. She followed it.

"Which group of initials did you say you were with, again?" the sheriff asked, clearly losing his patience. Nathan Dogberry had been sheriff in these parts for almost 15 years. At least that was what he liked to point out repeatedly in this conversation. The one thing that was clear is in 15 years he'd gotten really good at being almost no help at all.

"I ain't with any initials, sheriff." Charlie quipped back sharply. "That's Agent Bowman here."

"FBI. Sheriff, I'm with the FBI." Grant said. "You saw my credentials. As did your office watchdog, in the lobby, before you." he could see the sheriff become upset at Grant referring to the older front desk clerk in that way. Grant figured you had to get your wins where you could. "I'm here to help. We're here to help. We've told you the reports we've gotten, how about you tell us where you'd like us to start first. How about that? Which would be the most helpful to the Adams County Sheriff's Office? The lake, or the dead cows?"

The sheriff seemed reset by Grant's authoritative tone. He adjusted his posture, sat up straighter, and really looked at Grant. "That is a good approach, I should think, Agent Bowman." he conceded. "Would you look into the lake incident? It was enough when it was just stories of a creature in the lake, but now we have one missing girl."

"I don't see why we cannot do that." Grant said, looking to Charlie for confirmation, he nodded. "We'll get on that right away." he reached for the door. "Good day, sheriff."

Outside the sheriff's office was a small bank of desks for other officers, and for everyone's favorite people, IT. The information technology group was three people, two of which were out today, but that didn't stop Grey from making friends with the one remaining person. Donna was an older woman who doubled as a member of IT, as well as the support for the 911 operator line. She was a brilliant, 72 year old spitfire, and she was loving every minute with Grey.

"My dear, I simply couldn't." Donna said, as she did exactly the thing she claimed unable to do, and gave Grey access to the computer next to her.

"Thanks, Donna." Grey said. "Which website did you say that was?" he asked, while furiously typing in his own desired commands. They had been talking about everything under the sun, and settled on penguins. Who doesn't like penguins, right? Well it turned out Donna was not a fan. More than that she had verified documentation that proved her point regarding the "vile monochromatic birds" as she called them.

She gave Grey the web address and he typed it in. "Alright, let me see what it says here." he said as he pretended to look over the site. While Grant and Charlie attempted to get aid, or at least insight from the sheriff, Grey was the backup plan. He had presented himself as a system tech from the regional internet provider, and claimed he was there to verify their automated upgrades went correctly. "Ooo.. Oh my." he said, continuing to pretend to read the website. In the corner of his monitor he watched the status bar reach 100%.

"One more thing, sheriff." came Grant's voice from down the hall. "You will contact us if any new reports come in, yes?"

Grey couldn't hear the sheriff's reply, but watched as Charlie stepped through the door of the office, and into the hall, an amused look upon his face. Time was up, and he needed to go. It was at that moment that Grey realized Donna was speaking to him again.

"I tried to tell her, you know, a girl her age. There are special items made for that sort of thing, and some for other things. Nonetheless, I didn't think that was a safe activity for a person's butt. Who am I to judge? Just grandma, or aunt Don-Don." she mused. "In the end it works out. But oh, silly me. Is that working out for you dear."

"Yes. Thank you." Grey said, removing his usb module, and shutting down the computer. "I'd say you were right." he said with a smile. "I'll also never look at penguins the same way again." he grabbed his bag. "Donna, it has been a treasure. Please reach out if you need anything from us, okay?"

"Certainly will." she replied. "Thank you for the conversation."

Grey caught the eyes of one of the officers in the back as they rolled in their sockets. He felt a sense of success at that, and smiled at Donna. "Take care, Donna."

Outside Grant and Charlie waited in the van, Grant started the van as Grey approached. Before Grey could get the sliding side door closed they were already moving.

"Conversation went that well, huh?" Grey asked.

"We didn't get any new information about the happenings in the area." Grant said.

"He didn't look like a very friendly guy." Grey said.

"I'd sooner shit on his lawn than ask him for help again." Grant said.

"Damn right." Charlie agreed. "He was a fucking prick."

"Good thing we won't need to." Grey said, as he plugged in the usb module to the onboard computer system in the back of Grant's van. He turned a couple dials, and flipped a switch. The speakers crackled to life with all the communication coming in, and out, of the sheriff's office.

"Well damn, Grey" Grant said, sounding impressed. "That may be overkill, but it is impressive."

"Give me a minute and I'll have it cycling through the computer to catch any chatter about werewolves, ghosts, and whatnot." Grey said.

"Damn unsettling." Charlie said.

"I tell you all the time, Charlie." Grey said in his best 'you didn't hear it from me' voice. "Someone's always listening."

"We headed back to the motel?" Charlie asked Grant, not giving any additional encouragement to Grey's statement.

"Yeah. I think the sheriff said one thing correctly." Grant said. "We should start with the lake. Though between all of us we could split up. Maybe check out this place called Hell's Gate at the same time."

"I'm game for whatever, brother." Charlie said. "I just hope everything is good at the motel when we return."

The trail Ifotia followed got warmer, and warmer. There were chemical smells in the air of a sour sweet kind. Human's always used smelly things to clean themselves, and she presumed it was another cleaning agent, but for what she did not know. She stepped through a pair of double doors. As she did the air filled with the chirping, singing sounds of children laughing, and screaming. There was a part of Ifotia that enjoyed the screaming. It reminded her of simpler times.

Families moved around in towels, entering and exiting the space. Ifotia could see a large basin of water that ran the length, and width of the room, sunken into the floor. The heat source was near, and she continued. She was still presenting in her black shirt, belted denim pants, and boots, yet all around her these humans pranced about in their wet undergarments. Ifotia felt confused, yet as she walked past a mother addressing the needs of her young girl she heard the mother say that the "swimsuit had to stay on in the pool". Swimsuits must be what these shiny, water friendly garments were.

Ifotia rounded the corner and she saw the heat sources. Against the wall were two, much smaller, circular basins of water, and they were boiling. Heat spilled up from the splashing water. A man sat alone in one, while the other was empty. Fascinated, and attracted to the heat, Ifotia approached. She stepped up to the empty tub, watched as the bubbles came up, broke the surface of the water, and released hot air into the room.

"They're great," said the man from the other pool of water.

"What are they?" she asked.

"Don't tell me a pretty thing like you has never been in a hot tub before."

"Hot tub?"

"Yeah!" the man exclaimed. "Motels and hotels have the best ones. Get yourself a swimsuit and try it out. You won't regret it."

As the man settled back in his hot tub, he seemed to watch to see what she would do next. Ifotia agreed that she needed a swimsuit, and willed her appearance to change. Starting at her toes a ripple moved across her feet, up her ankles to her legs, to her hips, her body, to her shoulders. As the ripple moved it replaced the shirt, pants, and boots with a simple black one piece swimsuit like the one she observed the mother wearing. Wisps of smoke like particles floated up away from her, and she could feel she would need more ash soon.

"The fuck was... Damn lady." The man stumbled over his words as he climbed from the pool. He retreated to find his towel. He clearly was intending to leave, and he looked scared.

Behind Ifotia there was more commotion as the families seemed to find now an appropriate time for their own departure. This was of no matter for Ifotia, she was going to enjoy the pool. The hot tub. In moments the once roaring ruckus of the room was silent except for the sounds of the facilities motors, and pumps. Ifotia stepped down into the pool.

From the treadmill Bob noticed through the large glass panes of the wall that people seemed to be evacuating from the pool area. Soon he heard them as they exited, and headed towards the lockers. Their exchange of questions of "What was that?" and "What is she?" caught his ear. "Oh my." he said as he stepped from the treadmill.

The water was warm. Almost cool. It was certainly not a hot tub as advertised, and Ifotia was not impressed. She certainly couldn't see what the man was enjoying so much about it. She did enjoy the bubbles while they lasted. The water was also welcoming, and she found the sensation against her body a soothing one as she lowered herself into the pool. It simply wasn't hot however.

"Hey, um, Ifotia?" came Bob's voice.

"I'm over here, Bob."

Bob came around the corner from the pool, and saw Ifotia's head just above the edge of the hot tub. "What happened in here? Everyone was leaving. Is... is everything alright?"

"Yes. Everything is fine, except for this not hot, hot tub."

"The people were running out. They seemed scared." he said. His words stopped as if someone else had interrupted him. It was then that Bob noticed Ifotia was in a swimsuit, and not her previous self-made outfit. "Did you. Did you change in front of them?" he asked.

"I needed to wear a swimsuit for the water. I heard the rules." she replied. A look of discontent came upon her. "This water is not hot enough."

Bob moved to say more. To encourage Ifotia out of the pool, and back to their room, before motel management got involved. All Bob could think of is how upset Mr. Grant would be if things went south before he returned. Bob would have said all these things, he would have done all he could to help, only as he moved to speak he was hit with a gust of painfully hot steam. The explosive force of steam thrusted him off his feet, back through the air, and into the pool behind him. He hit the water, surprised, and grasped for purchase.

Hands grabbed Bob, and pulled him from the water. Cahya, and Nikolai, set him down on the cool tile, and waited as the steam lifted. As it did they saw her. Ifotia stood, looked perplexed, in a hot tub now completely void of water.

CHAPTER 7
MIDNIGHT WARNINGS

Chaotic flashes of blue, red, and white strobing lights filled the air, reflected off the cars, trucks, and exterior of the motel. The parking lot looked like a disco, if a disco was run by local police, and fire department personnel. It was bright, loud, and took place in the middle of the afternoon. Grant, Charlie, and Grey had heard the call in the van as they made their way back to the motel. They had been passed by the emergency vehicles as the first responders raced to the scene. With each second that passed, the tension in the van increased. Something was wrong.

Calmly, as if everything were normal, and there weren't police and fire fighters everywhere, Grant parked the van in the spot nearest their rooms. He was a professional after all. It seemed to Grant that all the interest was focused around the main building where the office and gym facilities were. That was a relief. Meant they were nowhere near their rooms. They got out of the van, and headed inside.

Grey opened the door to their room, and he and Charlie stepped inside. Grey heard Charlie exhale as they entered. "Hey guys!" Grey said. "What's with all the fuzz outside?"

Inside the room Nikolai reclined in the furthest bed, fully clothed, looking relaxed, and comfortable. In the closest bed, Cahya reclined similarly, a towel over his head, and he snacked on a bag of chips. Bob laid upon his stomach on the pull out mattress. He was wet, head to toe. All three of them faced toward the television where one of those manufactured, next American world pop music tart shows played. Grey didn't see Ifotia anywhere in the room.

Next door, Grant entered his room, left the lights off, and locked the door behind him. A light blinked from atop the night stand. Grant walked over, retrieved his communication device from the night stand, and sat on the bed. He flipped the device screen up and turned it on. The small device illuminated the dark room. Grant started, drawing his handgun, and pointing it at the figure sitting in the lounge chair across from him.

"Hello, Grant. I need your advice." the figure said.

Grant exhaled a calming breath, removed his finger from the trigger, and calmed down. "God damnit, Ifotia. You ought to know not to sneak up on a person like that." he said.

"I needed to talk to you in private." she stated plainly. "I need your advice."

"There are better ways to go about it is all I'm saying." Grant said, and turned on the bedside lamp. "What do you need? And please tell me it has nothing to do with the fleet of police, and firefighters outside."

"Why are you wet?" Charlie demanded of Bob. His tone was something like a parent perplexed by the new displays of intelligence put on by their teenage child. Charlie let go of his initial question and asked what he really wanted to know. "Where is Ifotia?"

Bob explained everything to Charlie, his words fumbling out like he was, in fact, that teenage child caught red handed for the first time. "And I didn't know she was going to explode the water, and launch me into the pool, Charlie. She didn't do anything wrong. She just didn't know how to do things right."

"Charlie." Nikolai interjected in his calm way. His baritone voice was like smooth chocolate to the ears. "No one saw us. Or saw her. We were away from there before another soul entered."

"Was there property damage?" Charlie asked, their faces looking at him confused. "Was the hot tub damaged? We need to know these things."

"No. I do not believe so." Nikolai said.

"Ah, I did not see. But I would be happy to revisit the scene and investigate if you would like me to." Cahya offered.

"I doubt that will be necessary." Charlie said. " Thank you though. Where is she now?"

The room went quiet. Long enough for the silence to have a presence in the room. Bob shrugged as if to say he didn't know, and laughter could be heard coming from the room next door. Not just any laughter. Charlie could swear that it was Grant laughing... with a woman.

"You changed right there at the hot tub?" Grant asked again. "I bet the look on that guy's face was priceless." he said, continuing to laugh. They both collected themselves, Grant took a breath. "You could have hurt Bob, though." he said sincerely to Ifotia. "You need to be careful as you acclimate to this world. You can do things we do not come close to understanding."

The door between rooms opened up, Charlie stepped across from the group room, into Grant's room. "Did she tell you what happened?" Charlie asked.

"She did. Pretty damn funny if you ask me."

"We were almost made." Charlie said. "What the hell were you thinking?"

"The water was not hot, Charlie. I simply wanted to experience a hot tub." she said.

"That clearly worked out well."

"Relax, Charlie. No one was hurt." Grant said.

"Lucky us." Charlie quipped. "I called down to the front desk, asked if everything was alright. Sounds like the pool area is closed down. Something about a water main malfunction, and one of their hot tubs melting."

"Melting?"

"Melting." Charlie confirmed. "You're lucky we don't have to move motels."

"That was not my intention." Ifotia said with remorse. "Would you be able to help with my other question, Grant."

"What is it?"

"I need to burn something." Ifotia said, noticing the rest of the group now listening through the open doorway. "Do you recall when I dressed myself?"

"You mean, when you manifested an entire outfit from nothing?" Charlie said. "Yeah, I'd say that was a not soon forgotten moment."

"It wasn't from nothing. It was from ash. When I use my power to burn, I can capture the ash and use it to create things." she explained. "When I changed to this." she motioned at her swimsuit. "I used the last of what ash I had available. I gather it would be best if I did not continue in this presentation as we move forward."

"I would be happy to help you burn things." Cahya offered. Ifotia looked at him hopefully. "We should do it away from the motel. Perhaps we could find a dumpster, or one of those overpriced fried chicken establishments."

"We're not burning down fried chicken... No." Charlie said.

"Ifotia, how much ash do you need?" Bob asked. Bringing a sense of normalcy and concern back to the room.

"To make clothing? Not much at all."

"Would a book do?" Charlie asked, his voice calm. Ifotia nodded yes. He stepped into the group room, and returned quickly with a book in hand. He tossed it on the bed. "This should do nicely."

"The Gideon Bible?" Grant asked with a smirk.

"No one here is reading it." Charlie said.

"Certainly not." Ifotia said.

"Where do we burn it?" Grey asked.

"I have an idea." Cahya said.

They left the motel room, collectively going outside with Ifotia. Cahya walked to the corner of the motel, and retrieved a metal trash can from near the laundry room. He dumped its contents into another nearby trash receptacle. The parking lot was quiet now. The police, and fire department vehicles were long gone. They moved behind what looked to be a utility building. It likely housed the main plumbing, and electric connections for the motel to the city. The small building blocked their group from sight of the roadway, and most rooms in the motel. Forming a circle together, Cahya set the metal trash bin in the center of their group.

Grey looked around for witnesses. "Everything looks clear." he said. Grant dropped the book into the can. The sound of it hitting the bottom created a louder clammer than anyone seemed to expect. "We're good. We're good." Grey said in an attempt to quell any concerns over who may have heard the noise.

Ifotia extended her hand over the trash bin. The bible burst into fire, the flames swirled in a small vortex. The light of the flames did not emit much beyond the metal bin. They were not the typical shades of orange and yellow, but of blue and green. The moment felt drawn out, as if the bible was slowly being whittled down. When in truth it only seemed long to them. The bible went from a readable book to scorched ash in a breath, and the vortex corralled the ash up to Ifotia's waiting palm. As the ash touched her hand the group could see it assimilate into her. As it did, her outfit began to shift. This time it did not go from feet to head, but from her outstretched hand, inward. Within seconds she was back in her black t-shirt, belted black denim pants, and black leather boots.

"Hot damn." Charlie said.

"What else can you do with that?" Grey asked.

"Truly impressive." Nikolai said, his voice one of sincere wonder.

"Can you use that to make weapons?" Grant asked.

"I am still learning what I can do." Ifotia said. "It has been years since I've used these powers here. There is no need for them in my home."

"Well you'll need to keep me informed." Grant said, rushed, as he remembered the message waiting for him in his room. "I need to head back in. You should get some rest." he said, and left the group.

"He sometimes talks like he's the oldest kid in the group, but isn't he your younger brother, Charlie?" Grey asked.

"Oh, Grey. You have no idea." Charlie said, and headed inside.

They respectively made their way to the motel room. Each of them went through their bedtime routines, brushing teeth, showering, or in Cahya's case, naked yoga. It looked a lot like the exercises women do to prepare for delivering their baby, at least to Charlie. When questioned about it, Cahya explained that his discipline allows him to sleep anywhere, so long as he can stretch. As fair of an explanation as it was, it left out any reason for being naked. Nonetheless they were all soon asleep.

Charlie took Grant up on his offer from the previous evening, and joined him in his room, where he had a pull out mattress. He got comfortable, forgoing a blanket, instead he used a sheet for coverage. He got hot while he slept, and knew a blanket would be too much. Charlie also chided himself as he struggled to get comfortable with the motel pillow. Too many nights sleeping on his duster he supposed. "What's it say?" he asked Grant without turning toward him. Charlie could see the glow from Grant's communication device reflecting off the walls.

"It's updates from the home office. I had sent them everything I knew earlier, and left the com here while we went out, so it could stay plugged in, and not miss their response." Grant explained. "The signal out here sucks. Anyways. They got back to me. Looks like everything is matching up. Now, we won't have a full moon for a couple days, so if there is a werewolf we likely won't hear anything until then. Gives us some time to look into the other activity areas."

"Sounds good. Where would you like to start."

"I'm thinking tomorrow we send Bob, Nikolai, Ifotia, and Cahya out to Lake Violet to check into that. There are mild, and steady readings coming from the area, but nothing spiking. Could just be a normal missing person scenario." Grant said. "While they are doing that, you, me, and Grey will go look into Hell's Gate."

"That already sounds like trouble. Hell's Gate."

"From what I have it looks like a private, gated residence. We'll probably go out there and find some new age hippies, burning sage, and trying to be one with the earth."

"Hell's Gate makes it seem more likely we will stumble upon animal sacrifice, complete with altars, and the promise of eternal torment." Charlie said.

"The name, Hell's Gate, refers to the actual gates of the place. They were designed, and built custom for this home by an artist, W. V. Hees. Guess he has work built into the architecture also, but we don't have photos of that."

"I'm game for whatever, Grant. This is your show."

"Yeah. I know." Grant said as if he were acknowledging the brightness of the sun. Without contention. "Glad you're here, Charlie."

"Me too, Brother. Me too."

"I'm happy you're here too, Charlie." said the voice again in Charlie's mind. It's sound was like an echo, and a thunderous boom all at once. Charlie wanted to move. To run. He wanted to fight. But he had no idea where the voice was coming from. "Soon. Charlie. Soon."

Before Charlie could get words out, he found himself standing on the shore of a lake, looking out over the water at a lone fisherman. The sun shone bright in the midday sky. Everything looked wonderful. Too wonderful. The man cast out his line, slowly reeling it in. Charlie couldn't help but think of days in his childhood, fishing with his daddy. Either from the dock, or from a friend's boat. He smiled, watched the man fish, and for a moment felt warm. He smiled. Then he watched as tentacles reached up from the water, the boat tilting back, its rear being pulled into the lake. The man screamed, a horrible, shattering scream, that was abruptly silenced. Charlie felt his smile melt from his face as he realized what he was seeing. This was Lake Violet.

As quickly as he saw the pieces of that puzzle fall into play he was finding himself in another place. Wooded, and surrounded by foliage. His hands felt wet and sticky. His vision flashed. He was looking at an altar, square with a circle, and unfamiliar runes carved into it. Blood, the same blood that was on his hands, flowed over the altar. His vision flashed again, now into darkness. Charlie heard screaming. He heard the sound of metal to stone. He felt power, and pain, and the sounds of the world changing around him. The darkness got darker, and he felt as if he were standing in a void, watching as little red dots started appearing all around him.

"It will be good to see you, Charlie." the voice came, and a sharp pain ripped across his face.

Charlie's eyes opened to a blur. The pain struck him again, and he heard the slap of Grant's hand connecting with his face.

"Charlie!" Grant was calling. "Wake up, Charlie."

Charlie knew another slap was coming, and got his hands up before he could get his mouth to move. He caught Grant's next effort at caffeine through contact, and stopped the slap. "I'm up. Stop hitting me, god damnit, I'm awake." Charlie said. "You saved me. Geez! You're a big damn hero."

"Fuck you, Charlie." Grant said jovially. "You ok? You were making a hell of a ruckus in your sleep."

"What time is it?" Charlie asked.

"Just about 6am."

"Excellent. Hopefully Ifotia's swimming adventure didn't cancel eggs in the cafe room." Charlie sat up, seeing the look of impatient concern on Grant's face. "Let me get some eggs, then I'll explain everything." Which he did.

Charlie explained his dream to the group between mouthfuls, and tried to help them understand he believed what he saw was connected to what they were planning to do that day.

"This changes things." Nikolai said.

"As much as I hate to agree with you." Grant said. "We need to be smart about this."

"Agreed." Charlie said, and looked at the group, his gaze settled on Ifotia. "There is something in that lake. If my sight was correct, then it is eating people, and that explains the disappearances."

"Are we still going in two groups?" Cahya asked.

"Yes."

"Just be on alert."

"I am not worried. I have fought all kinds of beast and monster. We will find the creature and destroy it." Cahya Said.

"I'm thinking the second part of my vision was of things that were, not of things to come. It just felt... different." Charlie said. "Grant, Grey, and I will go to Hell's Gate, it's not far from the lake, and will likely just be a sightseeing situation. We'll get in, see what there is, and get to the lake." he looked at Cahya. "I need you to not engage with anything unless you need to. No unnecessary risks, ok?"

"Absolutely, Charlie."

They set out. Bob drove the purple Windstar with Cahya, Ifotia, and Nikolai to Lake Violet. While Grant, Grey, and Charlie went to Hell's Gate. Before leaving everyone verified they had their cell-phones on, and they fully charged. They agreed to keep in contact, and not engage anything without being certain they could do so successfully. Grant watched the purple Windstar drive out of sight before continuing on their way.

"They'll be alright." Charlie said.

"Sure they will, but will we?" Grey said.

Charlie shook his head. The things Grey says sometimes.

"Grey, do me a favor, and grab that case from below the back rear panel." Grant asked.

"Sure thing, Grant." Grey retrieved the case. "What is it?"

"Hand it to Charlie."

"What is it?"

"Open it." Grant said, and Charlie did.

Inside the case he found a pristine, well oiled, specimen of beauty. One he hadn't seen in, what, at least three years. He pulled the custom M4A1 out of the case. He ran his hand along the length of the assault rifle from muzzle to stock. He was happy to see the notches he'd left on the barrel, minor inscriptions special to him from his time in the service when he first received his rifle. "Hey Betty." Charlie said, the way you'd say hi to a favorite pet that had nuzzled up in your lap of its own accord.

"Betty?" Grey asked.

"This is Betty, Grey." Charlie held the assault rifle up, showing it to him. "Damn, Grant. I didn't know you still had her."

"Almost lost her, but it worked out." Grant said. "There's extra clips, and a suppressor in the case. Plenty of ammo in the back."

"Thanks man. I definitely wasn't expecting this."

"I was going to give it to you under better circumstances. But based on what you saw last night, I think we're going to need it." Grant looked to Charlie. "You know this ain't no sightseeing trip we're on."

"Yeah." Grey agreed.

Charlie looked at Betty in his hands. Then out the window. He knew his brother was right.

The purple Windstar reached the lake. The sun shone brightly in the sky, and Bob used his hand to shade his eyes. There was no one at the lake. This was encouraging, and worrisome all at once. Was Charlie wrong, or were they late? Nikolai, Ifotia, and Cahya exited the van. As they started to look about, Bob stayed in the van. A growing sense of assurance formed in him. He turned to say something to Nikolai, and his eyes caught a truck at the edge of the lake. Beyond it Bob saw a small fishing boat trolleying out into the lake, with a single man in it. He was moving toward the middle of the lake, his fishing pole clearly visible. Just like Charlie said.

CHAPTER 8
HELL'S GATE

After more than a quarter mile of two lane blacktop, lined by rows of trees, and six foot deep ditches, Grant and Charlie arrived. "Welcome to Hell." Charlie mused as they pulled the matte black conversion van up to the entrance of Hell's Gate. It was a single door gate, affixed to a stone barrier wall. The gate loomed like the entrance to Jurassic Park. "Wonder what they keep in there?" Charlie said to no one in particular.

"I'm leaving the van here." Grant said. "We should go in on foot."

"Yeah. Element of surprise!" Grey said in his airy, raspy way. "Ya know. Like commandos."

"Weren't you in the army, Grey?" Grant asked.

"I can neither confirm, or deny that, Grant." Grey said, and received a sideways look from Grant. "A man is allowed to have his secrets."

"I think you got that saying wrong."

"Yeah, isn't it usually said a woman is allowed her secrets." Charlie said.

"We're going for gender equality here, fellas." Grey said in a snippy tone. Both Grant and Charlie chucked, and all three exited the vehicle.

"You bringing Betty?" Grant asked Charlie.

"Fuckin' right." Charlie replied, hoisting the pristine weapon to his shoulder. "Been apart this long, I'm not just going to leave her in the van."

"I figured as much." Grant said. "There's a shoulder strap in the case, next to the suppressor."

"Excellent."

"Are you good, Grey?" Grant asked, and turned to Grey. "I hadn't asked before we left."

"Oh yeah, Grant." Grey said while he rolled out a case that at once looked like a side carry gym bag. Few things are what they seem with Grey. He unsnapped some clasps, then rolled out the bag to display a full assortment of handguns, and close combat weapons. "Just give me a minute." Grey said, smirking. He pulled a belt from the case, affixed to it two holsters, three knife sheaths, their knives, a clasp for his EMF meter, and two ammo clips. He then tightened the belt about his waist. Grey also had on his standard army surplus attire, complete with a tactical vest, digital camo cargo pants, tucked into calf high boots. He filled the vest with additional gear, ammo, and a candy bar.

"You have any more of those?" Charlie asked, pointing to the candy bar.

"You feeling hangry, Charlie?" Grey quipped, and tossed him and Grant a bar each. "Gotta stay prepared." he said, as he placed two M17 handguns in their holsters.

"I don't eat those." Grant said.

"You gonna give us some, my body is a temple, bullshit?"

"My body is a temple." Grant said plainly. They all chuckled after a brief silence. "It's the peanuts. Just don't like how they taste in those." he clarified.

"More for me!" Grey said. He retrieved the rejected treat. He folded up his pack, placing the candy bar back inside it, and put the pack inside the van. "I'm ready." he said to Grant.

"Let's do this." Grant said, while brandishing his own weapon. Grant hit a button on the inside wall of the van, and a drone rose straight up from the van's roof. "To watch our six." he said plainly. With that the three men walked through Hell's Gate.

"This is not good. That is not good." Bob repeated to himself as he left the van, and headed toward the others. "Not good. Um, Ifotia? Ifotia."

"Yes, Bob. My, are you alright?" she asked.

"What is it, friend, Bob?" Cahya asked. "Are we not at the correct lake?"

"That's not it." Bob said. "It's that I think we are exactly at the correct lake."

Nikolai looked past Bob, and to the lake. From their vantage point at the back of the purple Windstar he could make out the boat moving toward the middle of the lake. "It is happening. Just like in Charlie's dream. Yes?"

"Yes." Bob confirmed, and watched Nikolai's face become like stone. Then, he was gone. Just, poof, gone, but without any poof. "Um... Where is Nikolai?"

Cahya looked from Bob, to Ifotia, clearly unsure of where Nikolai went.

"He is flying." Ifotia said. "Can you not see him?" she pointed. They looked and said nothing. "I can see him." she said. "That seems like a good idea. Better to see the whole lake up there." at those words she too lifted into the sky. Warmth, like the breeze over an open fire, passed around them in a whoosh. In a breath Ifotia was above the trees, and headed out to the water.

"What do we do?" Bob asked Cahya.

"We will go fishing." Cahya said with a jovial excitement to his voice. "If there is a monster in the lake, we will fish for it." he said, and he started toward the lake.

Bob watched him walk away, but not completely away. Bob saw that he was walking toward a small building near the road. The building had a motorcycle near the back of the building, but no cars or people could be seen out front. As he ran to catch up Bob then saw it was a bait shop.

"Afternoon boys, what can I do you for?" said the shop clerk in a clearly practiced manner. He was a middle aged man, perhaps in his late forties. His manner of dress was simple. The shop clerk had on jeans, shoes, and a t-shirt that read "It's 5 o' clock somewhere". His name badge read, Jim.

"Ah. Hello friend. I am not sure what you would do me for, but I am looking for bait." Cahya explained. "Do you have fish particles?"

The clerk shook his head, and looked put off by Cahya. It may have been the hat, but most likely it was how Cahya communicated. "I've got minnows and leeches. Would either of those work for you?"

Bob joined Cahya at the counter.

"May have needed to go to a butcher." Cahya said, mostly to himself.

"Could we, ah. Hello, Jim. Could we get an assortment of both?" Bob asked.

Jim nodded, and went about his business. He grabbed two 12 ounce plastic containers, each was semi transparent, and filled up near the cover with water. In each container the silhouettes of the leeches and minnows could be seen. "That'll be $10." Jim said.

Bob paid for the bait using the black card that Mr. Grant had given him for expenses. He mumbled to himself "Remember to use this card. Yes. Mr. Grant. I will, Mr. Grant." Jim was giving him an odd sort of look as he handed Bob his card back. "Thank you." Bob said as he left to join Cahya who had already headed outside with the bait. "Don't you need a pole?" he called out to Cahya as he hurried to catch up.

"A pole I have." Cahya replied. "It was bait I needed."

Bob was perplexed, he hadn't seen a pole. Cahya certainly wasn't carrying one at that moment, and he didn't seem to have had one in the purple Windstar. Bob was about to ask for clarification as he witnessed Cahya retrieve from his side shoulder bag a six foot rod and reel. Bob chuffed, stumbled for what to say. He settled on saying nothing.

"Keep the sun to your back." whispered Nikolai to Ifotia.

"There you are. Hello Nikolai." Ifotia said as they both hung suspended in the sky. "Why do I want the sun to my back?"

"He will be less able to see you." Nikolai said plainly. "You stay hard to see silhouetted by the sun. He will likely think you are a large bird."

"This is as Charlie saw." Ifotia observed. "Do you see anything of concern?"

"Not yet." Nikolai said. He watched Cahya, and Bob walk out to the dock. Cahya was waving. Nikolai followed his line of sight, and watched as the fisherman noticed Cahya waving, and pulled his boat toward the dock.

"Hello friend." Cahya said as the fisherman got close.

"Hey. What's up? Is everything ok?" asked the fisherman.

"Yes. Everything is well. My name is Cahya. May I join you in fishing?" he asked.

"Hell, I don't see why not. Fishin' is always better with company." he pulled closer to the dock. "Hope in. My name is Max." Max waited as Cahya joined him in the boat, and Bob did not. "You not coming?" Max asked.

"Not this time." Bob said. "I think I'll bird watch, or read a book. Maybe next time. Be safe." he said. Bob turned, and headed to shore. As he did he caught a shimmery motion under the water below the dock. He turned to alert Cahya, and Max, but they had already departed back towards the middle of the lake.

Nikolai saw it too, and in an instant his muscles tightened. The shimmer had come from the back of a long, large creature. The water obscured the finer details, but Nikolai could tell it was long, sleek, and dangerous.

"What is it?" Ifotia asked.

"The monster from Charlie's dream. It is here." Nikolai said.

Grey began to whistle, and caught himself. This wasn't the time for that. They had no idea what they were walking into, and who may be waiting for them. Grey really wanted to whistle.

They were thirty yards down a long, single lane drive. A light forest of pines filled the land on either side of the driveway. Sprinkled throughout were bushes, other kinds of trees, and the bright shining sun shone through. Mostly it was pines. Their lower branches were free of needles as there was little direct sunlight for them to grow. The wind hummed within the trees, and in the distance were the sounds of life, birds, and scurrying animals.

Grant put up a fist, calling for them to stop with the signal. Charlie approached.

"I heard it too." Charlie said. He looked back at Grey, using his hand, two fingers extended straight, he motioned in the direction they heard the sound. Then spreading his two fingers, he pointed to his eyes, then back out to the wooded space, pivoting his hand to the left and right, as if to tell Grey "Watch this space."

Grey nodded in understanding. "I got you." he mouthed back to Charlie.

"You cover my six. I'm going to see if I can draw out whatever it is." Charlie said to Grant, who nodded once. "If it ends up being a squirrel, or something, don't shoot me." he said, and stepped off the drive, and into the pine covered land beyond.

The soft crunch of pine needles came with each step Charlie took. Grey cupped the grip of his pistol in his hands, and watched intently. Charlie did the same two finger gestures, only pointing it forward. Grey, and Grant walked further down the drive in time with Charlie's own progression. The space seemed to get darker as they moved along.

Grey heard a crack from behind where they were focused. The sound came from behind and to his left. He looked, and saw two glowing read dots in the shadows beneath a brush. He looked at them, trying to work out what they could be. Then they blinked.

Grey involuntarily slipped a step, and bumped into Grant, who had stopped moving.

"Watch yourself." Grant said.

"Look, Grant. Towards that bush."

"I know, Grey." Grant said, not turning to look.

"Grant, you gotta look…" Grey had turned to insist Grant look at the bush, and stopped when he saw what Grant was looking at.

In the trees, upon the path, from every shadow, glowing red eyes looked at them. The increased darkness of their path was caused by the density of the creatures that hung from the trunks, and branches of the trees. It wasn't dozens of pairs of eyes, it was hundreds.

"Charlie!" Grant called out to his brother.

"I see them." Charlie said. "You good?"

"I'm tucked in like a thong on a fat man's ass." Grant said. "This feels hairy, and gross."

Charlie looked to his brother. "What do you want to do?" he asked at the same moment a creature that looked like a matte black cat from his nightmares, jetted out from behind the tree that was between Grant and Charlie. It hissed, a loud, violent scream, not leaving its perch on the trunk of the tree. "God. Damnit!" Charlie yelled, and backed away a few steps.

"We're backing up." Grant called.

"Yep." Charlie confirmed, and matched their progress of retreat, adjusted his trajectory, slowly moving towards the drive again. The little black creatures were now pressing toward them from three sides. They were in a sort of crescent moon formation, getting closer, and closer. "Distance?" Charlie called out.

"Twenty feet to us, 40 to the van." Grant said.

Charlie heard another hiss, and saw one of the matte black demon kitties had jumped near him. Charlie lifted Betty, and in a moment of impulse pulled the trigger. Bullets spit from the rifle. He hit the creature, and blew away chunks of the tree's bark, and meat. There was a moment of drawn out pause, that in reality was only a breath of time. Charlie looked to Grant in time to see hundreds of red eyes focused on him.

"Charlie, run!" Grant yelled.

The swarm of creatures converged upon Charlie. Branches snapped, and the churning sound of pine needles underfoot filled his ears. Charlie heard another scream, this time like a siren, as a small group of the creatures joined in together. Charlie heard Grey's voice but couldn't make out what he said. He ran.

Grey yelled for Charlie to "Duck!", as he retrieved two vials from his vest. Grey knew there was little time, and whether Charlie would duck or not, he had to take action. He crushed the vials in his palm, the tiny glass cutting his skin, and mixing his blood with the elements of both potions. Power filled his hand, warm and familiar. Grey said the words, and extended his other hand toward the creatures pursuing Charlie, yelling once more for Charlie to "Duck!"

Power, magic, flooded through Grey's body, through his hand, up his arm, across his chest, and out to his other hand where blue white light shot from Grey's outstretched palm.

A hum, all too familiar to Charlie, filled the air, and Charlie hit the dirt. There was nothing graceful about it. At best it was the tuck and roll of a career drinker on a holiday bender, it left Charlie on his back looking up for a brief moment. The blue white light extended out like webbing through the air over Charlie. The webbing caught the pursuing creatures, and interrupted their pursuit. Just as quickly as it caught them, they started to break through it. Charlie shuffled to his feet.

"Move your ass!" Grant yelled, himself almost to the opening of Hell's Gate.

Charlie ran, gripping tightly to Betty. His feet hit the drive, and Charlie heard the creatures scream, and he recognized they had broken through Grey's barrier spell. The rumble of the van's engine came from the distance, and Charlie ran. The screaming, hissing call of the demon kittens intensified, and he ran. His ears filled with the sound of his own breathing, and the pounding of heart. His vision blurred. What was happening? Was this the demon? His demon? The van roared. He was too late. His feet hit hard against the pavement. Thunderous vibrations shook his body with each step forward. He was too late. Something grabbed Charlie hard, pulling him violently off his feet. There was a rolling sound of metal on metal, a thunk, and click. The van door was closed, and he was inside.

They were moving, the van's eight cylinder engine being pressed to full capacity.

"Are they on us?" Grant yelled from the driver's seat. "Grey!"

"How do I know, Grant? You don't have rear windows!" Grey yelled back.

"On the console, hit the flashing button." Grant instructed. "Then on the monitor press view."

Grey did as instructed, and the monitor presented an aerial view of a slightly delayed transmission of them. "I see us!" Grey said. "Looks like we are buffering."

"Good." Grant said. "Do you see them?"

Grey watched, focused keenly on the footage. Then he saw the shadow approach the gate, the van pulling away. Then nothing. Not that there was no image, there was. He still saw the trees. Saw the van driving away. Yet as soon as the footage showed Grey pull Charlie into the van, and close the door, all the creatures vanished. Not fled. Not dispersed. They disappeared. "They're gone." he said to Grant, stunned.

"What?" Grant said, looking into his rearview mirror. "What did you say, Grey?"

"They're gone, man. Disappeared. Poof. El Vanisho! Gone."

Grant saw nothing in his mirror. He heard no more screams. "Call the drone back, Grey." he instructed. "Charlie, you ok?"

"Yeah." Charlie grunted. He felt like he was going to puke. "Nothing a little whiskey won't fix." he said, and dropped his head back against the hard wall of the van.

Grant laughed. He knew full well Charlie was spent from that run. But he said he was ok, and there was no time to argue. Whatever had just happened here was nothing they were equipped for. This whole trip to Iowa was increasingly becoming more than Grant expected. They needed to work as a group. Only right now, they were not. They were various parts of a potential whole, and even worse they were split in two. Grant knew he needed to get them to work as a team. Needed them to come together. Even with the vampire. They were going to need each other. They had to get to the lake.

CHAPTER 9
LAKE VIOLET

Shades of blue, green, and the vibrant yellow-white rays of the sun mixed, and reflected off the surface of the water. The wind blew softly, leaving subtle ripples on the water to compliment the swaying tree branches, and bending grass. The breeze was that cool, refreshing kind of temperature best to combat the heat of the sun. Sporadic cloud cover did little to dampen the scene. It was evidently an ideal day to die fishing in Iowa.

Nikolai waved his arms, trying to get Cahya's attention in the boat below him. He waved in vain. Having forgotten for a moment that he had made himself invisible. Currently it seemed only Ifotia could see him. He growled in frustration. The creature, whatever it was, seemed to be slowly swimming the outer perimeter of the lake, moving ever so patiently toward the center. Towards where Cahya sat, in a fishing boat, with the helpless stranger.

"Do not become angry, Nikolai." Ifotia said. "There must be something we can do."

"Go to Bob." Nikolai said plainly.

"But I wish to help you."

"You will be." Nikolai said. "Please, Ifotia, go to Bob. I will bring that creature to you."

"Then what will we do?" she asked.

"Stay alive."

Ifotia looked at the water. She could see the creature now, and tracked its movements. It seemed to bob up and down within the water, while never breaking the surface. As it would rise, the sun would illuminate upon its flesh a pattern. It would glisten with lines of luminescent green and purple, lined by gold. She watched. Each time the pattern looked more clear.

"Ifotia?"

She started, and realized that she had lowered herself close to the water. With a smooth stroke of her wings, she rose up to join Nikolai again. "Yes, Nikolai. What is it?" she asked.

"Where did you go, just then? Are you alright?" Nikolai inquired.

"There are lines upon the creature's back. On either side of his back." she said.

"His?"

"They look familiar to me, Nikolai. I didn't mean to go so close to the water. I only wanted to see them better." Ifotia explained. She didn't wait for a response from Nikolai. Instead she flapped her wings, only she didn't fly away this time, she simply disappeared. In a blink later she stood by Bob. Bob jumped when she appeared.

"Hello Ifotia. I had not seen you there." Bob said.

"I was not here, I was there." she said, pointing to the sky.

"Yes. Of course." Bob agreed. "Good you are here. I saw something in the lake."

"We saw it too."

"You did?" Bob asked for rhetorical confirmation. "Good. Good. I was just about to call Mr. Grant."

"I'm going to go out on the dock." Ifotia said as she walked toward the wooden platform.

"Sounds good." Bob said, and set to dialing Grant Bowman. The phone rang only once, then picked up. "Hello Mr. Grant." Bob said.

"Yes... Mmmhmmm... Yes. I understand... Um, Mr. Grant. Yeah. There's a creature in the lake, and Cahya is in a boat fishing with a man in the middle of it."

Grant disconnected.

"We don't catch much on Lake Violet." Max said. "Still, it's calm, and peaceful out here."

"It is that." Cahya agreed. "Reminds me greatly of the lakes around our monastery back home. I do miss them. It feels good to be fishing again."

"Monastery, huh?" Max said. "Where are you from?"

"My deepest apologies, my new friend. I am Cahya, tenth of my order. I am from the sect of the Open Eye. We are a peaceful community of warriors, sworn to protect the world from all manor of danger."

"Oh. Well, I'm Max Bahlenovich. I got a daughter, and an ex-wife. So I fish."

"Thank you for letting me join you, Max." Cahya said. "Is this lake dangerous, do you know?" he asked.

"You must have heard about the missing girl. Yeah, that happened." Max said. "Doubt it's the lake's fault. It's just a lake, right?" he said with ironic humor in his tone. "I don't know. Suppose someone else lost their dog here too. We all knew that story was bullshit."

"Why would you say that?" Cahya asked.

Max gave a light laugh. "They claimed some big ass fish ate it." he made a dismissive sound with his mouth. "Look at this lake. It's tiny. Ain't no way some fish big enough to eat a dog lives here, without it having been seen before."

Nikolai couldn't fully make out the conversation, but the creature's path was now mere yards from the boat. He positioned himself behind the man in the boat, so he and Cahya would be facing each other. He planned to make himself visible, and signal to Cahya that they needed to go into shore. In position, Nikolai made himself visible and appeared just behind Cahya's companion.

"Ah! Nikolai!" Cahya exclaimed.

Max appeared surprised. "No. I'm Max."

"Yes. Of course you are." Cahya said, still looking at Nikolai who gestured for him to stop and be quiet. "I got excited, is all. Nikolai... Nikolaiy. Nikolay is what I meant to say." he said, as Nikolai now gestured enthusiastically toward the dock. Cahya gave a subtle nod, and said to Max. "I thought I had a tug on my line."

"But you haven't casted off yet?" Max pointed out.

The water splashed nearby, drawing both of their attention. Nikolai didn't look. He knew what it was. The creature was getting prepared to attack. Invisible again, Nikolai glided down and forward, placed his hand on the throttle for the motor, and turned. The boat roared to life, all 10 horsepower of the small engine engaged. The man, Max, Nikolai thought his name was, screamed.

"What the hell is happening!" Max panicked.

Just behind them the water churned, writhing dual tentacles, and clawed arms extended from the water, and searched for the boat. The creature turned in pursuit. The boat's engine howled as it was pushed to its limits. The creature wailed a reply that carried in spite of the water, and waves. Its tentacles extended out as it pursued.

Cahya reached into his side shoulder bag, and retrieved from it a shining silver sword. He pressed by the panic stricken Max, and moved toward the back of the boat. One of the creature's tentacles came close, and Cahya swung with his sword. The creature pulled its limb away. "I recommend you hold on to something, Max." Cahya called out. The shoreline quickly approached.

Grant saw the boat as it bulleted toward the shore. He slammed on the breaks, the momentum of the van stopped after it had passed the edge of the parking lot, and out onto the grass. He slammed the vehicle in park and he, Charlie, and Grey piled out. While Charlie, and Grey seemed to move toward the shoreline, Grant opened the side-door to the van, retrieved the case that hung on the back of the driver's seat, opened it, and pulled out a MK 13 sniper rifle.

Grant climbed up to his sniper rack on the roof of his van. He laid upon his stomach, his right leg hooked out to the side for balance. Grant positioned his sight on the chaos happening on the beach.

The fishing boat hit land hard. Nikolai lost his grip, and tumbled out beyond the boat. He became visible as he came to a stop near Bob's feet.

"Hello Nikolai." Bob said, and helped Nikolai to his feet.

Cahya grabbed Max by his shirt, yanked him from the boat, and to the land. The water erupted forth from Lake Violet. One strong limb of the creature slammed down, and through the fiberglass boat. The creature roared a wet gurgly roar.

A sharp crack split the air, and the creature pulled back as one of Grant's rounds met its target. Two more shots came in quick succession. They hit true, and though the creature clearly felt them, it seemed unaffected by the attack. It wanted Max. It reared up on two powerful, lean front limbs. It's three pronged claws digging into the sandy clay of the shore. The creatures had two large eyes, gills along its neck, with a dangerous looking pronged fin that ran the length of its back. Its tail was like that of a shark's tail, decisive in its purpose, and extending out from his lower sides were two tentacles. As the creature roared again in protest it presented its gaping maw to them, filled with row after row of wickedly angled teeth.

Charlie dropped to his knees. Retrieved his salt from his duster pocket, and used it to make a circle around him. All the while he cursed himself that he kept forgetting to get a belt knife for moments like this. Charlie bit the inside of his mouth, drew blood, and when he could taste enough of it to be sure he was successful, he spat the blood upon the salt. Applying his will, Charlie said the words, and a circle of power formed around him. He reached out with his mind. "Charlie!" came his name in a scream. His heart jumped into his throat. This was not the time for this. He did not want to deal with his demon now.

"Charlie, listen." Ifotia said again. "I know what that is. Who that is." she said in a rush. "I saw the markings on his back. Only they aren't markings. It's Samarian."

Charlie collected his thoughts and he looked to Ifotia. "What are you trying to tell me?"

"It is Enki, of the Old Ones." she said, catching her breath. "That creature is the Samerian god of water. In part. I think."

"You think?" Charlie yelled.

The creature lashed out toward Nikolai, and Bob.

"You need to be pretty damn sure about things like this, Ifotia. What do you mean, in part?"

"I do not believe it is fully Enki. I believe this creature is a manifestation of part of Enki's power. Which is good." she said.

"How is that good?"

Ifotia looked at Charlie, her face more serious than he'd ever seen. "It means we may be able to kill him."

Charlie looked at her. This divine goddess, and knew she was right. He had never seen her look this way. His eyes met hers again, and watched as hers went hard. She turned from him, wings extended from her back. Vibrant, flowing, wings of fire. They were beautiful. In an instant she was in the air above the creature. She said his name was Enki. Charlie wasn't one to let a good tool go to waste. Reaching out with his will he could feel the circle still present around him. He was going to reach out to Enki, mind to mind, and see what might satisfy this creature's need.

He closed his eyes, and said the words. Charlie evoked Enki's name. Did it work? He looked to Enki, his will resolved to try again. As he opened his eyes he saw the god of water looking directly at him.

Grey moved. He rolled, and stopped. Adjusted, then moved again. He was going to need the creature to come further out of the water for this to work. Water was hell on magic. Where blood was the grand catalyst. Water was the neutralizer. "Nikolai, draw it over here!" he yelled. Nikolai, always so cool and collected, gave Grey just enough of a gesture that he knew he understood. Grey positioned himself to move again, and took the fifth mini-bomb from his tactical vest.

The beast roared. Its head moved to look away from Nikolai, Bob, and Max. Grey tracked the line of sight. It was looking at Charlie. One of the creature's powerful limbs dug into the dirt, pulled it forward, toward Charlie, and out of the water. "Yes!" Grey hissed to himself. He adjusted his position. It wasn't going to be perfect, but it would work. He hoped. He dropped the last mini-bomb, and decided to move toward Charlie. Grey tracked the beast as it moved into place. He pressed the detonator.

Five mini explosions erupted around the now moving creature. Each emitted bursts of blue white light. From the explosions, lines of power went out to each other explosion, and formed an encircled five pointed star around the creature. Then from those lines branched out more lines, until a dynamic webbing of power laid over the creature like a net to hold it down.

It let out a low, earth rumbling growl, its tail, tentacles, and one of its front limbs were bound. Half of the creature's head, and one front limbs still tried to move. The creature's eyes burned upon Charlie, who remained within his circle of power. As if in reply to the creature's protest a crack ripped through the air as Grant loosed another bullet from his rifle. Grey watched as the bullet connected, and the creature's left eye exploded. Grant was a great marksman, and the shot released a sense of relief within Grey. He breathed out, and watched as the momentarily limp monster in front of him surged with renewed fury. The beasts wounded eye moved, and stitched itself back together.

Charlie focused again. He put everything he had into the effort. Like lightning hitting right outside your home, the connection thundered into him with a physical torrent that was impossible to ignore. Charlie's mind filled with images of gold, silver, and young livestock. He saw an altar, heard the jingling of coins, and felt a gut deep need to give.

"Tribute." came a gravelly, hissy voice. "Tribute."

"What do you want?" Charlie asked the god of water through his mind. "Why are you here?"

All that came back was the word. "Tribute. Tribute. Tribute."

"What kind of tribute?" Charlie tried again. There was silence for a time. Charlie repeated. "What kind of tribute would satisfy you, Enki?" He could feel it, the attention grasped by using its name. There was a snap. He was losing his connection to the creature. Charlie heard only one word in reply.

"Blood."

Enki, the Samarian god of water, reared up. The lines of power over it moved from blue white, to a hot, radiant white. The beast's tail shifted. Long barbed spears shot forth, barely missing Bob and Max. The tail moved again. Another spear came forth, and caught Nikolai in the upper chest. He flew back off his feet. His body pinned to the ground by the force of the spear.

Cahya, sword in hand, charged the creature. His swipe was true, the silver blade inflicting noticeable wounds upon the beast's flesh. Cahya was between Enki and the lake and did not see the surge of water rise up to collide with him. Like a hand all its own, the water took hold of Cahya, and pulled him into Lake Violet.

"It wants a tribute!" yelled Charlie to those who could hear. 'A tribute."

Ifotia surged as below her Charlie pulled his rifle to bear down upon Enki. Grant too, continued to fire. She knew they would run out of projectiles before this shadow of a god perished. She had to act. Words from another time came to her. They were not foriegn, they were her words, her voice. She reached for them. Invited them to her lips.

She lowered to the earth, her feet pressed softly on the ground. Her majestic wings folded in, disappearing within her body. She could feel the shadow god's pain, its anguish. She stepped toward it. "I bring you tribute." she called out. The creature looked to her, in a sudden calm, both expectant, and riggid. Ifotia tossed a package in brown, wrapped, and tied paper.

"Not the bacon!" called Charlie.

The bundle rolled within reach of the creature. It reached out, took the offering, and consumed it. Ifotia heard Charlie's vulgar protest behind her, and ignored it. Calmly she stepped forward. Closer. Until she was within reach of the water god. She felt the earth vibrate beneath her as the creature growled out.

"Tribute." it said.

Ifotia took a last step forward, meeting Enki straight on. "Was that not enough?" she asked, to more growling. "I have more for you." she said, and she could feel the once far off words now rested inside her lips. She yielded way for them, and as they came forth a sword of fire, and power, formed in her hand. Ifotia thrust the sword forward with otherworldly speed. She thrust it forward, and up into Enki's throat. The blade erupted with fire out of the back of the creature's head. She watched Enki's eyes, watched for the irrefutable extinguishing of life. Then removed her sword.

They all watched as life seemed to breathe out of the creature, its limbs gave way to its weight, and the body fell to the ground. Little flakes started floating off the carcass. Few at first, and quickly giving way, like a seeding dandelion being blown apart by a child. In a short moment the once mighty beast was gone, and all its secrets with it.

"Cahya!" yelled Bob, pointing to the water.

Ifotia was already moving, like an angel of salvation, she rose upon radiant wings of fire. They watched as she dove into the lake. Her glow emitted mildly through the surface. It felt like minutes passed before she returned. She carried out Cahya's still body, and laid him upon the sand.

Grey was the first to reach them. He lifted Cahya's shirt, pulling it up to his neck.

"Do you know CPR?" Bob asked. "I only ask because I know CPR and..."

"Fuck CPR." Grey said, and slammed a needle tipped syringe into Cahya's chest.

Cahya's body contracted forward, his eyes opened wide as he

vomited lake water onto the ground, and Bob's shoes. He coughed, and struggled to collect himself.

"What else do you keep in that vest, Grey?" asked Charlie. Based on Grey's expression, he answered himself. "Yeah, I know. A man's gotta have his secrets." He headed over to check Nikolai's wounds. His friend had removed the spear from his body, and rested, bleeding, against the base of a tree. "You okay, buddy?" he asked, and Nikolai gave Charlie a thumbs up.

Grant breathed a sigh of relief at what he was seeing through his scope. A vibration came from his left thigh. He pressed his bluetooth ear piece to accept the call. "Yes." he said.

"Agent Bowman."

"Yes."

"Well done at Lake Violet." the disembodied voice said.

Grant started. How did they know they were at Lake Violet? But all he said in reply was. "Yes."

"We have resources for you at the Adams County Historical Society regarding your remaining points of interest. Do hurry. The full moon is in just two days." the voice said, and disconnected.

CHAPTER 10

BEER AND PIZZA

The scene was the kind of calm that only exists after you almost die. It was a feeling he knew too well. Mortality endangerment, or not, there were still matters that should always be taken seriously. "Look! I'm going to tend to Nikolai, and then, goddess or no, we're having a conversation about the proper treatment of bacon!" Charlie said firmly to Ifotia as he walked through the door with Nikolai draped over him by one arm.

"What did I do?" she asked.

"What..." Charlie started to repeat back to her, stopping himself. Instead he continued to the bed to set Nikolai down. He placed a pillow below Nikolai's head as he reclined lengthwise on the bed. "You alright, bud?" Charlie asked Nikolai.

"It will be alright, Charlie." Nikolai said. "I simply need rest." he said. The wound where the spear hit him was directly below his left clavicle bone. It was not bleeding, not like a normal person's wound would. Yet the injury gaped open, a grotesque reminder of what happened.

"I know. I know." Charlie said, only having listened halfway. "I'm going to get you something to help." he turned to the door, and yelled. "You need help with Cahya?"

"No, I got him." Grant called back from the doorway. "He ain't too heavy. In fact, I'd say he's lighter than he looks."

"That's the benefit of healthy living, my friend." Cahya said softly.

Grant laid Cahya down on the left side of the same bed as Nikolai. He looked at Nikolai lying there. A feeling of concern struck him. Was it wise to lay a weakened Cahya next to that monster? Doesn't injury make animals more dangerous? For a moment he thought to move him. The other bed was open. Or he could kill Nikolai, and finally be done with it.

"Grant?" Charlie said. "Grant, you ok?"

"Yep." Grant said, meeting Charlie's eyes. "I'm fine. Where are you going?"

"I'll be back. Going to get something to help them heal." Charlie said.

"What do you plan on getting?"

"Probably best you not know, brother." Charlie said. "I'll be back soon. Mind if I use the van?" Grant tossed Charlie the keys. "Thanks, brother."

"Charlie." Grant said. His brother turned to look at him. Grant thought to say to be careful, or to stay safe, or even to make some crack jab at Charlie just to get a smile out of him. But he refrained. "Don't damage my van."

Charlie made a "Psh" sound as he smirked, and left.

Nikolai laid in the bed and looked up at the ceiling. He would have given anything for a ceiling fan at that moment. His body was warm, almost hot. Was it from the wound? Perhaps the beast left venom on the spike? Surely it couldn't be the wound alone. He had suffered worse than this. This was a stubbed toe when compared to what the Turks did to him during Romania's war of independence. He was still surprised that certain parts of him grew back. Still he was increasingly warm. Nikolai took a breath, and attempted to put himself into a more comfortable state. It must have helped, because he noticed it wasn't his whole body that was warm. It was just his wound.

"Try not to move." Ifotia said softly.

Nikolai turned his head enough to see Ifotia had extended one of her hands, and was holding it directly above the wound. "What are you doing?" he asked.

"You were hurt. I should have acted sooner, and perhaps it could have been avoided." Ifotia said. She could see on his face that her reply was not satisfying to him. "I think I can heal you."

"You think. You are not certain?" Bob asked. His voice, typically soft and kind, broke through the silence like thunder.

Nikolai noticed then that everyone in the room was watching them. All except Cahya, who took that moment to start snoring deeply. Nikolai looked at Ifotia. Her eyes glowed subtly, and her face registered a kindly, concerned expression. Nikolai took a breath. "Thank you." he said.

"Yeah, thanks, Ifotia." Grant quipped. "If anything is going to kill him, it's going to be me." he said, then opened the door to his room. "Tell me when Charlie gets back." he said, and entered his room, closing the door behind him.

"Grant needs to learn to let some things go, ya know?" Grey said.

"Yeah." Bob agreed. "Mr. Grant is a great guy. I'm sure he didn't mean it."

"He has said such things before. Remember, also, his response at the diner." Ifotia said.

"Yeah. I do remember that." Grey said. "Really intense." he said, recalling the look in Grant's eyes when Charlie spoke to him at the diner. "Hope Charlie get's back soon. Where do you think he went?"

"To get blood." Nikolai said, gently moving Ifotia's hand away, and sitting up. The area where the wound was had healed over, and only bruising remained. "Thank you, Ifotia." he said, not looking at her.

"Are you better?" she asked.

"I am."

"Please do tell me if I may help further." Ifotia said.

Nikolai's stomach fluttered. He kept his eyes from her. From her beauty. From those eyes. She had healed him. With her warmth. Her fire. He wanted to be burned by her. To embrace possibility, even if it meant pain. She was so beautiful. "I will." he said finally. "Excuse me." Nikolai left the room, and went out onto the walkway balcony.

"He ok?" Grey asked, looking at Bob, and Ifotia. "He didn't seem ok."

"Would you please help me with this?" Bob asked Grey, extending a corner of a blanket to him. Together they covered a heavily snoring Cahya, and tucked him in snuggly. "Thank you." Bob said to Grey.

"Yeah, man. Of course." Grey kind of kicked the floor like he wasn't sure what to do, or how to propose it. "You guys hungry?" he asked eventually.

"I'm not a guy, but I could eat." Ifotia said.

Grey chuckled at her response. "It's just a saying. Never-mind. I saw a pizza place just down the block. We could walk down, and get pies for everyone. If you want?"

"That would be splendid." Bob said. "Will you join us, Ifotia?"

"I would like that." she said.

The three of them left together. As they exited the parking lot of the motel, they saw Charlie return. They explained where they were going, and Grey confirmed the pizza Charlie would enjoy.

Charlie parked the van, and approached Nikolai who was leaning against the rail of the walkway balcony. "What the hell are you doing out of bed?" Charlie asked. Nikolai cut him off by opening his shirt to show the bruising on his chest. The wound was gone. "Holy shit. How did you do that?"

"Ifotia did it."

"What did she do, exactly?"

"Not sure." Nikolai said with a shrug, taking from Charlie the thick plastic pouch he had offered to him. "I was focusing. Laying in the bed." he took a drink. "I was so warm. Did not realize initially it was her. By the time I had, I was like this." he said, and gestured at his healed chest, while he tipped back another mouthful.

"Well, shit. That Ifotia is sure full of tricks. You see how she finished off that thing?" Charlie asked, then realized how silly it was to have asked Nikolai that. "Heh, I suppose you didn't. Being as you were bleeding, and pinned on your back an all." he leaned in close to Nikolai. "Sword of fire. Conjured it up from nothing. Never seen anything like it. Seemed to take its toll on 'er though." he clapped Nikolai on the left shoulder. "I'll let you finish that up. Best Grant don't see you." he nodded at the pouch. "Toss it when you're done, would ya?"

"Thank you, Charlie." Nikolai said with a nod.

Inside the room Cahya was snoring. Charlie walked over to him, slapped one of his feet through the blanket. "Wake up old man." he said kindly. "Come on. I got you some medicine."

Cahya stirred. His awakening was like watching cold molasses drip from a spoon. Once it seemed like all of his faculties were aware they were attempting to awaken he took a sharp breath. Cahya behaved like an old carburetor motor striving to turn over. Cahya's eyelids opened, and closed, a number of times, as his eyes grasped for focus. There was a crack, a hiss, a pop. The smell of hops, and fermented wheat filled the air in his nostrils. Cahya lifted his head to find Charlie. "Medicine?" he asked hopefully.

"It isn't the 'good stuff'. Afraid they don't sell that in Iowa." Charlie said. He extended his hand to Cahya, who took the offered item. "Still. If I recall correctly. This should help you recover just fine."

Cahya's fingers searched like excited blindfolded children in search of their prize. They found the tab, and pulled it open. Crack, hiss, pop. The aroma, full and sweet, filled his nose. He brought the can to his lips, and poured the sweet nectar in. It was everything he needed. He was so consumed by the rewarding flavor that he didn't hear Grey, Ifotia, and Bob return. He didn't smell the pizza. There was only this. Peace. Comfort. Beer.

Three thuds rang hard against the wall. A moment passed, and Grant opened the door that connected their rooms. Grant's eyes, no not his eyes. It seemed his whole being reacted as he found the pizza. Grant smiled. "One moment." he said, and turned away. Not a minute passed before he returned with the chair from his room. He positioned it in the doorway for himself to sit. As Grant grabbed a slice for himself he saw Grey pass Charlie a full box. "What's this special treatment?' he asked.

"Any of ya'll can have some." Charlie said, pulling open the box. "Grey asked what I wanted, and I told him."

"You didn't get pineapple on your pizza did you?" Grant asked, knowing full well what the answer was. He watched as Charlie proudly retrieved a slice of pepperoni, sausage, with pineapple. "You're disgusting."

"Refined, brother. I am refined. For I know the value in complimentary flavors, and the truth that pineapple does belong on pizza."

"He's riding with you, from now on, Bob." Grant said to the room.

"Alright, Mr. Grant."

"He's kidding."

"Oh. Okay, Charlie." Bob said, sounding more perplexed.

"Hey." Charlie said. "Why does he get called Mr. Grant, and I'm just Charlie."

Bob shrugged. "I don't know. Because we were friends." he said, sounding more like he was asking, than telling.

"You do know his last name is Bowman, don't ya? He's Mr. Bowman." Charlie offered.

"I like the sound of that, Charlie." Grant said. "You can call me Mr. Bowman."

"Oh, fuck off." Charlie said. "I was just wondering. Thought I'd ask."

"Now you know." Grant said, earning snickers from Grey, and Cahya.

"Don't encourage him." Charlie said to the two amused cohorts. He noticed then that Ifotia was sitting on the bed, where Nikolai had been, and not eating. "You get any pizza, Ifotia?"

"Not yet, Charlie."

He moved closer to her. As much as that was needed in a single room space. He offered her the box with his pizza inside. "You're welcome to have some."

"Grey said he wasn't sure about your pizza." she said.

"Why would he say that?" Charlie asked, looking directly at Grey.

"Ah. No offense, or nothing, Charlie. I like pineapple fine. Mostly with ham, myself. I'm just not sure about the sausage." Grey said.

"Try a piece." Charlie said to Ifotia. "If you don't like it, don't finish it." he extended the box, opening the cover for her. She took one piece. "Excellent!" he said.

Ifotia hadn't tasted anything like it before. The warm softness of the cheese and crust, combined with the complement of flavors, was delightful. The pepperoni was zesty, the Italian sausage savory, and both were complimented by the sweetness of the pineapple. She ate it, and she loved it. She had another piece, and another. As she devoured her fifth piece she noticed Charlie watching her. Their eyes met, but she looked away, and noticed Nikolai was also in the room.

"What was that thing today, Ifotia?" Charlie asked, calling her attention back to him. "You said you knew it."

She looked to the room. All of them watched her. "His name was Enki." she said eventually. "Or, more accurately, it was an echo of Enki. Enki is the Sumarian god of water. I believe the creature we fought today was an echo of the essence of Enki."

"What makes you say that?" Bob asked.

"If it had been the full Enki, we would all be dead." she said.

"Dead?" Grey asked. "Even you?"

Ifotia thought for a moment. "No. I would not die. I would cease to be here. In this realm. We wouldn't have defeated Enki." she paused. "Though Enki would never have been behaving the way that creature was. He loved his people. That thing was just an echo."

"Echo or not, how was it here?" Grant asked.

"The Old Ones." she said simply. "They are coming. Fighting to break through the barrier between realms. They want to see humans in fear of them again. To revert the natural order of things."

"That doesn't sound too good." Grey said.

"It will destroy this world." she looked at Charlie. "It would bring Armageddon."

"And that's why you are here." Charlie said, more than asked.

"Yes. That, along with your prayer, brought me here." Ifotia said.

"I wasn't praying." Charlie snarled to no one in particular.

"Efforts were already being made to get me here, in your world. When you called out, I was drawn here." she looked to the others in the room, her eyes rested finally on Nikolai. "I believe I am supposed to be here."

"That's all well and good, but it doesn't fully answer my questions." Charlie said. "What was that flashy sword trick you pulled? Hmm? How many other things can you do that we don't yet know about?" he demanded.

"I can do that." Ifotia said as if ticking off options on a list. "I helped Nikolai heal." she paused.

"Yeah."

"Yeah." she agreed. "I'm not sure of all I can do." she admitted. "I have areas of my memory that are full, vibrant, and rich. While others are dim, and hollow." Ifotia looked to Charlie again. "I didn't know I could call the sword, or banish the echo, until the words came to me, and I remembered. I also didn't recall how much it would drain from me until the power had been taken."

"You'll need to be careful." Cahya said. "One's cup may runneth over, and may be poured out, but a broken cup is never filled."

Ifotia nodded. "Thank you." she said.

"Looks like it will be another mystery for us to learn together." Grant interjected.

"What do you mean?"

"I got a message from the company. While I was on the van."

"Good. Bad. Otherwise?" Charlie asked.

"I'd say odd." Grant said, looking at his brother. "They knew what we had done."

"What do you mean, 'they knew'?"

"Down to the minute, Charlie. They knew where we were, and that we had just killed that beast."

"Oh man." Grey whispered harshly to himself.

"I'm telling you all this because we need to trust each other. Three of us are connected to different organizations, and groups. Then we got a monster, a vagabond... I love you, Charlie," he motioned to Ifotia, "and a goddess." Grant looked at each of them. "As much as Grey will hate to hear this, we're being watched. We're likely being directed. Worst case, we're being manipulated."

"Yeah. I do not like that at all." Grey said.

"Nor do I." Cahya agreed. "The sect of the Open Eye does not treat their chosen in this way."

"I don't think it's your people." Grant said to Cahya. "Or yours, Grey."

"I certainly hope not."

"That is something we will need to address later, to find out who is pulling the strings. For now we know this. People are getting hurt." Grant's voice took on a firm, resolved tone. "I don't care if people are trying to pull my strings. What I care about is we are here, and we have a job to do. I need to know that I can count on you." he looked at Nikolai. "That you will see things through, as a team." turned back to Charlie. "We'll get answers, but I need us to finish the job. Are you in?"

There was silence for a long moment. Not a silence of fear, or question. A silence of connection, of focus, and resolution. Each person's eyes met the other 's eyes. There were subtle nods. And if one paid close attention, they would have seen the longer than needed connection between Ifotia, and Nikolai. They would have also noticed Bob's clenched fist, as he himself became settled on what was to come. Charlie saw it, and gave Bob an approved look, then looked to his brother. "Where do you want to start next?" Charlie asked Grant.

"The message I received directed us to visit the Adams County Historical Society, and reminded me that the full moon is just a couple days away." Grant said. "So tomorrow, we're looking into what's been killing those cows." his voice lowering. "Then we're going wolf hunting."

CHAPTER II
THE LOWE FARM

There are common ways people typically start their mornings. Some people get their exercise in. Some enjoy drinking coffee. Other folks eat breakfast. Then there are those who detest mornings, no matter their routine. Charlie was craving the motel's offering of an all you can eat breakfast that included fresh eggs. Before he could partake Charlie had to finish what they were doing first. It was important, after all. When it was done, and they were on their own. Charlie was getting eggs.

"I've got a full house, a straight, and two pair, jokers wild." Charlie said.

"Very good." Grant said. "What about you, Grey?"

"Well, I've got four of a kind, twice, and a small flush."

"With my two straights, and the couple three of a kind I've got over there, we should be set." Grant said.

"I think you're right." Charlie agreed. "What?" he asked Ifotia, who watched on with a lost look on her face.

"I do not understand." she said.

"Me either." chimed in the pair of Bob, and Cahya.

"We're preparing." Grant said. "We do know what we're walking into next."

"Preparing." Bob said. "Through poker?"

"It is a game they play." Nikolai interjected.

"I know what poker is." Bob said.

"No. No. Bob, this is not real poker. They are using terminology from the game to describe their available ammunition." Nikolai said as if it were obvious.

"Yeah! Since I use pistols. Primarily. I have four of a kind, twice, with my clips." Grey explained, showing the eight full clips to the three of them. "And a small flush." now pointing out his knives. "Ya know?" he asked. "It can be confusing. Charlie thought it up, and taught it to me. Didn't know Grant knew."

"That's because Charlie didn't think it up." Grant said, giving an 'I got you sucker smirk' to Charlie.

"Oh, was it you, Grant?"

"Our daddy thought it up. Taught it to both of us." Grant explained. "Never could figure why he never just said what things were, but it was fun, and made the task enjoyable."

"The man had his secrets." Charlie added.

"Grey explained it correctly. Each term relates to our cache of weaponry and ammo." Grant said. "That is also why I listed the most hands." he smiled wide. "I have the most weapons."

"I think I understand. Thank you for that explanation and examples." Cahya said.

Bob nodded, an expression of concern still hung upon his face. He looked from one man's collection of items, to the next. Then back. Charlie caught his eye with a 'what's your problem' look on his face. "I do have one more question." Bob said.

"Spit it out."

"Well, you see. I follow now how the name applies to the type of weapon, or ammo, and how in order for it to fully make sense the other people would have to know what the other guys have in advance." Bob paused like he watched the pieces click together.

"That's a pretty clever way to communicate status in a fight without giving away your actual inventory. Hmm... I like that."

"What is your question, Bob?" Grant asked.

"It's for Charlie. You see. As much as I understand, I still cannot think of what you would mean by jokers wild." Bob said.

A snort came from Grant, and a light chortle from Grey, as Bob's question registered. Charlie gave Bob a tight half smile. The kind that only moves part of your mouth, and rarely shows teeth. He tightened up his bag, his weapons and ammo inside, and tossed it up onto the bed by Bob. Charlie rose from where he, Grant, and Grey had been sitting as they inventoried their supplies. Bob stayed seated on the bed, watched Charlie, and waited for an answer. Charlie put his hands in his pockets. Eventually his hands located what they were searching for, retrieved it, and tossed it in Bob's lap.

The item was not large, and not small. Nonetheless, its smooth surfaces made it difficult to grasp as Bob fumbled it in his hands. He looked up at Charlie.

"Jokers wild, Bob." Charlie chuckled. "Good morning, ya'll."

"Where you off to?" Grant asked.

"Gonna go see a man about some eggs." Charlie said. "I'll meet you all by the vans when you are ready to go." he said, and left the room.

Bob ran his finger along the curved edge of the smaller metal item. The polish was dull, and it appeared to be old. He held it up to Grant. "Jokers wild?" Bob asked.

"That's Charlie's favorite flask." Grant said. "Must mean something. Him leaving it with you."

Contemplation and interest washed over Bob, and he looked at the metal flask with recognition, and pride in that moment. "You may be right, Mr. Grant. You may be right."

After necessities were cared for, and Cahya was thoroughly satisfied that he would never beat Nikolai in leg wrestling, they piled into Grant's van, and the purple Windstar. Grant knew they needed to go to the Adams County Historical Society, as directed by the ominous voice on the phone call. They weren't starting there, however. Their first stop was going to be Lowe, and Offerman farms, where the cows were mutilated.

About 45 minutes North West of the motel they located the Lowe farm. It was like something off of a tourist postcard. A slight roll to the ground allowed the eye to follow the fields into the distance, broken up sporadically by collections of trees. The Lowe home itself rested upon a pristine patch of land, well manicured, complete with a large red barn, and two smaller red shed style buildings flanking the home. Also, like the postcard photos, there was no one to be seen.

They pulled into the driveway, and parked their vehicles. Grant moved around the van to talk to Bob in his purple Windstar. "I don't see anyone." Grant said.

"We didn't either." Grey offered from the passenger seat of the Windstar.

"We need to spread out, but not spook anyone." Grant said, looking past Bob. "Ifotia, Nikolai." he paused, his mind getting settled, that he was about to directly ask Nikolai to do something. His stomach turned. "Walk the perimeter, and keep an eye out for anything suspicious." Grant turned to Bob. "You, and Grey, approach the house. See if anyone's home."

"Yeah!" Grey said. "I'm bringing my EMF meter."

"Keep it subtle." Grant said. "I'm taking Charlie, and Cahya, with me. Good?"

"Sounds good, Mr. Grant." Bob said.

Grant left them to it. He, Charlie, and Cahya moved from the van, and began walking onto the grounds. "Barn?" Grant whispered to Charlie.

"Yep."

"I will walk the outside." Cahya offered.

Grant gently placed his hand on his pants pocket, an easy distance from his sidearm, should it be needed. As they drew close to the barn they heard a low rumble, almost like a growl. Grant shouldered the door, bursting in, his gun drawn. Charlie hot on his heels.

"Howdy there, boys." said a middle aged, gentle looking man, as he shut off the generator near his workbench. "You sure know how to make an entrance."

He heard Charlie's own low growl behind him, as he put his gun away. "Our apologies, sir. Are you Mr. Lowe?"

"One and the same."

"We umm... We thought there may have been danger." Grant said.

"You're here about the cows, huh?" Mr. Lowe said.

"We are." Grant reached for his wallet, and his fake FBI identification. "We're with the..."

"The FBI. Yeah, the sheriff phoned a couple days back. Said you may be by."

"So helpful." Charlie muttered.

"What's that?"

"The sheriff." Charlie said, swallowing what he wanted to say. "He is a helpful guy."

"Yeah. Nathan is a fair sheriff. I grew up with him, so you know, that forms a man's view of things."

"I'm sure it does." Charlie said.

"Enough of that." Mr. Lowe said. "Let me show you the cows."

"They're still here?"

"Yep. Sure are." Mr. Lower confirmed. "I couldn't process them after they were attacked." He opened a rear door to the barn, and led them out. "No butcher in the state worth their spit would have touched them."

"So they were attacked?"

"Sure hope so. Otherwise I'm in trouble."

"Why do you say that?"

"Insurance doesn't cover negligence. Besides, I don't know what else leaves tooth marks like these."

"Hello!" came Cahya's cheerful warm voice.

"Mr. Lowe, this is Cahya. He is a member of my team." Grant explained.

"Pleased to meet you, and please, call me Bob." Mr. Lowe said.

"No can do, Chief." Charlie said, to a perplexed looking Mr. Lowe. "It's no disrespect. Fact is, we already have a Bob on our team, and it'd get damned confusing calling you both Bob."

"It's just our names." Mr. Lowe said.

"That it is, Mr. Lowe."

Mr. Lowe gave another look to Cahya's unconventional outfit of flowing garments, a tunic, shoulder bag, and wrapped footing. Then he looked to Charlie, in his black, thigh length duster, black denim jeans, and black leather boots, with a dark gray t-shirt. He addressed his words to Grant as he said. "Unconventional uniforms for federal officers, huh?"

"Can't believe everything you see on television."

"Suppose that is true." Mr. Lowe said, and resumed their walk. "I figured you, and the big guy, to be some kind of Molder and Scully team."

"Really?" Charlie asked, a laugh caught at the back of his throat. "Which of us is Scully?" he asked, and received a smack from Grant.

"He is, clearly." Mr. Lowe said, as he pointed over his shoulder at Grant. "Speaking of, I never caught your names."

"I'm Charlie Blackwater, and this beautiful skeptic is Agent Grant Bowman."

"But you're not an agent?"

"I'm a consultant." Charlie said. "Grant is the professional. He calls guys like Cahya, and me, in to help where he thinks we can, Mr. Lowe."

"Ok. That makes sense. Though you can call me, Bob. Can't imagine you would be around here long enough for that to become an issue with your other Bob." Mr. Lowe said. The guys were quiet like they were waiting for the other to speak up first. "Wait." Mr. Low said. "You think there is more to this than animal attacks, don't you?"

"What would give you that idea, Mr. Lowe?" Grant asked.

Mr. Lowe seemed to endure a sharp, and quick internal debate before he spoke again. When he did he squinted like you do when you're looking into the sun, only he wasn't facing the sun. It was like he was uncomfortable with what he was about to admit to. "Ya know, Sheriff Dogberry?"

"Sheriff Dingleberry?" Charlie quipped. "We've met."

"Dingle.. Heh. I like that." Mr. Lowe said. "Anyways, Nathan never was a good listener. He was a bullheaded young man, and he's no better now. I like him well enough. But when he came up here to look into my claim for the insurance company, he seemed convinced about what he'd find, before I'd shown him anything. Don't get me wrong. He probably did me a favor over all. Doubt the insurance company would have processed the claim based on my information. I'm surprised the FBI is even here. Didn't think he'd call you out, thought for sure he didn't listen to the thing I said." Mr. Lowe paused. "Nathan is a fair sheriff." he said, as if to reassure himself.

"He didn't call us, Bob." Grant stated plainly. He knew his words would burst whatever comfort bubble was forming in Mr. Lowe's head. Still, he said what needed to be said. "We experienced first hand how skilled of a listener Sheriff Dingleberry is not. We want to listen. Tell us what he was unwilling to hear."

"First, I'll show you." he said, as he reached down, and pulled up a tarp. The plastic covering made a cracking, rippling sound as he whipped it back. The surface shimmered in the sunlight. As it moved it revealed a large hole, filled with the bloated, decaying bodies of Mr. Lowe's cattle. The revealed sight brought with it a gut churning stench that wafted up into the air around them. "Sorry about the smell, boys. Not much can be done about that."

"Fuck." Charlie muttered from under the hand placed over his mouth and nose.

"How many were lost?" Grant asked.

"Sixteen." Cahya said.

"Very close." Mr. Lowe said. "There are sixteen in this grave. We've lost 18 in total." he looked at Cahya. "How did you know?"

"I just knew."

"When did it happen?" Grant asked. "We heard it was two attacks, roughly 28 days apart."

"Yes, that is correct. During nights of the full moon." Mr. Lowe said. At that moment they all started as a dark, shaggy, barking dog bound around the barn toward Mr. Lowe. "Oh, quiet you mutt." he called out, and knelt down to pet the affectionate animal. "Frank, this is the FBI. Fella's this is my boy, Frank."

"Well hello there, Frank." Cahya said. He knelt to pet the dog. "He is a beautiful breed."

"He's mutt. Some kind of shepherd dog, and a breed that barks too damn much. He is perfect for the farm."

"He is, in fact, twenty six percent Australian Cattle Dog, fifty eight percent Border Collie, and sixteen percent Chocolate Labrador Retriever." Cahya shared casually. "Unfortunate about the Chocolate lab. They are not the brightest of the canines. Likely why he feels the need to bark frequently." he said to no one specific, and continued to pet the gregarious dog.

"How does he?" Mr. Lowe said to Grant, a thumb pointed at Cahya. At that moment Bob, and Grey, rounded the barn. Their arrived captured Mr. Lowe's attention, and stole away his question. "Who's this now? I see the wife sent you with lemonade."

Bob, and Grey, were indeed carrying multiple mason jars of a sweet smelling yellow liquid. They handed them out to the group, with each having carried three beverages, there was one for each man. Mr. Lowe motioned them back toward the barn, and away from the smell. Cahya remained near the grave, as he pet, and conversed with Frank.

"Mr. Lowe." Grant said. "This is Grey, he is our tech specialist, and Bob, our transportation specialist."

"I'm also a handyman." Bob offered. "I can fix most things, but specialize in automobiles, HVAC systems, and general carpentry. I noticed your front door could use some attention."

"Thank you, Bob." Charlie said, cutting him off. "As good as this lemonade is, and it is good. Kudos to your bride for such a treat. Can we get back to that grave of wasted steaks you have stewing outside?"

"Yes, of course." Mr. Lowe said.

"The wounds. Those aren't typical wolf bites." Charlie said.

"I didn't think so either. After the first attack I was suspicious. After the second one I was certain." he lowered his voice conspiratorially. "I saw him."

"Who?"

"The creature. I was here when it attacked."

"What was it?"

"Are you sure? I don't need to be laughed at again." Mr. Lowe said. He looked to each of them, and received only sincere looks of interest. "It was a werewolf," he said finally.

"Are you worried it will come back in the next full moon?"

"I'm not worried. I'm certain it will. That's what I'm doing in the barn. Preparing for that eventuality."

"Why are you certain?" Grant asked.

"Only me, and Rick, have had our stock hit. I've asked around. It's only us." Mr. Lowe explained. "It isn't me, or my wife. Means it's gotta be coming from his household. Could be him."

Charlie could sense the tension rising in Mr. Lowe. Not an overly dangerous feeling, but a solid one that should not be ignored. "Mr. Lowe." he said as soothing as he was able. Which for him is a lot like the difference between a regular mallet, and a rubber mallet. It may be rubber, but something is still hitting you. "What night of the moon did it come?"

Mr. Lowe seemed to pop back into reality a bit firmer. "It was always the second night, when the moon was at its fullest."

"That's what, in two days?" Grant asked.

"Three." Grey said. "I, ah. I looked it up." he said, showing his phone.

Charlie nodded approval to him, and looked back at Mr. Lowe. "We're going to be back here in three days, and we'll be in and out over the next couple of days. We're going to stop this thing for you. Alright?"

"Alright." Mr. Lowe said. "How can I help?"

"You need to keep your home safe, and move all your remaining cattle into that central corral out there." Grant said. "When it comes to three nights from now. I need you inside, keeping yourself, and your wife safe. Understand." Grant could tell by the look on Mr. Lowe's face that he did. "Thank you for talking to us, and please, thank your wife for the lemonade." he said, and set his mason jar down near the entrance back into the barn. Grant passed through the barn, and traced his steps back to the van.

The others shared similar sentiments, and followed Grant. Bob stepped up to Mr. Lowe, a bright smile on his face. "Hello Sir. I understand your name is Bob as well."

"Yes, hello, Bob. I'm Bob Lowe." Mr. Lowe said, and extended his hand to Bob, who shook it.

"My name is Bob Doe." he said, and chuckled when he realized how similar their names were. "Are you a Robert that goes by Bob, or are you a Bob, Bob?"

"I'm a Bob."

"Wonderful. I am also." Bob said. "Wouldn't it get discombobulated if we were around each other often, with everyone trying to talk to us." Bob chuckled. "Who would they want? Bob or Bob? And they can't use our full names, or even our last names. Do you want Lowe, or Doe? Ha! That could get tough."

Mr. Lowe was laughing now, as he caught the wisdom in Charlie's words.

"Ha! I didn't catch that. Did you catch that? Discom-BOBulated."

They both gave way to laughter. A horn honked, and Bob excused himself, handing Mr. Lowe his mason jar, now void of any lemonade, and raced to the purple Windstar.

The team left, and opted not to visit the Offerman farm at this time. They had seen the farm that had suffered the most deaths to its livestock, and they needed to get to the Adams County Historical Society before it closed for the day.

As they drove, Charlie listened to Cahya go on and on about how wonderful it was to visit with Frank the dog. He expounded on each detail that Ifotia, and Nikolai missed out on. What Charlie didn't miss is how close the two sat to each other, and how comfortable Nikolai looked. It was a welcome distraction from the replay of the gore in his mind. The shocking devastation the Lowe family had suffered. He wondered to himself how this was all connected. The watching big brother, the shadow god at the lake, Ifotia's appearance, and how involved was his own demon? How much had Charlie's own choices contributed to what they were dealing with.

"Soon, Charlie."

He heard it, and he jumped. Not dramatically, but that kind of start you feel when a car cuts you off a little too close, and your heart feels like it tripled in size. That was what he felt. It was the voice, but whose voice was it?

"Are you alright, Charlie." Ifotia asked.

"I'm solid." he lied. He was far from solid. The thought of catching a nap between the Lowe farm, and the Historical Society, was robbed from him by the images that flooded his mind each moment he closed his eyes. The bodies of those cows opened up, bloated, and laid bare. The bite marks that looked to be three times the size of a wolf's bite. He'd never faced a werewolf before. Cahya said he had, and claimed it was not so bad. But there is a pattern with Cahya's stories, and Charlie was convinced that no matter what happened, or what Cahya faced, so long as he lived, the experiences were not so bad.

Charlie adjusted in his seat. He watched the telephone poles go by. His eyes tracked the up and down rolling of the barbed wire fencing, and he joked to himself that it doesn't take much to keep corn in. He soon found himself dozing off. The world went black to Charlie, it was just the hum of the engine, the wheels on the road, and once again the voice in his mind saying. "I'll see you soon, Charlie."

CHAPTER 12

HISTORICAL SOCIETY

"He ate how many?" Grant asked.

"He ate twelve."

"Regular cheeseburgers, or quarter pounders?"

"They were regulars. Still, he ate twelve in one meal."

"Where does he put it?" Grant asked. "Cahya isn't that big of a guy."

"That he ain't." Charlie agreed. "Hell, you see all the shit he pulls out of that bag of his?"

"I have. It's concerning." Grant said, and he and Charlie gave way to laughter.

"Hey guys?" Grey called from the back of the van. "Where are we?"

"We're about three minutes from the Historical Center. Why?" Grant said.

"Because three of our sensors just lit up, and my EMF meter is going crazy." Grey explained. "Something is close."

They pulled into the parking lot of the Adams County Historical Center, twenty minutes remained before closing. As pleasant as the drive was, Charlie struggled with why they had to drive all the way here, and lose their whole afternoon. He figured there were any number of things they could have been doing instead. This wasn't a sight seeing venture. Besides, the Historical Center wasn't much to look at. This far into Iowa, there just wasn't much to look at. More than that, Charlie didn't like Grey's update. If something was close, this wasn't the place Charlie wanted to deal with it.

Parked, they unloaded and gathered at the stairs to the Historical Center. Bob looked uncertain, and Nikolai looked occupied. Ifotia had her now common look of inquisitive interest. While Cahya remained in his state of almost perpetual zen, Charlie noted he was standing very close to Ifotia. She did save him from the lake. A reality that still lingered upon Cahya. Next to Charlie, Grey had his EMF meter out, a single earbud in to listen to something, and muttered to himself. Charlie nudged him with his elbow.

"Hey. Yeah, Charlie?" Grey said.

"Pay attention."

"Right. Right." he said, and removed the earbud.

Grant spoke to them in a calm, controlled voice. "We each see things a little different," he said. "Ifotia claims divinity, while I'm bound more to what I can explain through evidence, and science." Grant took a breath. "Fact is, we've already seen some things on this trip that I have no way to explain. Yet, I know they happened. So here we are. Before we go inside, we need to be on the same page."

"What seems to be the concern?" Cahya asked.

"He's worried we're being worked." Charlie said.

Grant looked at his brother, and rolled his eyes. "It ain't quite that simple."

"The hell it ain't."

"Listen." Grant asserted, interrupting Charlie, and focused back on the group. "Let's walk through this quick, ok?" they all nodded in agreement as Grant continued. "How'd we end up together?"

"Charlie called me here." Ifotia said, sounding excited to contribute.

"Right, and the rest of us?" Grant asked.

"Well, see, you called me. Well, not me. You called Charlie, or for Charlie. Never-mind. You called, and I answered, and you said you needed Charlie's help. So we came." Grey said. "We, as in, us. Nikolai and me. Seeing as we were with Charlie already. Yeah. That's how we got here."

"Cahya was already with me because we had just finished a job." Grant said.

"That was a dirty job." Cahya said. "I do not know when I will be able to eat burritos again."

"Burritos?" Grey asked.

"Never-mind that." Grant interrupted. "The only other piece is I was told to get Charlie."

"You were what?" Charlie asked.

"The company knows we're brothers. They keep an eye on family, and seeing as you were already on their persons of interests list."

"Three times."

"The number of times is unimportant." Grant said. "The fact is they knew. Get that. They knew where they were sending me, and they told me to get you to come with."

"I don't know if I'm comfortable with that." Charlie said.

"Yeah. Not cool." agreed Grey.

"It gets better." Grant said. "We're here, going to the Historical Center, because they directed me to go here."

"Yeah, we knew that." Grey said.

"What I hadn't explained was that their message to come here was sent to me moments after we killed the shadow god at the lake." he paused, made eye contact with each of them. "I'm talking, while you were jamming epinephrine into Cahya's chest, I was getting a call. They knew where we were. Exactly where we were. They knew what we had done. It sounded like someone informing that call had eyes on, and was tracking our movement."

Grey jumped. Moved himself a step back, and looked up and down the area around them. "What are you trying to say, Grant?"

"I'm telling you everything I know. I'm saying that the company is acting weird and I'm not sure who to trust. I'm choosing to trust each of you." Grant said. "Grey. Cahya. I need to know what you've heard from your people. And don't play coy, I know you've heard from them. Pretty sure you check in multiple times a day, Grey." he said, and looked directly at Grey. Then turned to Cahya. "And I've known since Budapest that the Sect of the Open Eye sends you daily messages. They were sending you messages twice a day in Jabuti." Grant took a breath, and collected himself. "I cannot explain with my science, or proof based evidence, what we are dealing with, but we were all at the lake. We all saw the farm. We are in the thick of it, and I am asking... I am needing your trust."

"It's ok, Grey." Charlie said softly to his friend. "Tell him everything."

Grey, uncertain, stepped side to side. He positioned himself back among the group, and looked to Grant. "Yeah. Ok. Alright, Grant." he said, and cleared his throat as he typed something quick into his cell phone. A beat later each member's cell phone either beeped, vibrated, or lit up. "I sent you the information I've been getting. Specifically the last update I received three hours ago. I should be receiving another any minute. They send me one every three to four hours."

"I'll read it later." Grant said. "Give me the cliff-notes."

"There's more here than we've been told." Grey stated plainly. "Either your people at the company are uninformed, or they're lying to you." he sniffed. "Or themselves." Grey gave his head a sharp shake, like he was resetting his own focus, and then the torrent came. "They know about Ifotia. Knew as soon as she arrived. We hacked the mainframe. Iowa isn't alone. Don't know how many yet, but there are more. Energy spikes. Rips in reality. There's concern that Ifotia is a danger. Her arrival signature was similar to the ones tracked in Iowa. The trouble here is three months old. But the major EMF event took place about ten days ago."

"Ten days?"

"Mmmhmm." Grey affirmed.

"That was when I was first asked to start looking into these things." Grant said.

"Not surprising." Grey said. "When the spike of energies happened, that was when we hacked the company, and started keeping track of everything."

Grant seemed less bothered than anyone expected. "Do your people know what we're up against?"

"Not yet." Grey said.

Charlie bumped Grey. "Tell him."

"Ugh. Ok." Grey conceded. "What Charlie is referring to are my EMF readings. When we were at the Museum of Weird my meter spiked. Ifotia saw it." he looked to her for support, and she nodded in affirmation. "I didn't tell her at the time, or anyone really, but I'd seen readings like that before."

"You had?" Ifotia said, sounding hurt, that he had kept that from her.

"Yeah. Sorry, Ifotia." Grey said. "I'd seen them before in Florida. With Charlie." he paused for a moment to swallow. "I saw them when Charlie made his deal with the demon."

"Well shit." Grant said.

"Do you think we are dealing with a demon?" Bob asked, apprehension in his voice.

"That is something we will need to determine." Grant said. "Cahya, do you have anything you can share?"

"Nothing more than what Grey said. Beyond that, in the area that we're in, the Sect senses the presence of a great power." Cahya said.

"What do you recommend we do next?" Charlie asked Grant, and the rest of the group.

"Whoever is inside is expecting us, I'm sure." Grant said. "Problem is, I don't know if the people at the company are on our side or not"

The sliding side door to the van opened, and Charlie pulled out a couple items from his bag. He looked at the group as he closed the door. "Let's go introduce ourselves." he looked to Nikolai. "Stay out here, keep watch. Okay?"

"I will do as you ask, Charlie." Nikolai said.

"I will aid him in this effort." Cahya said.

"I would like to come with you, Charlie." Ifotia said.

"You are." Charlie said. "I need you to stay close to Grant. Grey, you watch my six."

"Will do, Charlie."

"What would you like me to do, Charlie?" Bob asked.

"You're coming in with us. You know we're shit at talking to normal folk. We need our one part translator, two parts public relations guy with us."

"We have a translator?" Bob asked. "I've always wanted to know more languages."

"I'm talking about you, Bob." Charlie said, shaking his head. "Ready?" he asked Grant.

"Let's do it." Grant said, and they moved up the stairs, and inside the Historical Center.

The entrance was one of warm hardwood, and glass doors. The doors glided open with ease. Their footfalls clapped off the tile floor. Beyond the foyer, in the initial lobby was a sign that read: The Adams County Historical Society Welcomes You! The subtext read: Please address any concerns to Maxwell Johnson, Society Director. There were some small groups, families, finishing up their time in the Historical Center. The building was more empty than it was full.

"That's the guy we need to talk to." Grant said, pointing at Maxwell's name.

"I'll catch up." Grey said. He moved away, towards an adjacent room.

"Looks like what we want is downstairs." Charlie pointed at a guide on the wall.

Grant, Ifotia, Bob, and Charlie took the stairs down one level, and found their way to the office of the Director, in the information center. The lower level areas were dim, with overhead lights turning on in response to their movement. They found Director Johnson's office. It was locked. No lights on, and a sign on the glass that read "Out of office".

"Well that makes no sense." Grant said. He checked his phone, and the communication logs. He had his information correct. Adams County Historical Center. Talk to the Director, Maxwell Johnson. "Damnit, Charlie. I don't like this." Grant hissed quietly to his brother.

"We better collect Grey, and skedaddle."

Back on the main level, they found Grey walking the perimeter, focused on his EMF meter. The light on it blinked in a steady rhythm. Between them, and where Grey explored, was an information booth, with a younger looking man stationed behind the counter. A sign hung above the desk that read: Questions?, and it made Bob chuckle. The things you miss when you think you know where you're going. They approached the counter, and left Grey to his mischief for the moment. As they approached the younger man looked up from his work, and noticed them.

"Agent Bowman." the young man said in a pleased tone. "I am happy you were able to make it here so quickly."

"I'm sorry. Do we know each other?" Grant asked, his posture straightened, and alert.

"No." the man said. "We have only just met."

"Then how did you..."

"The company told me you would be on your way." He stood up a bit straighter. "Forgive my manners. I should introduce myself. My name is Josh Rahtlu. It is a pleasure to meet you all."

"Our instructions were to meet Director Johnson." Grant said.

"Yes, that would be preferred, I'm sure. Director Johnson is... away, at present. I am here."

Charlie stepped next to Grant. He didn't like the feeling of this Josh fella, and was certain the less time they spent jaw flapping with him the better. "What do you have for us?" he asked.

"Ah, Charlie Blackwater. The ever so forward vagabond."

"Hey now." Charlie said. "I prefer dinner before pet names."

"As I said, I knew you were coming. I was... looking forward to it." Josh said. "You, Charlie. Grant. Bob. Even inquisitive Grey, over there. I knew you would be here. They didn't mention you." he said, looking at Ifotia. "Who might you be, you exquisite beauty."

"She's with us." Grant interjected, cutting off Josh, and interrupted Ifotia before she could answer, and possibly say too much. Grant could see from his expression, though controlled, that Josh didn't enjoy being interrupted. "Josh, is it? Let's cut to the chase. Hmm? We got two full days at best. What do you need to tell us?"

A tingling sensation moved up Charlie's leg, across his spine, and he felt his right fist clench. He wasn't in control. He looked at his fist. Looked to Grant, who was speaking to the information boy. Every fiber of his being wanted him to strike his brother, but why? He breathed. Found a spot on the wall to focus on. Something to ground him, and he fought the urge. His eyes burned as he focused on the pattern in the wallpaper. Breathe. Breathe. The wallpaper moved, a face turned to look Charlie eye to eye. "Punch Grant Bowman in the face." it said to Charlie, and in the shock of the moment the compulsion gained purchase. Charlie pivoted, his arm shot out, and his fist struck his brother in the head.

"What the hell, Charlie?" Grant asked in surprise.

"Gr..Grant." Charlie stuttered. "That wasn't me. Excuse me." he said, and walked to the far side of the same room Grey was in. His heart pounded in his ears. Grasping for release, Charlie called out to the spirits. No circle, no elements in place, he simply willed for them to hear him. They answered like a symphony orchestra. The thrum of power that reflected back on him knocked Charlie to one knee.

"You've got nice friend's, Charlie."

Charlie opened his eyes, found himself in a black space, the only light shone upon the area encircling him. In the shadows beyond a figure moved. "What do you want?" he asked.

"You owe me, Charlie. It's about time you paid up." the voice said.

"I need to know my friends will be safe." Charlie growled, his suspicions becoming more sure.

"Your friends. Oh Charlie, are you trying to make another bargain with me?' the voice laughed. "Remember what happened last time. Wait." it chuckled more. "You can't."

"We are trying to save people. Just let us do our job."

"Save people. No. Charlie, you are interrupting our fun." the voice hissed. "Not to worry. Things are looking all the better by the minute."

"What are you talking about? What do you want?" Charlie demanded.

"Lives. Blood. The usual. Do look forward to the coming days, Charlie. It will be like old times."

Charlie squinted in pain as light filled his eyes. He felt a hand slap his shoulder. Charlie looked, and Grey was next to him. He hand haplessly slapped his shoulder, as Grey stared in shock toward the information desk. "Grey. Buddy, what is it?"

"That man." Grey said, looking at Josh Rahtlu. "That's the man I ran into outside the bathroom at the museum."

Charlie turned to look at the information desk, his brother still spoke with the information boy, Josh.

"You clearly know less than us." Grant said to Josh. "We should really be speaking with Maxwell Johnson."

"Perhaps this portfolio will help clarify things for you, Agent Bowman." Josh said, as he handed the collection of information he had been referencing their entire conversation. "Though before you go, I do wish you would tell me your name." Josh asked Ifotia.

"My name is Ifotia." she said without hesitation.

"Ifotia." he repeated, as if tasting the word. "Beautiful. That's Sanskrit isn't it? Divine offering, I believe, is the meaning." Josh looked at Ifotia. "Fitting."

"Do you at least know anything about Hell's Gate." Grant asked, and it seemed to recapture Josh's attention. "You know the one, near Hangerford, Iowa. Has a large gate design by some artist."

"W. V. Hees." Josh said matter of factly. "I absolutely adore his work. Died too soon if you ask me. But, as they say. Live as a heathen, die gloriously."

"What?" Grant asked. "No one says that."

"I can tell you that it was a site of great events." Josh offered. He ignored Grant's response. "It is one of five other similar locations throughout the United States. I wouldn't go there."

"No shit Sherlock, we were there. Almost got killed by these cat-like matte black monster things."

"The Mekal." Josh said, acknowledging. "Precious creatures."

"Alright fam, we are outta here." Charlie said as he, and Grey, walked through the room.

"Charlie, why so soon?" Josh asked.

Grey's EMF meter began to chirp from his pants pocket.

"Grant." Charlie said firmly. "Grab the kids."

"Let's go." Grant said.

"Guess we're off." Bob said to Josh. "Thank you again for your help."

"My pleasure, Bob. See you again soon." Josh replied.

"Oh, Okay. Sounds nice." Bob said. "Take care."

Near the door a twinkling caught Charlie's eye. He turned to see the shimmer again, on a map hanging on the wall. He stepped closer, looked quickly. On the map it showed the state of Iowa, the rural area they were in, and other key locations. Charlie looked at the shimmering, twinkling shape. It was his double circle of power, with the runes. The spirits were trying to still answer him. He looked toward the information desk. Josh stood, and watched him. The lights had dimmed, and at that moment only Charlie and Josh were in the building.

"Be seeing you soon, Charlie." Josh said in that now all too familiar voice.

Charlie thought to reply, but didn't. Behind Josh, in the shadows by the stairs, and within the adjacent rooms, small pairs of glowing red eyes began to appear. Dozens of them. Charlie said nothing, kept his eyes on Josh and backed out of the building.

"What the fuck was that, Charlie?" Grant asked as he jumped in the van. "What is up with Grey?"

"Look!" Charlie said. He pointed toward the Historical Center.

The sun was setting, and shadows covered the building. As they backed up Grant watched with Charlie as pairs of red eyes began shining from the windows, the entryway door, and from the bushes about the building. "Shit." Grant said.

"Call it my gut, but that was a trap." Charlie said as they turned on to the road and sped away. "We were being set up."

"What's wrong with Grey?"

"Let's get to the motel." Charlie said. "If what I saw as we left is true. We're going to need to prepare."

"What did you see, Charlie?" Grey asked weakly from the back.

"I saw my circle of power, with my runes, shimmering back at me from a map of Iowa."

"Where on the map." Grant asked.

Charlie took a breath and said. "The Lowe farm."

CHAPTER 13
SALT AND BLOOD

The young man working the check-in counter at the motel was less than amused when Grant came in to reserve another room. It was almost one o' clock in the morning, but it could have been three in the afternoon for all it was to Grant. He was in full Agent Bowman mode.

"I need the room below us. We're in 213." Grant said to the young man.

"I'm sorry man, that room is occupied." the clerk said.

"Which room, closest to that one, is open?"

The young man typed. His struggle with alertness was real. "Umm..." he hummed to himself. "Room 117 is available."

"I'll take it." Grant presented his company credit card. The transaction was processed. The young man handed over the keys, and Grant exited the reservation office. He found Charlie waiting outside for him. "Room 117." he said.

"That's not the room below us." Charlie said.

"I know."

"You do recall that I explained that for this to work we need one of the rooms below ours."

"We have it." Grant said as he started walking toward their rooms. "At least we will have it."

Charlie knew that tone of voice, and could only shake his head. He followed Grant to room 113, the room most directly below their own. As they drew close Charlie saw Grant pull his wallet from his pocket. At the door, Grant struck the door with three firm knocks. Charlie recalled a similar situation they'd been in together in Georgia. Hopefully, this would go better.

The door opened to a worn looking older man. "Yeah. Um, what is it?" the man asked.

"Please pardon the late interruption, sir." Grant said, sounding oddly professional. "We need to ask you to switch rooms to 117."

"At this time of night? Are you serious." the man asked.

"Completely." Grant said.

There was no uncertainty in Grant's voice. His kind, assertive approach seemed to awaken the man, who appeared to want to argue, and comply all at once. "This is ludicrous." the man said. "Are you with the motel? You don't look like motel staff."

"We are not with the motel." Grant stated directly, and before the man could contest further he brandished his fake FBI identification. "FBI."

The wind appeared to leave the man's sails and he dragged. "You're FBI?" he asked, almost bashful.

"What is your name, sir?"

"David. Uh, my name is David."

"Get your things, David." Grant said, looking past him into the room. He saw another body in the bed inside the room. He looked down to meet the man's eyes. "Now, David."

Charlie stepped alongside Grant. "I can take it from here." he said with a smile. He took the key for room 117 from Grant, and stepped into the room. Flicked on the light, and an undeniably artificial light filled the room. A person's eyes never quite adjusted to fluorescent lights like this. Their odd, off white, greenish blue haze was for the eyes what a hangover was for the stomach. Charlie did his best to emulate the oddly professional voice Grant used. "Let's go, people. Chop! Chop!"

The body in the bed stirred. "What... David? David, what is going on?" it grumbled.

"Come. Come, dear." David said. "All is well. There was a small mistake, and we need to switch rooms."

"At this time of night?"

"Sooner you move. The sooner you get back to sleep." Charlie held out his hand. "Your room key, please?" He collected the key to room 113 from the couple, and escorted David and his mostly asleep companion down to room 117. "The room's on us. Enjoy your stay." he said as he left them to return to sleep. Grant had hoped the gesture would help put them at ease. Though Charlie knew first hand that they would be sitting up all night, thankful they survived a brush with the FBI. Charlie had agreed they should pay for the couple's room. Still he enjoyed the visual of the couple laying awake at night. It's the small joys, afterall.

Meanwhile, in their room, Grey, Nikolai, Cahya, and Ifotia had already cleared away space in the middle of the room. The bed turned on it's side, and leaned against the wall. The dresser moved to the corner, the nightstands set on top.

"How's this look Charlie?" Grey asked.

"Why are you asking me?" Charlie said. "I learned all this stuff from you. At this point I'm just guessing." he looked at the space. "Do you think circles here align with the ones above?"

"It does." Nikolai said.

"Yes. I think it matches up too." Bob offered.

"Bob." Charlie said, only then sure Bob had returned. "Were you able to get the things I needed?"

"I was. Though there are reasons we aren't supposed to go to big box stores at this time of night." Bob said. "It is all that was open."

"Thanks for going."

"You're welcome, Charlie." Bob said, handing over the plastic bag.

Charlie removed one of the large canisters of salt from the bag, and tossed it to Grey. "You comfortable with this?" Charlie asked him.

"Yeah man." Grey said. "Cahya is going to run support on me." he looked around. "Is Ifotia going to support you?"

"I think I'll need her to."

"This may be the wrong move." Grey said.

"You know what you saw. I believe you." Charlie said. Thinking briefly of what he himself saw. Those red eyes. All moving in and surrounding Josh within the Historical Society. So many eyes. Charlie looked to Grey. "We must try."

"You're right, Charlie."

"Let's begin." Charlie said, then raised his voice to the rest of the group. "We're running out of daylight here folks. We wait too long, and this dog won't hunt."

Grey, and Cahya, returned upstairs with Bob. Nikolai, and Ifotia, stayed with Charlie. Charlie took out the remaining canister of salt, and began laying down his two circles of power according to the premeasured markings from Grey. Once the circles were down, Charlie placed candles at the five points of the star. In the room above he was certain Grey was doing the same. Everything was in place, candles were ready to be lit. Once Grey was set up, Bob would call Nikolai, and with the call on speaker, Charlie and Grey would activate their circles together. Charlie's working theory is with the two circles placed above each other, if activated together, would create one unified circle. It would allow them to utilize their shared power.

"Charlie." Grant called from the entry of the room. He stepped in and closed the door behind him.

"Watch the salt!" Charlie said. "Just, sit." he said, gesturing to a chair in the corner. Grant sat. "What is it? Are we good?" Charlie asked.

"You sure this is the right move? Grant took a seat in the chair.

"It is the necessary move."

"Because you think that boy at the Historical Society is connected to the demon?" Grant asked. "Your demon?"

"Yes." Charlie said. "He is either connected, or he is the demon."

"Wouldn't you know if he was?"

"I don't know. Which is the problem." Charlie said, frustration in his voice. "I don't remember everything, Grant. Specifically, I don't remember anything from around that time. I've never really had cause to know more than I do. I made a deal with a demon, and at some point I knew it was going to come a calling for its payment. I didn't know when." Charlie's hands formed fists at his sides. He exhaled deeply, his eyes lost in the middle distance. "Figured if I focused on knowing my powers. On learning them. If I focused on being powerful... Well, then when the demon returned I could fight it off." he paused, and looked to Grant. "I think I was wrong."

"What are you not telling me, Charlie?" Grant asked, having seen the concerned look on Nikolai's face from the corner of his eye. "What is it?"

"Tell him, Charlie." Nikolai said. "You don't talk to Grey or I about it. Tell Grant. Everything."

Charlie's shoulders fell, the way a beast of burden looks after the yolk is removed. Like Nikolai's encouragement was the permission that Charlie needed. "I have dreams, Grant." he said. "They come, and go. Overall they've been easy to manage. Over the last couple weeks they've been bad. Hell, the night before Ifotia showed up, I woke up in the woods behind where we were staying." he juggled the salt in his hand. "In the last few days, they've been worse. I'm hearing him, the demon. The prick is taunting me. Says we'll be seeing each other soon." Charlie's voice took on a deep, angry growl. "Talks like it's watching us." '

"What will this do?" Grant asked, gesturing at the salt on the floor.

"I need to remember, Grant. I need to remember what happened, why I made the deal, and if in remembering there is something that can tell us how to defeat this motherfucker." anger filled Charlie's voice. "It took my memories from me for a reason. My thought is these joined circles of power will allow Grey, and I, to both search my mind for answers."

"What about Cahya, and Ifotia?"

"They are going to be here to support us." Charlie said. "They're here to pull us out."

"Pull you out?" Grant asked.

"Pretty much. This is what could be called big magic." Charlie said with a shrug. "I know I've never done anything this big. Not sure what could go wrong."

"Damn, Charlie. What if this kills you?"

"Don't think it will come to that. Besides that's why I need you to be here to pull the fire alarm if things look like they are going sideways."

"Why the fire alarm?" Grant asked.

"It will set off the sprinklers." Charlie explained. "It's like electricity. Same reason the world feels clean after a heavy rain. The water defuses magical energy, grounding it. Plus, if you pull the switch, and turn on the sprinklers, it will dissolve the salt circles."

"Couldn't I just kick them out, and break them?"

"You could... technically." Charlie tossed the empty salt canister away. "That might kill you."

"Bullshit, it's salt, Charlie."

"Salt that will be helping to hold back an unmeasured amount of magic. Magic built up by the combined efforts of the four of us." Charlie said, a serious look on his face. "The sprinklers will dissolve all four circles in as close to unison as we're going to get with our present circumstances."

"How'd you learn all this, Charlie?"

"Grey's help, plus a lot of trial and error." Charlie said, smirking. His face took on a serious look again. "I'm willing to bet it's all connected. All of it. The shadow god, the creature attacking the cows, the reason the demon is harassing me. Hell, those little black cat looking things that tried to eat my face. It's all connected, and I don't know for sure how we beat it. I damn well know I'm not going in there without being as prepared as possible."

A look passed between Grant and Charlie. Resolution, support, and love washed over their faces. Grant nodded once. "I'll be here, brother," he said. "I'll be right here when you get back, and we'll finish this together."

Nikolai's phone rang. "Hello Bob," he said. "Yes. I knew it was you. I was expecting your call." he shook his head. "We are prepared here. I am placing you on speaker."

"Good approach to doing this." Bob's voice came through the phone. "I suppose I should put my phone on speaker also."

"Good plan, Bob." Charlie called out.

"Oh! Hello, Charlie."

"Can Grey, and Cahya hear me?"

"Hey Charlie!" came Grey's voice. "We're reading you loud and clear, buddy."

"You sure you're good with this?" Charlie asked.

"It isn't the most exciting way to spend my night, but yeah man. I'm sure."

Ifotia moved close to Charlie. He felt her hand upon his arm. "I hadn't realized until this moment that you're a little taller than me," he said.

"Just a little." Ifotia replied with a smile. "Are you ready?"

"As ready as I'll ever be." Charlie said, then raised his voice. "Light the candles." He could hear the click of the lighter popping through the phone, and in a small way pitied their process as he watched Ifotia light all five of their candles with little more than the pivot of her finger.

"All lit, Charlie." Grey said. "I'm ready when you are."

Charlie pulled a knife from his belt. He saw Grant tense, and Charlie raised his hand to calm him. "On three, Grey." He placed the blade against the skin of his left palm, and pressed. "Three..." Blood formed upon the meaty flesh. "Two..." Charlie knelt near the inner salt circle, allowed drops of his blood to fall upon both circles. The outer first, then the inner circle. "One." he said firm and loud, at the same time applied his will to the task. He could feel a warmth behind him, it came through Ifotia's hand upon his arm. Tension filled the air, like the pressure of a door closing on an airtight room. Charlie could sense Grey's familiar power above him, as well as Cahya. So much power surrounded him. He could hear Grey's voice come through the phone, joining his own, as they said the words.

SOMETHING ABOUT THE FLORIDA SUN MADE IT BRIGHTER THAN OTHER PLACES. At least that was how Charlie saw it. Though it may be brighter in Hawaii, he reasoned to himself. It was a typical Tuesday all in all. The plan was to meet his daddy, and brother for drinks at some hole in the wall bar in Indian Shores. Charlie liked the place. Liked its style. Something about it spoke to him. Didn't hurt that the walls were covered in old dollar bills, along with ladies bras, and panties. They only went to the classiest places after all.

Charlie arrived early. Took advantage of the opportunity to flirt with the bartender he liked. Enjoyed a few beers. Not the light ones the tourists seem to enjoy. Charlie enjoyed full flavored brews, and he never enjoyed just one. The time passed, no word from his daddy, and brother. He figured Grant and the old man could handle themselves, why worry? He'd stay put, enjoy another drink, and they'd know where to find him.

A man in a dark grey suit sat next to Charlie at the bar. Charlie never could figure why folks had to sit by him when there were plenty of seats available. Still, the man sat. He looked younger, definitely not old, and sharp in his suit. Charlie figured him for a businessman. An out of town businessman, judging by his drink of choice. Charlie ordered another beer.

"How long will you wait?" the businessman asked.

"Excuse me?" Charlie said.

"You look like you're waiting for someone. How long are you planning to wait for them?"

"Not seeing how that's any of your business." Charlie said.

"It may not be my business." the man said. "I thought I may be helpful and save you some time."

"You're gonna save me time, huh?" Charlie laughed. "How would you do that? Convince me to go home? I ain't waiting for some dame."

"No?"

"No."

"I do imagine a father and brother are worth more of an investment than some dame." the man said.

"What did you say?"

"See here, friend. I only mean to help."

"What did you say?" Charlie asked again, anger giving way in his voice. The alcohol stirred the flames as it were. You see, Charlie's brother, Grant, was a Federal agent. His daddy was retired. Still, Grant would bring his daddy in to consult at times. Help him with cases. Kept the old man outta trouble, and it was what brought them to Florida. Now, they're three hours late, and some fancy man in a suit was sitting here talking shit. Charlie saw red. "I suggest you exercise your right to speak, and do it fast, before you lose it forever."

The businessman smiled, and finished his drink. He stood, and turned to Charlie. "Why don't we speak outside?"

Rage filled Charlie as he grabbed the svelte man by his tailored dark grey suit. In one smooth motion he lifted the businessman from his feet, and introduced his back to the hardwood wall twelve feet to their left. "What are you playing at?" he growled at the businessman. "You waltz in here, scootch up next to me, and start spitting foolish words about my kin." he boiled inside. "You best start explaining yourself. Who are you? What does this have to do with my family?"

The businessman took a breath. His eyes met Charlie's. "My name is Joshua. I'm here to offer you my help."

"Your help?" Charlie said in an amused growl. "The fuck would I need help from you for?"

"Because your father, and brother are going to die, Mr. Blackwater. Depending upon what you choose to do, I may be able to help you save one of them."

CHAPTER 14

FAIR DEALS

According to Joshua, Charlie's daddy and brother were thirty miles away at The Florida Aquarium. They were supposed to meet a contact in Tampa. The contact selected this location. Charlie and Joshua completed the forty five minute drive to the aquarium in less than thirty. The Florida Aquarium closed at 5pm. They arrived close to six o' clock to an empty lot. Minimal lights still illuminated the facility. Charlie parked his Caprice in a spot near the entrance to the parking lot.

"We're here. Start explaining." Charlie said to Joshua.

"They're not here yet." Joshua said.

"There ain't nobody here, smart-ass." Charlie gestured to the open parking lot. "I'm about out of patience with you."

Joshua opened the passenger side door, and stepped out of the car. Charlie watched him walk to the front of the vehicle, and lean against the hood. He vacated the car, and moved to stand by Joshua.

"They aren't here yet." Joshua said.

"Where are they?"

"On their way."

"Why are we here if they're not here?" Charlie asked.

"Your father, and brother, are involved in things beyond their understanding." Joshua said, ignoring Charlie's question. "It's no problem telling you this because once you accept my offer, you won't remember this conversation in the least."

"You're not making any sense, boy." Charlie growled at the younger looking man.

"Boy?" Joshua said amusedly. "Oh, Charlie. I am eons old. I was there when your kind was formed from clay." his face took on a somber look. "I was there when your kind were chosen above us." a hard crisp edge came to his voice. "And I'm here now. To make a deal with you. Because it is some of the only entertainment we have left. We can't return home. We aren't allowed to mate. Sure, we can share in pleasure with your kind. That momentary bliss. Void of all reward." Joshua lowered his head, gently moving it from side to side. "Even when we were able to procreate, our offspring were born sterile. Sterile. Can you imagine the utter pain we felt? The realization of how unimportant we were compared to you. Humans."

Charlie felt confused. What in the world was this guy going on about?

"Of course, to address that we were pulled home, and forced to watch as all of our progeny were killed in a massive act of genocide. You all just call it a flood. Not just those silly Christians either. So many know it happened, and continue to be ok with it."

"What the hell are you going on about?" Charlie asked.

"Of course, Charlie. I digress. Let us get back to you, and our deal."

"Lets." Charlie said, unsure of what to make of Joshua's ranting.

"Allow me to show you something." Joshua said. Before Charlie could respond Joshua's right palm was against Charlie's forehead.

Power, and sensations rushed into Charlie. It felt like diving into a warm pool. The water, both cool, and comforting to your pores all at once. He felt the power flow from Joshua's hand, over his head, shoulders, body, until everything else ceased to exist. Charlie had never felt anything like it. A unique feeling at this stage of life. Significant, considering the amount of awareness altering things Charlie had experienced. The sensation settled upon him, like a blanket. Like a blanket of thorns.

Pain surged, and awareness flooded Charlie. He saw his daddy. Blood stained the collar of his daddy's shirt. It looked like he was trying to say something, but Charlie couldn't make it out. His daddy had a handgun in his hands, and a rifle slung over his shoulder. If not for the blood, he'd look like a businessman with a score to settle. In that moment, he looked spent, panicked, and something Charlie had never seen, he looked scared.

Charlie tried to go to him, and couldn't. His arms were bound by chains. The chains wrapped around his wrists, and pulled his arms out to his sides. His shirt was gone. He could see by the bruises on his body that he had been beaten.

"Grant." his daddy said. "Grant, son. I'll get you loose, and we gotta run."

Charlie watched his daddy go to work on his restraints. He was Grant, but what had happened to him? Where were they? He had to figure out where they were. His eyes jetted throughout the space. It looked like a storage locker, or warehouse. The darkness skewed how well he could see the walls. One arm was loose. Charlie heard the chains clatter to the floor.

Movement. A soft impact. Footfalls on the pavement. Charlie heard them, but his daddy didn't seem to notice. Too focused on his task, perhaps? Movement, this time Charlie saw it. In the shadows. There were multiple figures, and they were surrounding them. Charlie tried to say something. His daddy looked up at him, proud to have released his other arm. It was all too late.

Dark figures hit his daddy. They pulled him to the edge of the light, and held him. His daddy struggled against them like a mad dog to no success. Time seemed to slow down. A tall, slender figure stepped confidently into the light. As it did, Grant noticed his daddy's pistol was on the ground near where he was standing.

"We advised you to let it go." the tall woman said. Her skin shone a satiny pale softness. Her hair hung in deep, brown ringlets. "There is nothing you can do to change what is happening. Still, my soft heart wanted to give you a chance to walk away. Now you have given me no choice."

Charlie moved to speak, his words caught in his throat. The tall woman had raised her hand, and in an instant the figures that held his daddy hissed, and roared. They showed their fangs. Hands gripped at his clothing, as they bit down into his daddy's flesh. Blood poured out of the wounds, the vile creatures sucked, and lapped it up hungrily. Charlie knew them for what they were. Vampires. He tried to cry out, only to gurgle a fading sound. It was then that he realized he was being attacked. One vampire had bitten his neck. Another near his shoulder. He was on the ground. He felt another set of teeth dig into his thigh, through his pants. Above him stood the tall, pale, brown haired woman. She looked... regretful. Whatever she said to him, Charlie didn't hear her. He was not able to try to read her lips, as everything went black, and Grant died.

The blanket of power moved from atop Charlie. Disoriented, he tried to collect himself. It took longer than he liked. Soon, however, he had his bearings. They were in the parking lot of the aquarium. The sun was setting, and they were alone. They. Joshua was still standing in front of him. Charlie lunged at him. His hands sought to grab him, and slam him against the hood of the car. They connected. Charlie surged, and found himself without purchase. His back slammed against the hood of the Caprice. Over him, holding him down, was Joshua.

"The fuck did you do to me?" Charlie demanded through slurred speech.

"I know that can be disorienting." Joshua admitted. "It is still the easiest way. To your credit, you handled it better than most. Be thankful you were not John, on Patmos. At ninety years old, the poor soul almost died. Alas, daddy's boy always knows best and insists on having it his way."

"Those creatures. They killed…"

"Not yet." Joshua interrupted. "Not yet, Charlie. They will try, however. Seems your brother is just a bit too good at his job. Isn't he? Alas, it works well for our plans, so I want to help you."

"How does helping me help you?"

"That is all a bit above your pay-grade, isn't it, Charlie." Joshua said, and released his grip on Charlie. "Let's just say that what my brother showed John, in his revelation, wasn't the half of it. No. That lacked all style, for as creative as it was. But it's not for you to be concerned with. You want to save your family, yes?" Charlie nodded. Joshua continued. "I offer you a deal."

"I'm listening."

"You saw what they are up against."

"Vampires." Charlie said, shaken still by what he witnessed.

"Yes, you know their kind. Don't you? You have a friend in one of them, I'm told."

"How do you know so much?"

"Listen carefully, Charlie. I do not enjoy repeating myself." Joshua said. "I can give you power. Power enough to stand against them, and I dare say save at least one."

"One?"

"Listen." Joshua asserted. "I will give you power. Yours to keep for as long as you live, and to use how you like."

"But there's a cost."

"Oh, Charlie, you are so adorably precious. Of course there is a cost. Everything in life has a price. Everything. Including me." Joshua said, pointing at his own chest. "You'll owe me favor in return, Charlie. You'll owe me a favor, anything I ask, whenever I ask it."

"What…"

"No." Joshua interrupted. "No. You'll know when it happens, and you'll comply, or you'll die. Simple as that." he said with an almost friendly smile. "Ah, and your memories, of course."

"My memories? What the hell do you mean, my memories?"

"I can't have you walking about spewing your recollections of this conversation. What I've told you. Shown you." Joshua said. "Certainly not. You'll remember what you need to, while you need to. After you've used your new abilities to save your family, you'll forget."

"This is a shit deal." Charlie said.

"It is the one you have. At least you get a choice. It's not like I'm evicting you from heaven."

"One question." Charlie said.

"We have time, I'm curious to hear it. What is your question?"

"You're claiming to be an angel. A fallen. That makes you a demon."

"Are you asking me or telling me, Charlie? Yes. I'm a demon. What is your question?"

"What is Hell like?" Charlie asked with a chuckle. "Pretty sure I'm headed there eventually. Figured might as well ask."

Joshua looked at Charlie. Looked at him like he was a mathematical puzzle to solve. It felt like he wasn't going to answer until he said. "There is no Hell, Charlie. There is only life and death. Isn't that what father said? I place before you life and death, the blessing and the malediction, and for your part, choose life. All that doesn't matter anyways, Charlie. That wouldn't be your destiny either way."

"Start speaking sense, or you're destined for another ass whoopin'." Charlie said, ignoring the unamused, confident look on Joshua's face.

"Have you ever played chess, Charlie?"

"I have."

"Of course you have. Now imagine chess, but not with a light and dark pitted against each other. Instead varying shades of gray. Dozens of sets on one large board, all squared off to face each other. Can you picture that?"

"I can." Charlie said.

"You are a piece, as am I." Joshua said, pausing. "You are in a different set than I am." he paused again, a pleased look upon his face. "Oh, that is good. That is a good explanation, Charlie. It is too bad you will not remember it. Nonetheless. There it is. You have a destiny that would never lead you to Hell, if it even existed. Now, do we have a bargain? Time is waning."

Charlie nodded. "Yeah. I don't see where I have another choice. I can't let them die."

"Too right, Charlie. Always so noble." Joshua said. "Come here," he instructed, leading them away from the car. "Don't need any avoidable explosions after all." Joshua drew a circle upon the pavement. No chalk, or any writing element present. The line seemed to come directly from him. He stood up when finished. "Step into the circle, Charlie." Charlie did as asked, after he was inside Joshua continued. "Give me your hand." Charlie extended his hand, and Joshua pricked a finger drawing blood. He held Charlie's hand over the circle. They watched the drops of blood hit the pavement. "Do you have any other questions for me, Charlie?"

"No." Charlie said. "If you've fucked me, I will come for you."

"There is no need for that, Charlie. This is all on the up and up. Besides, you and I will have plenty of opportunities to come for each other when the war starts."

"War?" Charlie asked.

"Be seeing you, Charlie Blackwater." Joshua said.

Light filled Charlie's eyes, while he heard a deafening silence. All at once he perceived existence. Not simply the perception of existing. Rather the steps, and elements involved to form existence. He saw light form from nothing. The vast, black blanket of space sparkled to life with stars, and galaxies. He felt when love happened. Knew without question why it had such unfathomable power. The earth formed before his eyes. Plants, animals, the winds, and the churning sea all came to fruition. He saw them. The eyes that watched. The celestial beings observing their playthings. He saw all of it, and it made him burn.

Power flowed through his veins. He opened his eyes, and saw his hand had gripped into the blacktop of the parking lot. It looked like he had tightened his grasp around a thick blanket. Charlie fell back from his crouched position. His butt hit the pavement, and he pushed himself away from the circle until his back rested against his car. Joshua was gone. Charlie jumped to his feet, the lot was still empty. No sign of anyone, and the lights of the facility were now extinguished, except for those odd fire safety lights.

Charlie checked his watch. It was two in the morning. As he got in his car he heard his cell phone vibrate. It was Grant. He answered.

"If you'd turn the volume on your ringer, it'd be easier to get a hold of you." Grant said.

"Grant!" Charlie exclaimed. "Grant, you're ok! Are you ok?"

"Of course I'm ok. Dad's ok too. Are you alright?"

"Yeah." Charlie said quickly. "I'm good. Where are you now?"

"We're at the Tampa Marriott. Where are you?"

"I'm close. Just, umm… give me a couple minutes."

Grant gave him their room number, and they hung up. The Caprice roared to life and Charlie raced to the hotel. When there, he left the keys with the valet, and hurried up to his brother's room. They were on an upper floor. No doubt in a premium room. Charlie knew his daddy wouldn't have it any other way. Always pointing out he'd lived too long to deliberately accept bullshit. Charlie knocked on the door.

"Hey, Charlie boy!" his daddy said, opening the door. "Come in. Come in."

Charlie entered the room. It was every kind of comfort, and smelled of linen, and lavender. It was a three room suite. A bedroom to either side, and a center room that had the couch, bar, and food amenities. The overall color scheme was cream white, very opulent, and elegant. On each of their bed's they had laid out their weapons, supplies, and ammo. This gave Charlie concern. For a moment he hoped that everything with Joshua was a bad dream. He hoped his daddy and brother were ok, and it was over. No harm, no foul. He was wrong. They were preparing. Meaning, what Charlie saw, was still yet to happen.

"Charlie!" Grant called from his room. "Where the hell were you this afternoon?"

"Where the hell were you?" Charlie responded. "I was there, and you never showed."

"Whatever man, we were there. You weren't" Grant said. "Typical."

"Now, Grant. We may have been at the wrong location." their daddy said. "There are a few bars to pick from around here."

"Yeah, I suppose." Grant said.

Charlie kept his mouth closed. What had happened? Did they miss each other? What had Joshua done?

"You ok, son?"

"Yeah, daddy. I'm ok." Charlie hugged his father. "Man it's good to see you." he looked to his father's bed. "Are we counting hands?"

"We were." his daddy said. "Grant is all straights and flushes. While I have two full houses, a couple straights, and jokers wild." he said with a wink.

"Of course you do, daddy." Charlie said. "What are you getting set up for?"

"Meet tomorrow with an informant." Grant said. "This is big Charlie. Could connect a lot of dots on this one."

"Need another hand?" Charlie asked. "I mean, my schedule is open and I've got nothing else going on."

"I have Bob driving for us. You know him, right?"

"Bob is 'good people'."

"He is." Grant agreed. "So we have that covered. I'd happily have you join us, but you know how the company feels about you. Shit, they'd probably be pissed you're even here. Saying something like how I should arrest you."

"That's all a misunderstanding." Charlie said. "It'll blow over."

"Maybe. Still, I need to be careful. It is my job, Charlie."

"I understand." Charlie said. "I'm hearing things is all. Not sure that it's connected to your work, but I'd rather be close, than have you go alone." Charlie kept going before Grant could reply. "We'll keep it off the books. I'll trail you, and stay close. Just in case. Sound good?"

Grant, amused, shook his head. "Yeah, Charlie. Plenty of plausible deniability there."

"Good." Charlie said, not wanting further discussion. Grant would never believe what he'd experience anyway. His brother was a facts and numbers guy. Either science proves it, or it's in question. There was no way Grant would buy that he'd just made a deal with a demon in an effort to save them from a vampire attack. That is completely based in science. Isn't it? "I'll leave you boys to it. Love ya, daddy." Charlie said.

"Love you too, son."

Charlie closed the door, and took the stairs down. His knees wouldn't be the most pleased with this choice, but Charlie was fresh out of people to punch in the face, and the release of energy would do him good.

He tossed and turned all night, and into the morning. The stress of the coming day weighed on him. He awoke to a beeping in the early afternoon. Charlie had placed a GPS locational relay on the grip of one of his daddy's guns. It beeping meant they were on the move, and he needed to be also. Charlie made a mental note to thank his buddy Grey for gifting him such cool toys.

Charlie dressed, and went into the bathroom to care for personal needs before leaving. As he washed up he noticed his hands were black. They were covered in a sooty ash like material. He had it on his face, and his clothing as well. No doubt everywhere he had touched was contaminated. Charlie showered, cleaned himself thoroughly. He redressed, and as he grabbed his boots he noticed his bed looked in disarray. He knew he had slept rough, and thought it would be good to fix the bed before he left. After all, making one's bed always helped with starting the day off right.

He put his boots on, then turned on the light to evaluate his bed. His GPS relay continued to beep at him. Typically such an insistent anything would rake at Charlie, causing him great distress. At that moment, it was a minor concern. Especially when contrasted next to the burned sheets on his bed, and the ash marks in the shape of wings that extended up the walls, and on to the ceiling.

CHAPTER 15

FAREWELL FLORIDA

Some days call for a soundtrack. On days when you know you're about to face off against an untold number of vampires, in order to save your family, it's one of those days. Charlie started the Caprice, and turned on his Led Zeppelin playlist. He gave himself a look in the mirror. Looked deeply into the reflection of his eyes. The rhythm of Cashmere filled the car. It was going to be that kind of day.

Charlie pulled over about half a block down from the parking lot of the hotel where his daddy and brother were staying. He was early. He knew he was, because he knew how Grant and his daddy operated. This was perfectly fine. Charlie had to make a call. He dialed the number, and his call was answered on the second ring. Charlie explained the situation, and what he needed. It wasn't going over well.

"I know it's risky. Given the circumstances you're the only person I can trust with this. Not to mention, in this situation." Charlie said. "If I had a choice, I would do it differently. I don't have that choice. Can you do it?"

"I will do it, Charlie." said the voice on the other end of the phone.

"Thank you." Charlie felt a little relieved. "We'll be at the Florida Aquarium around sunset."

"Of course, Charlie." the other caller said. "I will follow them, and be there when you need me."

They said their goodbyes and ended the call. Charlie dropped the hand that was holding his phone to his lap. He laid his head back against the low headrest of his seat. As he exhaled a deep breath he contemplated the vision he'd seen. How they had restrained his brother, and the look on his daddy's face as the other vampires grabbed him. Charlie ran a mental inventory of the weapons he'd grabbed before he left home. At that moment the passenger door of his car opened. His heart thundered in his chest, and he moved for his pistol as the figure sat down.

"Calm down boy." his daddy said, as he settled into the seat. "If you were so worried, you should've locked the doors."

"Why you sneaking up on me like that?" Charlie asked. "What the hell are you doing here?"

"Sneaking up on you? Ha!" his daddy laughed. "I walked clear as the morning sun. Right there, from the front of the hotel," he pointed, and Bob's purple Windstar could be seen parked in the front entrance pick up area. "I walked open as a church on Sunday, straight up to your car." his daddy looked at him. "The real concern is why didn't you see me. You ok, son?"

"Yeah, of course I am." Charlie said. "I was lost in thought for a moment is all."

"What were you thinking about?"

"It was nothing. I should have been paying attention."

"Do you think I'm stupid? That I was born yesterday?" his daddy asked. "Do not insult me by trying to baffle me with bullshit. You're a Bowman." his voice became stern. "Act like one, damnit."

In that instant Charlie was sixteen again, sitting in the front seat of the Caprice with his daddy. He couldn't lie to his daddy. He had to tell him something. What could he say? That he'd been given a vision by a fallen angel, a demon, and because of that vision he made a deal with that demon. Sure, that would go over smashingly. Especially the part about everyone dying, and being eaten by vampires. Charlie had to say something. He could feel his father's eyes burn into him. "I'm worried about how things are going to go down." he finally said.

"What has you worried?" his daddy asked. "Grant is a professional, and I'm not exactly new at this work. We know what we're doing."

"Call it a gut feeling." Charlie said, hoping it was close enough to the truth to not tip off his daddy's bullshit detector. "What if things go sideways? What if this is a bigger mouthful than you can chew? I'm worried daddy."

"Oh, Charlie. That is always a possibility. Can't let that kind of fear shake you. Ya know?"

"I know, daddy." Charlie felt a humble acceptance weigh on him. "I don't want anything to happen to either of you. I don't want to lose you." The purple windstar started to move toward the street, and Charlie put the Caprice in drive to follow.

"Hey." his daddy's voice came out sharp, commanding, and Charlie put the car in neutral. "Look at me." and Charlie did. His daddy's eyes were void of question, or uncertainty. Their hard blue grey appearance seemed to cut deep into Charlie's very soul. "When it's our time, it's our time. You know this. I love that you care, son. I truly do. I love your heart. All your life you've lived with your heart on your sleeve. There's a time and a place for that. Now's not the time." his daddy took a breath. "You gotta get settled on this, and get settled right fuckin' now. If we gotta go to battle, we go. If we die, we die. You listen to me when I say this." he pointed at Charlie. "Listen, and listen good. Whatever happens... If it comes between saving me and saving your brother."

"Save my brother." Charlie said, completing his daddy's point.

"Ya goddamn right." daddy said. "And don't think you're cute, finishing my sentences." They shared a smile between them. "I'm serious though, son. If we fight, we fight. If we die, it's an honorable death. You understand?" Charlie just nodded. His daddy continued. "I know you do, son. I know you do. You're a good man."

Charlie put the Caprice in gear, and pulled out onto the road. The Windstar was not in sight. He wasn't worried. Bob had a pension for adhering strictly to the speed limit, or most other rules. Charlie was confident he could catch up. As he switched lanes to pass someone taking a right turn he saw his daddy looking at him. "What?" he asked.

"I'm proud of you, son." his daddy said.

Charlie didn't know what to say. "Thanks." he muttered.

"You've become your own man. There isn't much more a father could ask for in his son."

Warmth spread over Charlie. A deep, undeniable sense of fulfillment settled upon him. He'd long wanted to hear those words from his daddy. Hearing them today, knowing what was to come, hurt as much as they fulfilled. "I'll back up Grant, daddy." he said. "You watch your six. Okay?"

"I'll be fine, son." his daddy reached over. His sleeve moved up his forearm. Charlie saw the runic tattoos that he knew ran the length of his daddy's arm. They intertwined with Celtic and Norse knotwork. They were beautiful tattoos which represented a faith, belief, and strength that they would need. His daddy squeezed Charlie's forearm. "I'll be fine."

They pulled into the aquarium's parking lot, Charlie finally saw the purple Windstar. Something looked off. The Windstar was not parked right. Bob was driving for Grant, and Bob had a way about him. He would never have parked his beloved van even the least bit askew.

"Do you have a weapon?" Charlie asked. His daddy had already retrieved his semi-automatic pistol, and had it at the ready. "Good." Charlie said to no one.

Charlie parked the Caprice nose to nose with the minivan, and he and his daddy got out. The passenger side sliding door to the Windstar was open. The passenger window was broken. Internal items looked rummaged through. On the ground near the Windstar appeared to be spent gas shells. There were no bullet casings that Charlie could see. No blood either.

"Charlie!" his daddy called.

Charlie moved around to the driver's side. His daddy had removed an unconscious Bob from the vehicle. They rested Bob on the ground, his back against the rear driver's side wheel of the Windstar.

"Bob! Bob, come on buddy." Charlie shook his friend.

"Give him a second, son. He looks like he was drugged."

"It was gas." Charlie said. "There are spent shells on the other side of the van." he put a hand on either of Bob's shoulders. "Come on, Bob. I need to know what happened." he said.

As the words left his mouth his mind filled with images. The Windstar pulled into the seemingly empty parking lot. Grant told Bob to park by the lamppost. Four black SUV's appeared suddenly. Bob tried to pull away and was stopped by a fifth SUV that pulled in front of them. He heard Grant yelling commands. The glass broke. Gas filled the Windstar. Charlie heard Bob ask Grant what to do. Yelled out for him. "Mr. Grant!" The world came back to Charlie and Bob's eyes were wide, opened, and focused on his own.

"What did you just do?" Bob asked.

Charlie didn't know how to explain it. "Bob. Are you okay? Where is Grant?" he asked.

"Mr. Grant?" Bob said. "They did it. They took him." the panic seemed to rise like bubbles to the surface of a pot of hot water. "Charlie? Charlie, what happened? I could see it again. Like it just happened." Bob looked at Charlie. "They took him, Charlie. Mr. Grant is gone."

"Stay calm. Calm down." Charlie attempted to console Bob. He looked at his daddy. "What do you want to do?" he didn't need the words. It was all over his daddy's face when they looked at each other.

"We find him, and cause harm to whomever took him." his

daddy said as plainly as someone orders from a menu. Albeit, he ordered it angrily from that menu.

A ringing came from inside the Caprice. Charlie excused himself and went to retrieve his phone. His daddy stayed with Bob by the Windstar. "Yep." Charlie said as he answered his phone.

"I am with them. Charlie." the caller said. "They have Grant."

"No shit! I'm at the aquarium. They left Bob." Charlie said. "Where are they going with Grant?"

"I have sent you the address." the deep baritone voice replied. "I must go. I am being watched." The line disconnected.

Charlie's phone emitted a dinging sound. He pulled the location up from the text message, and routed directions. "Daddy, we gotta go!" Charlie called out, as he moved to where Bob rested.

"Here." his daddy said as he tossed a shotgun to Charlie. He was already headed to the Caprice. He carried his own shotgun, and had two hatchets attached to his belt. "Let's get movin'!"

Charlie didn't argue, or even speak. They left Bob rested against the Windstar as they rolled away. Charlie saw in the rearview that he had gotten to his feet by the time they'd reached the end of the parking lot. Directions came out of the phone, and advised them to turn.

"Is that where they are?" his daddy asked.

"Nearest I can tell. I got a tip."

"A tip? What the hell is going on here, boy?"

"Do you believe in ghosts, ghouls, monsters?" Charlie stole a glance at his daddy. "Do you believe in demons?" he asked. His daddy stared at him and said nothing. "Look, I'm going to explain this, and you need to trust me." he switched lanes, and increased speed. "We're going into a trap."

"Sure as hell is what it feels like." his daddy said. "How do you know it's a trap?"

"I was warned." Charlie said, and knew right off that this wasn't a good enough explanation. He shook his head, disappointed with himself. "I was given a vision, daddy. A demon showed me what was to come, and offered me a deal."

"Odin's beard, son. You made a deal with a demon?"

"I didn't have a choice." Charlie said. "In the vision you both die."

"All father." his daddy muttered to himself. "What are we up against?" he asked, with no emotion present.

Charlie knew he was settled. He didn't expect his daddy to be settled so easily, but he was settled. "Vampires." he told him, mimicking his daddy's calm.

"What was the deal you agreed to?"

"The demon said he'd give me the ability to save one of you. But I plan to get us all out of this."

"You'll remember our agreement." his daddy said sharply.

"I called in help, daddy."

"Charlie." his voice came out hard, and matter of factly. "You will save Grant." they met eyes. "You will do this."

That was that. Charlie knew it. They didn't say another word the rest of the drive. The sun was setting when they arrived at Charlotte Harbor. The GPS directions guided them to an abandoned building off the Kings highway, near the animal hospital. Charlie saw the five black SUV's. He pointed them out to his daddy.

"There's going to be a lot of them." Charlie said.

"Are you ready?"

Charlie didn't reply. They parked about a hundred yards away. Charlie got out of the Caprice, and moved to the trunk. Inside were his tools. His daddy stepped up next to him as he opened the trunk. A small arsenal of weapons laid inside.

"Good set up." his daddy said.

"You and Grant ain't the only ones who work." Charlie said with a smirk.

"Is that my..." his daddy started.

"The very same." Charlie confirmed, and handed the blade to his daddy. He closed the trunk, his selections made. "Let's go get my brother."

They made their way inside the derelict building. It was gutted. No drywall. Just open studs, and half complete rooms. Looked more like a warehouse, or storage locker, than the office building the exterior presented. More than anything, it looked just like what Charlie had seen in his vision. There were only emergency lights that illuminated the hallways. Sounds of muffled impacts, accompanied by grunts, came from within. Charlie gave a nod, and followed his daddy as they moved further inside.

At an intersection of hallways a single guard stood watch outside a door. The sounds of impact were louder here, and they could hear voices. The voices sounded eager, and demanding. Charlie could see the hallway had accesses at both ends. He signaled for his daddy to wait. Charlie then rerouted to approach the guard from the other end of the hallway. He walked confidently towards the guard.

"Hold up, friend." the guard said when he noticed Charlie. "You can't be here, this is private property."

"Damn right it is." Charlie agreed indignantly. "Who the fuck are you? And where is Stephen?"

"I'm afraid I do not know anyone named Stephen. I'm going to have to ask you to leave." the guard said, his hand moved to his gun.

"Sure you do." Charlie continued. "He's average height, likes to keep his hair shorter." only a few long strides remained between him and the guard. "You gotta know him. You'd probably like him."

"You think so, sir." the guard said, clearly not amused by Charlie's banter.

"Absolutely." Charlie asserted. "Hell, you may even relate to him. He did play that bitchy vampire in the Blade movie, after all."

The guard's entire demeanor changed. He pivoted, bared his fangs, and looked like he was about to pounce on Charlie. That was until the long, sixteen-inch blade Charlie had handed to his daddy, jetted out from the vampire's neck. In a smooth motion, the blade twisted, and swiped to the left. The creature's head made a hollow thud as it hit the ground. It was followed by the sound of collapsing limbs, and rubbing fabric, as the body gave way to gravity.

Charlie's daddy was wearing a smile of accomplishment when they saw each other.

"Decapitation." his daddy said. "It's the only sure way to know their dead."

"How do you know that?"

"I know a lot of things you don't know, son. Deal with it."

Charlie was going to say something smart, and sassy back, but stopped. He looked at his daddy. Saw the blood on his collar. Just like in the vision. His daddy pulled a handkerchief from inside his jacket and presented it to Charlie.

"Damnit, boy. Wipe yourself off. I didn't mean to get its blood all over you."

Charlie took it, and wiped off his face. Specifically around the eyes. "How do you want to do this?" he asked, already knowing the answer.

"I'll go in first." his daddy said. "You follow. You know what's going to happen. Let's see how it plays out."

"I don't know if..."

"Charlie." his daddy interrupted. "We're doing this." he looked at Charlie. "I love you, son."

Charlie's stomach dropped. He heard the words. Time seemed to slow as he watched his daddy enter the room. No doubt to find Grant bound by chains. Surrounded by vampires. He heard the words. Possibly the last words his daddy would ever say to him. The door was closed, Charlie heard footsteps, and voices came closer. He slipped inside the room, and softly guided the door closed.

Inside the room was dark, save for an overhead lamp that swung from the ceiling. Charlie stayed close to the wall. He moved as far as he comfortably felt he could from the door. He didn't want to be directly inside the room if the door opened again. Charlie positioned himself near a stack of building materials and surveyed the room. Under the light in the center of the room was Grant. His arms pulled out to either side. Bound by chains, and pulled up, just above shoulder level. Charlie froze. It was exactly like his vision. His brother hung there, beaten, bloody, and helpless. Charlie watched, unmoving as his daddy came out of the darkness and approached his brother. His daddy went to work on freeing Grant. Charlie's breathing tightened, and he shifted. One hand was free. Charlie needed to act. He couldn't move. Then the shadows shifted.

They came out of the darkness. Surely some came through the door. Charlie hadn't heard them. Two figures hit his daddy, and pulled him away from Grant. Then she was there. The tall woman. Her skin was milky white, her hair a deep brown, satin cascade of ringlets. Charlie was running out of time, and had to act. He didn't know what to do. Charlie panicked. His breath was short. His skin beaded with sweat. His heart pounded in his ears. Charlie needed to act. He gripped for his gun. Time slipped away. This was all going exactly as the vision showed it would. What was he supposed to do?

"You won't need that." said a voice within his mind. "Say the words." it instructed.

Like stone forming from mist they were there. The words were there. In his mind he could see them, hear them. He knew what he had to do. Charlie said the words.

Light filled the room. Every fine detail on display. The vampires searched fruitlessly for the source of this light, but were too slow. Charlie was already upon them. He moved with the wind. A torrent of wind moved through the room. It churned, and pushed Charlie forward. His fist hit one creature's jaw. The snap of breaking bone ripped through the room. Charlie pivoted, moved upward, and caught another vampire by the collar of its jacket, thrusted it up into the ceiling.

Two other vampires moved to flank him. Charlie's eyes were on the vampires who held his daddy. The one on the left nodded to Charlie, and pulled back its hood. Nikolai took one of the hatchets from Charlie's daddy's belt, and buried it in the face of the vampire next to him. The two vampires moved upon Charlie. He was ready. They grabbed him. Charlie could hear the tall woman yell. He grabbed the two vampires by their throats. Moved to look over their shoulders, and made eye contact with the vampire woman. He maintained his gaze with her as two lightning bolts cut through the ceiling, and ripped through the bodies of the vampires in Charlie's grasp. He maintained his glare with her as their bodies fell in ash.

"Charlie!" Grant called out.

Charlie turned; saw his brother fall below the onslaught of three vampires. Charlie growled words of power to himself. A smile filled his face as the three creatures atop his brother were ripped apart from within. Their blood, and visage spraying out. Charlie threw the shotgun to Grant. "Stay alive," he demanded. Grant simply nodded in confusion at the mayhem. Charlie turned, and looked for his daddy.

In the distance he saw him, he fought back to back with Nikolai. Charlie smiled. He knew Nikolai didn't like this kind of work. Still, he felt good knowing he could count on his old friend. They were surrounded, and Charlie needed to get to them. He called upon the wind again. Yet as he moved forward he felt a shove, and collided with a half finished wall.

"You came." hissed the tall female vampire. "You are a difficult man to find, Charlie Blackwater."

Charlie pulled himself up from the ground. "Who's looking?" he said defiantly.

"The Old Ones come, and we are promised our time in the light." she cried out. "The fallen one said he could get you here. I am happy to not be disappointed."

"The night is still young." Charlie said, and flew at her.

The vampire mother moved, parried to the left, and struck Charlie in the face. It was like being struck by a stone, and a pillow at the same time. He recovered quickly, and surprised himself in the process. Charlie watched her, and could see her minions were watching her as well. As if her next move was the next move for them all. The creatures watching moved in a mimic of her own motion. For her part, the mother moved like a predator preparing to strike.

Heavy boom's filled the room as Grant began emptying the

shotgun into the heads of the distracted vampires. Charlie could also see his daddy and Nikolai, in their continued combat with their assailants. They were tiring, and wouldn't last much longer.

The vampire mother moved upon him, and her minions moved in kind. This time it was Charlie's turn to evade. Within him he saw more words, and he gave them voice. He extended his hand toward the wave of vampires who advanced upon his daddy. Power surged out of Charlie, and disintegrated every vampire in its path, along with the walls beyond.

The shotgun clicked. It was empty. Charlie heard Grant call for their daddy. Another vampire came upon Grant from behind. Charlie lashed out, and sent power into the vampire and blew it to particles. Once again the surge of power cut through the walls beyond. A wood beam swung down, and hit Grant in the head. He collapsed unconscious to the ground.

"You're pathetic." The vampire queen hissed at Charlie. "So much concern. So much empathy." she stepped closer to him. "You can do what you will with my children." she said with a chuckle. "It will matter not, once I have your blood."

Charlie yelled out. "Time to go, daddy!" and stepped towards where Grant laid on the floor.

"You do not know from whence you came? You do not know who you are?" the vampire said. "That will not do. Let us free you of your distractions." she flipped her hand at the wrist.

Charlie felt power move through the air. He followed it with his eyes instinctively, and watched as a wood board lifted from the floor, moved quickly, and impaled Nikolai, thrusted through him, and came out the chest of Charlie's daddy.

"No!" Charlie roared as the two men collapsed together. The board held them in their shared defensive stance.

The vampire mother began to laugh a rich, full laugh. Her spawn that survived encircled Charlie where he stood. "Yield, boy." she demanded. "Yield, and I will do you the courtesy of sharing all with you before you die." Her eyes looked upon Charlie with a confidence reserved for mountains.

Charlie was unimpressed. He wasn't scared. He wasn't confused. He was furious. He didn't think. Didn't question. He simply did. He saw the vampires step back. He saw their eyes shift from hunger to fear. They had tried to trap him. They tried to kill his brother. They killed his friend. His daddy. He saw them again in his mind's eye. Charlie said the words.

Wings extended out from him. He rose up from the ground, and hovered over them all. They looked like statues, frozen in time. Mist came in through the open holes in the building. The mist crawled up the walls, across the ceiling, and filled the floor. Tiny flashes of lighting shot from one collection of mist to the next. He saw the vampire mother shift uncomfortably. She moved to raise one hand to him, as if to ask him to hold. He didn't hear her words when she first spoke them.

"We yield!" she called out loudly.

Charlie looked at her, at her minions, her children. Bile, and anger filled his throat. "Yes, you do." he said in a growl only loud enough for her to hear.

Thunder shook the building's foundation, and like grasping hungry hands, lighting exploded out from the mists. In a strobe of flashing light and sound, the room erupted. Moments later, Charlie's feet rested again upon the ground. Every vampire was dead. Their bodies were everywhere.

Charlie rushed over to Grant. He was alive, but injured. Charlie placed his hands upon him, and light shone from between them where they touched. Grant became more alert, and looked as if to see Charlie for the first time. Together they then moved to check on their daddy, and Nikolai.

The wood board had been pulled out of them. They both laid there bleeding upon the floor. Nikolai's blood was a dark, almost black color. While their daddy's blood was rich, and red. Charlie pulled their daddy up, draped him over his shoulder. Grant placed himself under his daddy's other arm, and they moved to the door. Nikolai laid unmoved.

As they passed through toward the exit Charlie heard something. "Get him outside," he said to Grant. They repositioned their daddy between them. Charlie released his hold. Grant gave him a nod. Charlie nodded back, took the sixteen-inch knife from his daddy's belt, and walked back into the room.

He followed the sound to find the vampire mother on the floor. She gasped for breath, struggled for purchase, as she hoped to live. The mother was on her stomach. She tried poorly to move toward the door. Her hands clawed at the wet floor. Charlie moved up to her without a sound. He grabbed a fist full of her hair. Wrenched her head back so she could see his face. The blade in Charlie's hand began to roar with red hot flames. Her eyes went wide. He plunged the blade into her neck. It sizzled and popped as he pulled it through her flesh. There was a pop as he cut her spine, and removed her head.

Charlie stood. Blood covered him and the floor. He dropped her head unceremoniously to the ground. He looked toward where Nikolai's body lay. He was gone. "Shit." he cursed, as he ran to catch up with his brother.

Grant and their daddy were outside. Their daddy propped up against a tree when Charlie arrived. "Daddy. Dammit. I'm sorry." Charlie dropped to his knees next to him. He put his hands upon his daddy. Hoping for something. Perhaps like what he was able to do for Grant. There was a slight glow, and then nothing. Charlie felt so tired.

"Hey." came his daddy's voice. It was weak, airy, and wet, but it was his nonetheless. "It's alright. This is a good death." he said. He reached up, patted Charlie on the cheek. "Let it be. You did good."

"I should have been able to save you." Charlie's words gave way to tears.

"No." his daddy said. "Because you will need to save us all."

"What?" Charlie said, confused by his daddy's words. "What did you say, daddy?"

"I can see them, Charlie. My father, and mother." his daddy said. "I see them, Charlie, and they welcome me." he looked to Charlie. "They are proud of you. I am proud of you."

"Daddy?"

"I have to go. They bid me, come." his daddy said. "Thank you, my son." he said. His hand fell, and rested softly upon his lap. His chest no longer raised. His eyelids hung heavy, as his eyes looked forward at nothing. Their daddy was dead.

Charlie wept.

Leaves crunched, and a stick snapped nearby. Charlie looked, and saw Nikolai. He bled from the open wound on his abdomen.

"Nikolai, are you ok?" Charlie asked. There was no response.

"You know him?" Grant asked.

"This is Nikolai, he was protecting daddy."

"He did a hell of a job. Charlie, he's one of them!" Grant said.

Charlie looked at Nikolai, who was feet away. "Are you ok, Nic. What do you need?"

Nikolai looked up at Charlie. His eyes were white, like the first winter snow. "I am sorry, Charlie," he said.

Charlie couldn't understand why he would feel the need to apologize. He had done all he could. Everything he had been asked to do. Charlie thought to assure him of as much when Nikolai leaped forward. His body collided with Grant. They fell to the ground. It clicked in Charlie's increasingly slowed mind. Nikolai was a vampire, and had suffered massive wounds. He needed to heal. To heal he needed to eat. Charlie moved. Three gunshots cut the night air. Bullet holes were visible on Nikolai's back from where the shots exited his body. He collapsed off of Grant.

"Grant!" Charlie called.

Grant struggled to his feet. Once standing, he shot the remaining portion of bullets into Nikolai's prone form. Charlie collected his brother, and together they carried their daddy back to the Caprice.

~

Vomit gushed forth from Charlie. It hit the wall, the dresser in the corner, and it broke the circle of power. There was a snapping sound as the contained power released, and expanded outward. A corresponding thud came from upstairs. Charlie figured that it was Grey, and Cahya, as they experienced the release of power.

Hands slid around Charlie, helped him up. "You did well." Ifotia said.

Charlie looked to his brother, who remained seated in the chair in the room. Their eyes met. Tears ran down Grant's face. It was then Charlie felt his own tears. Grant gave Charlie a nod of acknowledgement; they knew. They both remembered the pain, the loss, of what happened in Florida. Everyone knew now. Charlie made a deal with a demon, and failed to save his daddy.

Now that demon was in Iowa, toying with them.

CHAPTER 16
COFFEE IN THE MORNING

Open curtains welcomed warm sunlight, and the five bodies in the room remained still. Cahya, and Grey laid in the bed farthest from the door. Grey laid appropriately in the bed. While Cahya laid in a contrary fashion, his feet toward the headboard. Each man wrapped in their own bedding. Grey with the comforter, and Cahya with a top sheet. An arrangement Cahya suggested, as he gets too warm at night, and had little use for a full blanket.

As the sun rose into the day, its light moved to touch the pullout mattress where Bob slept. He was wrapped in a flannel blanket, and his head rested upon a down feather pillow in a flannel pillowcase. These items were not provided by the motel. Bob had them with him in his purple Windstar. They were part of his ready supply kit. Which the group was happy to learn also contained various canned meals by a popular chef, and a couple bags of beef jerky. After the night they had, Bob was more than happy to share. Plus it meant he got to use his multi-tool utility knife. Never a bad day for Bob when he got to use his multi-tool utility knife.

In the remaining bed, curled up under the motel supplied sheet and comforter, were Ifotia, and Nikolai. Together they laid, their legs casually intertwined. They were not asleep. They had been, but both woke as soon as the light of the sun broke the horizon. When they awoke they found themselves in an unbidden state of caress. Arms draped over the other person, hands upon their bodies, and legs wrapped together. They were dressed, and no clothing amiss. Together they laid in the silence of the room gently in contact with each other.

Ifotia looked upon Nikolai in a new way. Really she saw Grant, Bob, and Charlie in a new light after the previous night. But she saw Nikolai die. Before that, she watched him choose to live, and to potentially give his life for his friend. She saw his honor. She saw how far he would go, and how completely he possessed the capacity to love. He was like fire, and he burned a radiant light in her eyes.

"Good morning." Nikolai whispered, not wanting to wake anyone in the room. After all, they needed to sleep, and not because he was certain they would most surely ruin this moment for him.

"Good morning." Ifotia whispered back.

Goosebumps, is that what they're called? Nikolaiy couldn't remember the last time he felt his skin do this. The tightening, tingling sensation moved over his forearm where her hand touched his skin. He could feel the tiny bumps form, and dissipate in response to her. His breath caught. He wouldn't have noticed had he not been eager to speak to her. Goodness, he liked her voice. He felt he must talk to her. An odd feeling, not being the most conversational person, still he wanted only to talk to her more. Nikolai swallowed, and allowed himself a moment to take a breath. "Did you sleep well?" he asked.

"I did. Though, I do not need sleep like the others might."

"The others?"

"Yes. Charlie, Bob, Grey... the others." Ifotia said. "I know you are different. I knew before last night. Though I understand more so now."

"Does that bother you?"

"No." Ifotia said quickly, then took a breath. Her eyes squinted as thoughts worked inside her mind. "I do not think it bothers me. I don't know if I fully understand, but it doesn't bother me." she said.

"I saw it too." Nikolai said. "I wasn't prepared for that."

"Did it bother you?" Ifotia asked.

Nikolai was quiet a moment, considered the question, and the color of her eyes. "Yes." he said. "It bothered me." he took another breath. "I do not think about that night often. I do not like the memory of almost dying." he moved his eyes from hers. The weight of his memories were heavy upon him. "Of having to kill so many. Nor to remember the experience of being so injured that I almost killed my best friend's brother." Nicolai met her eyes again. "To experience that again as clearly. It bothered me."

"You fought well." Ifotia said in an attempt to assure him.

"I did my best. It had been almost a century since I had fought anyone like that." Nikolai recalled the experience. "I had forgotten the smell," he said. "When you saw it last night. How did you see it?"

"I saw it in my mind, like all of us did."

"No, I am sorry. I mean, were you watching it from the outside, or were you seeing it from one of our perspectives." Nikolai clarified. "I saw it again, as myself. I watched, and experienced every moment as if I was reliving that moment again."

"I was Charlie." Ifotia finally said. As she did she moved her hand gently against the muscles of Nikolai's forearm. "It was as you said. I saw, and felt, everything as he did." she looked deep into Nikolai's eyes. "I saw his care for you. His concern. I felt his need to protect, and his pain of loss." tears formed in her eyes, and Ifotia lowered her voice more. "Did you know he knew you lived?"

"I had wondered. It is not something we have readily spoken of."

"Charlie's daddy had told him how to kill..." she paused. Felt out the word for the first time. "Vampires." Ifotia finally said. "He knew the only sure way to kill them was to take off their head. He could have told Grant. I do not believe he ever has."

Nikolai and Charlie had been through a lot together. The good, the bad, and the stuff they only hint at on late night television. For all intents and purposes Charlie was his best friend. Nikolai recalled that it was Charlie who sought him out after that night. He wanted to make sure Nikolai was alright. No matter how crazy things got, Charlie never quit on Nikolai. That is a big deal for a person who's been alive almost three centuries.

Ifotia's leg moved, and for a moment Nikolai could think of nothing else but her presence. She smiled at him. Like she knew what she was doing. Perhaps she did. Nikolai felt like a fourteen year old virgin catholic school boy, on holiday, seeing boobs at the beach for the first time. His ability to think was not improving.

Next door, in Grant's room, there were no open curtains. Only a fool stays up that late and then goes to sleep with the curtains open. The room was dark. Delightfully so. Grant laid in bed, sound asleep. His low basso snoring like a recurring echo. In the chair by the window, Charlie sat in silence. Spread upon the table next to him were his weapons, and personal effects. He'd already cleaned everything twice, and only needed to put everything together. He sipped from the paper cup in his hand. It was empty. He refilled it from the whiskey bottle on the table. Just enough. Once he finished this cup, they'd both be empty. He wouldn't be.

Charlie had been up all night. He told Grant he'd get some sleep. Sleep hadn't come. He went for a walk. Tried to clear his head, to move past the vision. The memory. Nothing was helping. He collected one of his bottles of whiskey from Grant's van on his way back to the room. Once inside, he found a paper cup from a dispenser in the bathroom. Said he'd only have a couple. Which on one hand was true. He only went through two cups, having to grab a second after the first became damp from liquid absorption. He poured the last of the whiskey in his mouth, and set the second, also damp cup down. He missed his daddy.

How could he have forgotten all of that? That was the question, the main question that taunted him through the night. It didn't make sense. So he occupied himself with activities that did. Guns made sense to Charlie. They had parts, they worked and didn't work based on the quality, and care of those parts. So Charlie disassembled, and cleaned all his tools. Polished his knives. Then polished off a bottle of whiskey.

Charlie stood up to head to the bathroom. There were simply unavoidable consequences that came with consuming that much liquor, and as good as he was, it was time to break the seal. This all would have worked much better had he remembered the drink to personal balance ratio that also came with whiskey. Charlie's third step was like stepping out into nothing. His foot moved from beneath him, and he plummeted forward. The impact of his body hitting the bed bounced Grant clear out of bed. They both hit the floor at the same time. A short moment later the door to Grant's room from the other room opened.

"Charlie? Grant? You ok?" Grey asked, not seeing Charlie in front of him on the floor in the dark room.

Cahya found the light switch. "My, I think Charlie may need some assistance," he said.

"Get him in the shower." Grant said, now on his feet. He pointed to the shower in his room. "And strip him so we can wash his clothes." he could smell urine in the air.

Grey and Cahya moved to pick up Charlie. Nikolai joined them for support. Ifotia stood in the doorway, a concerned look on her face.

"He'll be fine." Grant said to the question unasked.

"Are you alright?" Ifotia asked.

"Aside from the full contact alarm clock, I'm fine." Grant said. He saw the confused look on Ifotia's face. "I'm alright, Ifotia." Knowing things would take a moment with Charlie, Grant called out. "Hey, Bob?"

"I'm already on it, Mr. Grant." came Bob's voice from the other room. "I'll be back shortly with coffee, and pastries for us all."

"Thank you, Bob." Grant shook his head in amusement. As the door closed he mumbled to himself. "That fuckin' Bob."

"Was he not considerate?" Ifotia asked.

"What?" Grant asked, confused. "What is considerate about falling on to my bed, drunk?"

"Not Charlie." she said "Bob. Was he not considerate?"

Grant felt foolish. A sensation he particularly did not enjoy. "Yes, of course. Bob is very considerate." he said with confidence.

"Why then did you say 'fuckin', regarding him? Isn't that a term of disdain?" Ifotia asked.

"It can be." Grant understood her confusion. "Fuck, and the various applications of it can be diverse. In this case I was complimenting Bob. I said fuckin, but I could have said 'that great guy Bob' or 'that awesome Bob'."

"Why didn't you?"

Grant smiled. "Because, I didn't fuckin' want to."

Bob returned a short while later with a drink carrier full of coffee, and a box of assorted donuts. Charlie was clean, and a tad bit more coherent by that time. They all ate, Grant and Grey forgoing their coffee so Charlie could drink it. Not a completely selfish gesture, as even Grey knew he didn't always need coffee to add to his energy levels. For a short time they were all at peace. They enjoyed their banter, and the company of each other.

"It was him." Charlie finally said.

"Yeah." Grey agreed. "He's toying with us."

"I'm guessing you all saw what I saw last night. In one shape, or another?" they all nodded. "The chap we met at the Historical Society, he ran into Grey when we were at the Museum of Weird." Charlie sipped his third cup of coffee. "He is also the same sonofabitch I met in Florida. The demon I made a deal with."

"Do we think he is behind all of this?" Cahya asked.

"I'd wager it's a safe guess that if he wasn't, he is at least involved now." Grant said.

"So that leaves us with strange shadow kitty creatures, a possible werewolf threat, and a demon to tend with." Grey said, not at all enthusiastically. "Great."

"We need to assume they are connected." Charlie said. "We need to assume that if we can stop him, we stop all of this."

"How do we stop a demon?" Cahya asked.

The seven of them looked at each other and said nothing for a long moment. The room only presented the sounds of consumption, and the drinking of coffee.

"We trap him." Ifotia offered.

"Can we do that?" Nikolai asked.

"We can." she said.

"Yes, we can!" Grey said, giving evidence to why he never needs coffee. "We're going to need a few things, but we can do it."

"You're sure?" Grant asked.

"Yeah. I mean. I think so." Grey said.

"What is this flavor?" Ifotia asked, holding up her donut.

"Oh!" Cahya started, his mouth full.

"That's a glazed, cinnamon swirl, chocolate dipped, bear claw. Do you like it?" Bob asked.

"I do."

"There is one more in the box. I can get it for you if you'd like." Bob offered.

Before Ifotia could say "Yes, please." Nikolai had retrieved the box and presented the available donuts to her. "Thank you, Nikolai." She considered her options. "What is this one with white on top?"

"Cherry filled." Grant interjected. "Don't eat it, they're gross."

"They are not good?" she asked.

"Correct. They are not good. For you." Grant said with a smirk. "For me they are delicious." he finished, as he grabbed the last cherry filled donut.

The room filled with a chorus of uncoordinated sounds. Grey, Grant, and Cahya all reached for their cellphones. Or at least that is the easiest way to explain them. Grey's looked like an inter-cosmic communications device Frankenstein put together for him. Grant's looked like a tank could roll over it and leave it unfazed. Which is likely more true than not. While Cahya's phone looked the most mundane, and normal. Though he retrieved it from that bag of holding he carried with him. Which automatically made it suspect.

"What is happening?" Bob asked.

"Communication, from the Sect of the Open Eye." Cahya said.

"Yeah. What he said." Grey agreed. "Only no open eyes here. Just my people with information to share."

Grant said nothing. He focused on the message on his phone. The other two did the same. Grey finished his reading quickly, with Grant right behind him. The group waited for Cahya to wrap up his reading, though this seemed to involve some communication exchange.

"What do we get?" Grant eventually asked. As soon as he did, he saw Grey shift, and knew he should have given better direction.

"Well, my guys are saying there was a huge spike of energy here last night." Grey began. "We all know what that was. I mean that was us, right?" he looked at the group. "Only it wasn't. I mean yes, they saw our spell last night. There was another. Not quite as large. Looks like it came from the Historical Society. My peeps say it matched the energy signature they saw before. From a few weeks ago."

"That's good information. What about you?" Grant asked Cahya.

"The Sect is saying similar things." Cahya said. "My only additional information is that the Sect feels this is definitely a werewolf killing the cows."

"How do they know?" Charlie asked.

"From the blood I collected."

"You sneaky bitch." Grant said, chuckling. "You grabbed it while petting the dog." he said, and got a grin from Cahya.

"A boy is allowed his secrets, I believe they say." Cahya said.

The group gave way to laughter. "Oh shut it." Charlie said. "You're spending too much time with Grey."

"That's impossible." Grey said. "You can never spend too much time with Grey. I should know."

"Focus." Grant said. "The company sent me similar information. They also told me that the director of the Historical Society, Maxwell

Johnson, isn't on vacation. He isn't anywhere. They looked. Max Johnson is missing."

"Shit, do we have to find him too?"

"There may be nothing to find." Grant said. "We do need to prepare ourselves. We know what we're up against. Now we need to kick it's ass."

"I do not believe the demon gave you your powers, Charlie." Ifotia's words captured the attention of the whole room.

"What the hell do you mean?" Charlie asked.

"Yeah." Grey agreed. "You saw it. We all saw it. Charlie made a deal, and the demon gave him power to save his brother, and daddy."

"I do not believe a demon could give you the power you displayed." Ifotia said confidently. "I'm not certain. I simply do not believe."

"That's a real comfort coming from a divine being." Charlie said. "We can explore your theory later. Grey says he thinks he can trap Josh. What do we need to make that happen?"

"I'll need some elements. Five. All designed to draw, and ground him in place." Grey said. "I'll need Cahya's help with the spell, and I'll need something from you, Charlie."

"Well don't pick now as the time you try to become coy. Spit it out." Charlie said.

"Seeing as the demon is most deeply connected to you, you will have to be involved in the spell to capture it."

"Of course, but what do you need from me?"

Grey took a breath and said. "I'm going to need a bunch of your blood."

CHAPTER 17
A CELL FOR TWO

"Read the list again." Charlie reclined in his chair. They'd been through this twice already.

"Milk. Candles, lavender scented. A large stone. A large, long chain. Three liters of your blood." Grey read off plainly from where he reclined on the bed.

"Three liters? You see, that's where I have a problem." Charlie said. "You do know people start dying at that point, yes?"

"Oh, Charlie, you'll be fine!" Grey assured. "We won't need to take it all at once. Once we have the supplies, we'll do a pint at a time."

"You said you needed liters." Charlie clarified.

"Pints. Liters. It'll all work out." Grey said. "The metric system can be confusing."

Grant signaled from the door to his room. Charlie held up one finger to ask Grant to give him a moment.

"We're burning daylight here, Grey. Can you take Bob, and go find what we need?" Charlie asked.

"I would like to join them." Ifotia said, as she reclined on the other bed, and chewed on a strip of fresh, perfectly cooked bacon.

"You still have bacon?" Charlie asked in hopeful surprise. "I thought you sacrificed it all to the shadow god at Lake Violet."

"That was only a large portion. I would have never sacrificed all of it."

"Do you have enough to share?" Charlie sounded more insistent than inquisitive. "I would also like to enjoy the bacon I paid for."

Ifotia extended her left hand to Charlie, and offered him five slices of bacon. They were crispy, fresh, but not too hot to touch.

Charlie accepted them. He devoured a piece. They were delicious. Charlie had never tasted better bacon. "How much do you have left?" Charlie asked through a mouthful of savory heaven.

"How much did you originally give me?"

"Three pounds."

"I am unfamiliar with pounds." Ifotia said proudly. "Still, about one sixth of the original portion remains. Four portions went to the shadow of Enki. We've eaten a portion, and one remains." Ifotia sat back, she looked satisfied with her explanation.

Charlie took another satisfying mouthful of bacon. He looked to the others in the room. "Cahya, will you join them?"

"I would be most happy to accompany them in their efforts." Cahya said.

Charlie couldn't help but wonder if Cahya was ever in a poor mood. He was always too jovial, and agreeable. While never seeming the least bit concerned. Must be that sect he followed.

Before he could say anything, Cahya continued. "I would be most interested in helping Grey set up the trap. I think our magics would work well together."

"Yeah, man." Grey looked at Charlie. "I think that would work well."

Charlie gave them a look of approval and turned to Nikolai, motioned for the immortal to join him and Grant, and headed into Grant's room. After they were both inside, Charlie shut, and locked the door. He took another bite of bacon, and looked at his brother. "We gonna be cool?" he asked.

"Did you bring enough bacon to share?" Grant asked.

"No." Charlie held his remaining bacon close to his chest, and smirked.

"Then, we're not going to be cool." Grant said with a hint of sarcasm.

"Go talk to the embodiment of fire. Sure she can pull some out of her tinderbox for you." Charlie took a seat in the chair. Grant was on the bed, his back against the headboard. "Said she's got about half a pound left." Charlie said.

"I'll leave eating treats from her box to you."

"Hey, don't make it dirty." Charlie said. "Not sure how it works, or where she actually keeps everything, but the bacon is divine. So, whether she is divine, or not, I'm not concerned. The bacon is." he finished chewing, and looked at Grant, his voice sincere. "Besides, you know what I meant. Are we cool?"

Grant looked up at Nikolai who stood near the door. They had all established, whether inside the circle of power, or not, each of them had experienced the memory with Charlie to some degree. Grant re-lived it from his own perspective, with little extras added in from Charlie's point of view. For Nikolai it had been much the same. Ifotia said she saw things from an omniscient, Charlie focused, kind of perspective. While someone like Grey, or Cahya, who were not involved at all, experienced it from a kind of limited third person point of view, and followed Charlie through the memory. Grant hadn't realized how much he had forgotten. Especially the actions by Charlie to combat the vampires. Nor had he realized that Nikolai fought with them. With his daddy. Grant's eyes met Nikolai's, and he nodded. "Yeah, brother. We're cool."

Nikolai affirmed this with a nod, and said. "Yes."

"The others are going to get supplies for Grey's spell." Charlie said. "Think there's any benefit in us going out to the farm early?"

"I was leaning that way." Grant said. "I am itching to shoot something. Still, I was thinking we should head back to the Historical Society."

"Is that wise?"

"We might find something. Maybe a clue where Maxwell Johnson is?" Grant said.

"What do you think, Nic?" Charlie asked.

"It is always good to have more information than less. The full moon is tomorrow night. We do have time." Nikolai said.

"See." Grant said. "We're cool."

Three heavy thumps came from the exterior door to Grant's motel room. Charlie slid quietly toward the door, and peeked through the viewport. The figures were silhouetted by the bright light of the day. Still, in the odd wide angle of the viewport Charlie could make out familiar features. Like how the sunlight reflected off the badge on the caller's chest. Three more knocks came. Charlie moved closer to Grant. "It's the Sheriff," he said plainly.

Grant let out a deep chested sigh. This joker was the last person Grant wanted to deal with right now. "Hold on." he called out to the door. Charlie sat back down in the chair as Grant stepped to the door. Nikolai remained where he was. Grant opened the door.

"Mr. Bowman?" the Sheriff said before the door was fully open. He paused, as Grant stood in front of him. "I wondered if it was you. Good day, Agent Bowman."

"Sheriff." Grant said, omitting the Sheriff's name on purpose. "What brings you by?"

"We had concerned phone calls to the station last night, and early this morning. Many of the patrons here reported a disruption last night that kept them from sleeping." the Sheriff explained.

"That's unfortunate. I slept fine." Grant said, as he looked at Charlie.

"Same here. Slept like a fat baby in a fresh diaper." Charlie said.

"Good to hear you boys were not disturbed," the Sheriff said.

"Indeed. Thank you, Sheriff. We appreciate you checking on us." Grant said, and moved to close the door. "You have a great..."

"Now, one moment, Mr. Bowman." the Sheriff interrupted.

"Agent." Grant said.

"Right. Agent." the Sheriff amended, and gestured at the two officers with him. "We didn't stop by to see how you slept, exactly."

"Do you need assistance? I'm sure you can handle looking into some folk's sleepless nights. We have our plates full."

"As kind as you are to offer, Agent Bowman, we're not in need of your help."

"Excellent. Have a good day then." Grant moved again to end the conversation.

"You see," the Sheriff continued as if not hearing Grant. "What we found in speaking with some of the guests is that you strong armed a couple in the middle of the night to move from their room, and into a room you had just secured. Is this correct?"

"Strong armed is a bit of an exaggeration."

"What exactly were you doing last night, Mr. Bowman?"

"Agent Bowman. Thank you." Grant said firmly. "As for what we were doing, that isn't your concern. You made it clear at your office that you were not interested in the reports coming from your constituents, and you were not going to help us." Grant saw he struck a chord in the Sheriff's eyes, and continued. "Did you look at the room?" no reply. "Did you look at it?" Grant asked again, calmly, and confidently.

"We looked," said another officer.

"Was there anything in disarray?"

"There was not." the officer said.

"What is your point... Agent?" the Sheriff said.

"What is your's, Sheriff?" Grant asserted back. "We've done nothing illegal. Nothing is damaged. If you're quite done, we have work to do."

"You can go." the Sheriff said. "We weren't looking for you anyways."

Grant froze. This was always a worry for him. Even the best covers have limits. They have a defined edge where things get cloudy, muddy, like late 90's and early 2000's video games. Grant knew he had his skeletons. Hell, he wasn't really with the FBI, for one thing.

He was sure other members of his crew had things about their pasts they'd rather be left alone. Grant's stomach dropped as he watched the Sheriff turn to address his brother.

"Charlie Blackwater?" the Sheriff said.

"That's me." Charlie said. "But you knew that, because we met. Remember?"

"I remember." the Sheriff said. "Imagine my surprise when the FBI had never heard of you. Or, after we ran your photo and finger-prints, the system came back with a hit." he stepped toward Charlie. "You're wanted for questioning in Florida, in connection to a murder. Isn't that right, Charles Bowman?"

"My name's Charlie Blackwater, sir. That mess in Florida was settled." Charlie said. "I ain't wanted for shit. Unless you went and called the tequila twins," he laughed. "In which case, tell them they are welcome, and can keep the change."

"I'm going to need you to come with us," the Sheriff reached for Charlie's arm.

Charlie was on his feet in an instant. Fists clenched at his sides. At full height, Charlie was an imposing figure against any man. It was no different with the Sheriff, who had to look up to maintain eye contact with Charlie. "Don't." Charlie said commandingly. "Do not touch me."

"Charlie." Grant said. "Sheriff, back off. Okay?" he stepped up, near the Sheriff. "Charlie, go with 'em. I'll make some calls. They can make some calls, and find out this Florida business is misin-formation."

"I doubt dozens of dead bodies found in a construction zone is misinformation."

"You don't know what the fuck you're talking about." Charlie snarled at the Sheriff. "We're on a time table," he said. More to Grant, than to the Sheriff.

"Just go peacefully, Charlie. We'll figure this out." Grant said.

Charlie looked at Grant, their eyes shared a silent conversation of their own. What was the irony? How they pieced together everything they had. Charlie only just remembered all that took place in Florida. They are at their strongest position to move forward, only to have the Sheriff, and his goons show up to inquire about this. Not only that, but how the hell did they get his fingerprints? Charlie was careful. He wore gloves more often than not when in public, and he didn't recall touching anything in the office. He gave Grant a nod, then looked at the Sheriff. "Lead the way, Sheriff." The Sheriff appeared to reach for handcuffs. "You're not going to need those." Charlie said, his voice cold, and deep. "Let's just go."

The Sheriff chose his better senses at that moment, and he, Charlie, with the two other officers, headed to the squad outside. Grant watched Charlie slide into the backseat. He cursed to himself as they drove away. He stood, staring at the empty lot after they had gone. He didn't notice Nikolai step up next to him.

"Shall I follow? To keep an eye on Charlie." Nikolai said.

"Yeah." Grant collected himself. "Do that. I'll meet you there after I make a call." he paused. "Do you need money for a cab or anything?"

"No. Thank you, though." Nikolai said. "I should have no problem keeping up."

Grant watched as Nikolai stepped out onto the balcony hallway outside the room. He didn't move towards the stairs. Instead Nikolai stepped up onto the railing as easily as some climbed into bed. Then he stepped off the railing. Only he did not fall. Nikolai instead lifted into the air, taking flight. As Grant watched, the light of the sky seemed to refract around him, and in a moment Nikolai vanished. Grant shook his head, processed the situation. "Damn, I need to get out more." he said to himself. He took his phone from his pocket, dialed the number needed, and closed his door.

The ride to the station was by all accounts uneventful. Charlie was placed in a cell by himself, which suited him fine. His willing surrender at the motel seemed to calm everyone's nerves. When they got to the station the younger officer didn't search or frisk Charlie. This pleased him. Particularly as he reclined back on the bench in the cell, removed his flask from his jacket's inner pocket, and took a drink. The whiskey was good, smooth, with the right amount of bite. Just like he liked his women. Charlie smiled at the thought, and took another sip.

"Don't suppose you brought enough to share." came the soft, younger voice.

Charlie's heart went cold. He knew the voice. It was as familiar to him as his own face in a mirror. Especially having heard it as recently as last night. Charlie slid the flask away. He looked to his right, to the cell next to his. Joshua sat, reclined in a similar manner. He watched Charlie. "What do you want?" Charlie asked.

"I imagine I want similar things as you, Charlie." Joshua said. "I want things to go how I want them to go. I want to be treated fairly. To be... loved."

"Oh, fuck off." Charlie interrupted. "You're a selfish, manipulative, scoundrel who uses people."

"Well. Well, Charlie." Joshua said, as he stood up and looked toward Charlie. "You speak of me as if we were the oldest, and best of friends."

"You used me, and now you're doing it again." Charlie said. "Me, and my friends."

"You wouldn't have your brother if it weren't for me."

"As far as I'm concerned, you are why my father is dead." Charlie said. "I will find a way to stop you."

"You'll try." Joshua said with no emotion. There was a pause in the air. It lasted long enough for true silence to settle upon them. "How did you do it?" Joshua asked.

"Do what, dumbass?"

"Your little experiment. I know what you did last night. It was impressive. You gained access to your memories." Joshua paused. "Must have been an experience to see what you did that night so long ago."

Charlie fought back the involuntary visions of all those he killed. "I suppose you were pleased."

"How do you mean, Charlie?"

"That was what you wanted me for, wasn't it? You wanted me to kill all of them for you. To kill her." he looked to Joshua. "Why?" The single word question hung heavy in the air between them.

"Oh, I suppose there's no harm in telling you now. It was so long ago." Joshua's face was free of emotion. "Do you remember what I told you about chess?"

"I do."

"Much like in chess, the pieces in this game cannot eliminate their fellow pieces on the board. White cannot take out white, nor may black move upon black. Do you see?" Joshua smirked, watching the comprehension upon Charlie's face. "I could not kill her. You, dear Charlie, you clearly had no problem."

"Because you're both monsters."

"Because we share a lineage, Charlie. My father is her, what would he be." Joshua thought. "Grandfather, I presume. Yes. Her grandfather. Whereas you. Well, your grandfather is something else entirely."

"What did you do to me?" Charlie asked.

"In truth?" Joshua asked rhetorically. "Nothing."

"Bullshit!" Charlie leaped to his feet. He felt the familiar heat of conflict rise within him. In an instant he had moved from his seat on the bench, to the area of steel bars directly across from where Joshua stood. Charlie felt like he was close enough to grab. He grasped the bars instead. "What did you do?" he growled.

"I didn't do anything to you, per say. You might say I unlocked you, and set you free." Joshua said. "You see, not all we demons do is condemnable."

Charlie roared. His right arm shot through the bars. His hand grabbed Joshua by his jacket. Charlie pulled him close. "Enough word games. Speak clearly, or I will…"

"Gentle, Charlie, gentle." Joshua calmly observed Charlie's clasp upon him. "As I have said, the vampire mother, and I, share a heritage to the same father. It would throw things too far off balance if I were to have eliminated her. Where as you are of the other father. We, pieces of white, are staged upon the board against your pieces of black. Like Chess. Our pieces have been at war for lifetimes. It was too perfect."

Charlie's grip tightened upon Joshua's jacket. "Meaning I could eliminate you with no issue." he smiled. Charlie grabbed Joshua with his other hand in an instant. He pulled the demon hard against the bars. "You've said there will be time for that. I'm a patient guy. What I need to know now is why are you in Iowa?"

Joshua's eyes rested upon Charlie's for an intimate amount of time. "You have something we need, Charlie."

"Something?"

"Something. Someone. We'll be coming for it soon. I'll be coming for it, and you'll give it to me as promised. Or I'll come for you."

"I'm right here." Charlie said, his grip on Joshua tightened, and pulled Joshua against the bars. "I ain't giving you shit."

"Do not be foolish, Charlie. You do not recall your powers. You tease at them, and yes, now you remember having touched them, but you do not possess them." Joshua said, suddenly free of Charlie's grasp. He stood out of reach from Charlie. His gaze was sincere, yet stoic. "You do have influence, and access to something we need. I'll be coming for it soon enough." he brushed himself off, like he had been bumped by something dirty. "Enjoy your stay, Charlie. I'm sure the Sheriff will be along shortly."

Charlie yelled, and slammed his hand against the bars. Anger, furious anger, churned within him. He yelled again. "I'll kill you! You hear me? I'm going to kill you!" There was no reply, but Charlie thought he felt something. "I'll kill you! I am going to kill you!" The tension increased. Charlie felt like he was shaking.

"Charlie... Charlie." a deep, rich voice said.

"Charlie?" came a more questioning, inquisitive toned voice.

"Pick him up," said another voice. Charlie recognized that asshole tone anywhere.

"Grant, no. No!" Charlie said. "I'm fine. Give me a damn minute.

I'm fine." he opened his eyes. He was on the floor of his cell. Grey, and Nikolai, were tending to him. Grant stood near the door. The Sheriff was there too. "What is this?"

"Come on. Get him to the van." Grant said.

Nikolai took one arm, and Grey the other, as they helped Charlie up. "Let us go, Charlie." Nikolai said. The three men headed outside without another word.

"The only thing my brother is guilty of is having a few too many on a school night, and being far too kind for his own good." Grant said to the Sheriff. "I hope you're satisfied."

"I want you out of my town in 48 hours." the Sheriff said.

"We'll be leaving." Grant said. "Don't miss us too much."

Outside Charlie rested in the rear of the van, Grey sat in the front passenger seat, and Nikolai sat near Charlie. Grant opened the driver's side door, and got in. "That was nice and quick." Charlie said.

"Are you alright?" Grant asked.

"Yeah." Charlie said. "I'm fine. I had a vision. A visit from Joshua. Said he's coming for his favor."

"Well he's going to have to wait. We are running late." Grant said.

"Late? Where the hell do we need to be? Full moon ain't until tomorrow."

"You sure you're ok, Charlie?" Grey asked.

"I'm fine, why?"

"The full moon is tonight, Charlie." Nikolai said.

"What?"

"Yeah, Charlie." Grey confirmed. "Sheriff had you for 16 hours, and we have about five hours until sundown."

CHAPTER 18
FULL MOON RISING

It felt like a good night to die, a good night for something to die, by Charlie's estimate. The night felt like a scene ripped directly from a movie. The moon shone bright and full. Few clouds in the sky, and the sounds of crickets and frogs could be heard in each direction. It seemed all the world was painted in her soft white light. Charlie loved nights like this. A person could see everything they needed to by the light of the moon. No flashlight needed. You could walk about and enjoy the night as is. He remembered how he, and Grant, would play army, or cops and robbers, under the full moon's light. Those were warm, good memories.

"What the hell are you smiling about?" Grant asked from the driver's seat.

Charlie had been smiling. He felt it when Grant asked, and hadn't noticed it before. Too lost in thought, he supposed. "What?" Charlie asked.

"You're smiling. Not saying nothing. It's creepy." Grant said.

"Fuck you. You're creepy." Charlie said with a chuckle.

"I liked your smile, Charlie." Ifotia said from the next row of seats. She, Grey, and Nikolai rode in the rear row seating of Grant's van. While Bob, and Cahya, had gone ahead to the farm in Bob's purple Windstar. "It is good to see you smiling," she said.

"Well, see?" Charlie said to Grant. "The goddess likes it. You can deal with it."

"She's creepy too. Doesn't count." Grant's quip elicited laughter from the group, including Ifotia.

"I was thinking about when we were kids." Charlie said after the laughter died down. "When Daddy would take us out to Grandpa Carl's land."

"We'd play cops and robbers?" Grant interjected.

"Yes, exactly."

"Ha! I do remember that." Grant smiled.

"Stop it."

"What?"

"You're smiling. Stop it. It's creepy." Charlie said, and everyone laughed.

The loose gravel of the dirt road shifted, and rumbled under the tires of the van. They pulled into the driveway of the Lowe Farm. Grant could see Bob, and Cahya, standing with Mr. Lowe on the front porch of the home. He parked the van, and looked to Charlie. "You ready?"

"Oh yeah." Charlie said.

The others in the van indicated their readiness, and they exited the van. Grey moved immediately to the perimeter of the property. Ifotia stayed close to Charlie, as did Nikolai. After Charlie selected the weapons he wanted they followed Grant, and walked to the porch.

"Are we set?" Grant asked Bob.

"Yes, Mr. Grant. We are all set." Bob said. "Cahya, and I set the perimeter sensors, just as Grey instructed us to. It was good to put my low voltage skills to use, and to use my multi-tool." he patted at his side where the multi-tool attached to his belt. "If anything large passes through the grid, it will trigger the lights."

"This is true." Cahya said supportively. "We tested it on one of the cows before sunset."

"Smart move." Grant said, clear approval in his tone. "Where are the cows?"

"We moved them to the center paddock." Mr. Lowe said. "Just like you wanted."

Grant looked at Bob. Bob gave him a small shrug. Grant hadn't asked for that, but it was a wise move. Keep the cows from the edges, away from the trees. It increases the chance that should something show up tonight, it will need to pass through the sensors to do so. "Nice work." Grant said, and gave a smile to Bob in front of Mr. Lowe. He made a good call, and Grant would respect that. Grant and Bob made eye contact. Recognition was there, Grant nodded once, and said. "Thanks, Bob."

"Yes. You are welcome, Mr. Grant." Bob said. A bright smile played on his lips. "Would you like some Lemonade while we wait?" he asked. "Anyone? Mrs. Lowe made it, and it is delicious."

"May need to hold off on that." Charlie said. "I'm not gonna just set, and wait." he collected the weapons he had entered with. "I'll be outside by the back of the barn."

"Charlie's right." Grant said. "Thank you for your trust, Mr. Lowe. Time for us to get to work." Grant looked at the rest of them. "Stay alert."

At that moment, Grey burst onto the porch. He was breathing heavily, sweat collecting on his brow. His eyes darted throughout the group. "Where is Charlie?"

"Calm down, Grey." Nikolai placed a hand on his friend's shoulder.

"Are you alright? What happened?" Grant asked. "Did you see something?"

Grey breathed. Tried to collect himself. He had clearly been running some distance. "I was near the back, by the woods." he panted. "I saw it. Moving in the shadows."

"The lycanthrope?" Cahya asked, eagerness to his voice.

"Yeah. Yeah, the werewolf. I saw it."

"Well that's good, Grey. We were expecting that." Grant said. "What has you spooked?"

"The wolf," he said. Interrupted again by his need for oxygen. "The wolf..." he tried again to catch his breath. "... it was trailed by dozens of red eyes."

Outside, Charlie positioned himself atop bales of straw by the barn. Grant wasn't the only one who knew how to use a long gun in this group. Charlie checked his weapon, the ammo, and positioned himself in wait. All the events of the last couple days had his nerves up, and he was ready to hunt. His eyes thought they registered some kind of red glow along the property line, but he dismissed it. He was here for the wolf. Charlie hoped he wouldn't have to wait long. His wish was granted as every light along the perimeter lit up.

The cows were as visible as if it were a summer afternoon. Charlie scanned the area with his rifle. He watched the tree line, panned left and right. There was nothing. No movement. No indication of what tripped the sensors. Charlie laid on his stomach, his feet toward the barn, straw bales on either side of him. He thought to reposition himself to see more to the left or right of the cows when he heard it. From the night came a sniffing sound, accompanied by a low, humming growl. The deep rumbling of the creature spoke of anticipation, and it sounded close.

The creature sniffed the air. Strong, insistent inhalations of breath that demanded information. Charlie froze. Would it be able to smell him? Charlie wasn't sure. He remained as still as he could, regulated his breathing. The straw crunched. The beast was close. Another crunch, the bale next to Charlie moved. No doubt from the weight of the creature against it. Another sniff. It was louder. There was no doubt about it to Charlie. The beast was right next to him. He recalled the sight of the dead cows. Their bodies ripped open. The savage, visceral, brutality of it all.

Charlie felt his heart pound within his chest. The rise of his fight or flight. Should he stay, or flee? He knew he only had one acceptable option. Even if he had wanted to flee, there was no chance he could put any safe distance between himself and the creature. He'd be easy prey. Charlie moved his finger, verified the safety was off on his rifle. It was. More sniffing. A louder crackle of sound, and small particles of straw floated down upon Charlie's head, and neck. He turned his head slightly. Charlie saw the claw of the creature grasped around the corner of the straw bale. He turned more to see the beast perched upon the bale, looked out at the collection of cattle in the field.

Charlie froze. The large wolf-like creature looked poised for mayhem. Ready to burst forth upon the fenced in cattle. Why was the beast waiting? Why wasn't it moving in for the kill? Charlie looked at the cattle. Was it too bright? Charlie saw it again. There was a red light beyond the cows. No, not a light. Lights. Small, red, paired lights. Eyes. Those were red, glowing eyes. Dozens of them. Adrenaline surged within Charlie. Things were about to get very chaotic, and very bloody. A warm liquid dripped onto Charlie. It landed upon his face, ran down from his right cheek. He looked back toward the wolf. It was looking down at him, its maw hung open, tongue lapped out, saliva dripped down. He heard the growl. Saw the muscles of the creature increase their tension in the moonlight. Maybe it wasn't a good night to die.

Charlie engaged all his muscles, rolled, brought his rifle up between him and the wolf. If wolf was a fair thing to call it. The creature was massive. Easily the size of a compact car. It looked like it could as comfortably move on two legs, as well as it could on four. Charlie's only hope was to get a shot off before the beast's teeth reached him. The thunder-crack of a gunshot ripped through the air. Blood erupted from the wolf's shoulder, and it fell back. Only it wasn't Charlie who had fired.

"Charlie!" called Grant. "What is your location, Charlie? Take the left side. Let's try to drive it to the middle." he directed the others. More guns went off. This time from the other side of the barn.

Charlie half stood, hopped down to the ground. "I'm here," he said. "Nice shot. You saved my ass."

"That ain't new." Grant quipped.

"That is a big beasty." Charlie said.

"He sure is." Grant agreed.

"It ain't alone." Charlie warned. Grant gave him a perplexed look, the two of them in close proximity to each other now. "I saw 'em." Charlie continued. "Eyes. Beady, red eyes. All along the tree line."

"They should leave us be, so long as we don't attack them, right?" Grey asked. "That's how it went down before."

"We'll find out." Grant said. "For now, we focus on the wolf."

The cows bleated in the background as the three of them rounded the barn. Cahya and Nikolai jogged up to meet them. There was no sign of the wolf.

"Where'd it go?" Charlie asked.

"I do not know." Nikolai said.

"When I drew my sword, it fled. Surely seeing it's power." Cahya offered.

"Surely." Grant repeated sarcastically.

The cries of the cattle rose. The group turned to see the wolf come out of the shadows of the forest. Faint traces of blood could be seen dripping down its shoulder. Though it didn't seem to favor the shoulder at all. The creature moved unencumbered toward its prize. The distressed calls of the cows grew louder the closer it got. The lycan circumvented the fence line, its movement as much a cat as it was a wolf. No sound could be heard beyond the calls of the cows.

Grant signaled the group to action. "Let's get this thing!"

The staccato sound of automatic rifle fire popped through the air. Small plumes of dirt spat up around the lycan as bullets hit the ground near it. Soft red puffs went into the air as bullets reached flesh. Grant expelled the magazine from his rifle, and smoothly reloaded the weapon. He reoriented on his target, and began firing. More rounds met their target as the creature launched its heavy body forward after the fleeing cows. Grant followed the beast through his scope. He was confident he'd hit it at least a dozen times, yet the large creature moved forward as if only encumbered by a stiff breeze.

The wolf howled. Grey thought it sounded like the bellow of a steam engine. The howl was deep, rich, and purposeful. It was angry. Frustrated with the team's interference. Annoyed by their presence. It moved as if it knew the land, knew the space well. Grey stopped as he saw the wolf notice him. He had tried to move around the creature, to set up traps, to slow it down. With the beast's eyes on him he couldn't move. "Charlie?" Grey called through their coms.

"Yeah Grey? You ok?" Charlie replied.

"It saw me."

"You ok?"

"Yeah." Grey paused. "I think I'm going to initiate the secondary protocol on the perimeter sensors."

"Not a good call, Grey."

"It's looking right at me!"

The beast roared, and Grey pressed the button. In a flash the perimeter illuminated, only this time it was not high lumen lamps. Instead condensed, powerful explosions went off. Dirt, pieces of trees, and plant life flew through the air. The lycan was surprised, and distracted. Grey had hoped for this, and used the opportunity to move away from the beast. Debris collided with the ground.

Grey activated the spells he had placed upon the ground between himself and the beast. Blue white light spread out like a web upon the ground. The wolf, aggravated and disoriented, moved to pursue Grey. It moved directly into the webbing of power between them. The tendrils of power clung to the lycan's feet. With each step they pulled at its progress.

"I will vanquish the beast!" Cahya yelled. He leaped over Grey, over the tendrils of power, his sword gleamed a bright white silver glow. Cahya raised the sword, brought it down upon the distracted beast. The blade struck true. Cahya sliced the wolf along it's left flank. Blood sizzled as it spilled from the creature's body. Cahya hit the ground, and rolled away from the wolf.

The beast swiped at Cahya. Cahya got his sword up in time for the blade to intercept the claw. The wolf closed his claw around the blade; its flesh sizzled on the silver weapon. A low, guttural growl crawled up from within the wolf. Light and fire played in the sides of its eyes, as it looked upon Cahya in hunger.

Fire. Cahya registered what he saw and rolled away. A burst of fire collided with the lycan's side, more power than heat, as it shoved the beast to the side.

Charlie raised his rifle. He looked down the sight, prepared to shoot, when he saw a figure. It walked toward the cows, from the opposite side of where the wolf was. It was carrying a ball of fire.

The fences melted away as Ifotia walked through them. In her hand she held a large log, now almost completely eaten away by fire. The ashes swirled in the air around her. She walked through another barbed wire fence. The tension of this line snapped open the enclosure holding the cows in place. They began to flee. Ifotia was unmoved by the cattle's retreat. She was here for the beast. The lycan moved in the shadows before her. The ball of fire faded, and last of the embers floated out from her hand as she watched the creature move in pursuit of its prey. Ifotia pulled the ash to her, as if breathing in a deep breath. Her skin, and eyes took on a subtle glow, as she took position to cut off the advancing beast.

"Are you ok, Cahya?" Ifotia asked.

"Thanks to you, I am well," he said. "Can you bring me to the others?"

Ifotia extended her hand to Cahya. He clasped his hand to hers, and in a blink they were standing next to Grant.

"Where did the explosions come from?" Grant asked.

"Grey is responsible for those." Cahya said.

Grant touched the communicator in his ear. "Grey, you better be breathing."

"I'm breathing." came Grey's reply, pushed between heavy breaths.

"Those explosions." Grant said. "I don't think that was helpful," he said, struggling to see through the slowly dissipating smoke that lingered near the ground.

"Yeah. Definitely not." Grey replied. His voice came across panicked, and rushed.

Grant looked toward Ifotia. "Can you do something about this smoke, fire goddess?"

"Yes, of course." she said, almost bashfully. Ifotia raised her right hand, focused, and extended her fingers. The particles within the smoke moved to her. She drew them in, leaving only a light, whitish mist in the air.

There was movement in the mist. The shuffle of the herd as they sought a safe place. The large silhouette of the wolf, clearly still getting its bearings. In the midst of all of that was the flailing, running form of Grey. He was running as if for his life. Pursuing him was a cascading avalanche of glowing red eyes.

CHAPTER 19

PRICES PAID

Charlie slammed the barn door behind Cahya. They had retreated to the structure to create a barrier between them, and the creatures outside. All were inside except Ifotia, who remained outside, and Bob who was inside the house with Mr. Lowe.

Grey pressed his hands against the wall of the barn as small impacts could be heard from the outside. Blue white light encircled Grey's hands, then rippled out across the walls of the barn. In an instant Grey seemed to surge, and then be drained of power. He lowered himself to the ground.

"Are you all right?" Nikolai asked.

"Yeah, Nic. I'm good." Grey said. "Slinging around more magic than I have been. Think it's draining me good."

"What did you do?" Grant asked.

"Protection spell. Should help keep the lil' beasties out for a minute or two." Grey said.

"We need a plan." Grant said to the group. "There are hundreds of those things out there."

"Hello, boys!" called a loud voice. "Do forgive the intrusion. It is not my interest to spoil your fun."

Grant and Charlie moved to the window. The glass was distorted by dirt and grime. Charlie used his shirt to wipe away a corner. Peering through he could see who spoke. He stepped away from the window, allowing Grant to look.

"Is that him?" Grant asked.

"That's Joshua." Charlie confirmed. He slammed his fist against a table top. "This just gets better and better." he growled.

"We're not ready to deal with him." Grant said.

"We are not." Cahya confirmed. "We were only able to collect some of the items needed before we retrieved Charlie from the sheriff's office."

Grant checked the ammo on his rifle, and looked to Nikolai. "We're gonna need to fight."

"I am ready." Nikolai said.

"Give me a minute." Charlie said.

"For what?" Grant said.

"Just give me a minute." Charlie walked to the far end of the barn. In the dirt of the floor he drew a circle with his finger. He knelt, closed his eyes, and applied his will. The circle closed around him. The air tightened, a soft ripple moved over the space, and opened his eyes. Charlie found himself in a dark void. The barn was gone. His team was gone. He was alone with the spirits.

"It isn't safe for you here, Charlie." they said.

"I need to know what I am missing." Charlie said. "How do we handle these things?"

Silence was his only response.

"The little black catlike creatures with the red eyes. How do we handle them?"

"My pets?" came a familiar voice. "They're perfectly harmless, until you harm them." Joshua stepped forward from the black void.

Charlie hands formed fists at his sides. "I'm going to kill you," he said.

"You're cute, Charlie. So honorable. So full of purpose." Joshua said. "I'm here for my prize. We made a deal. It's time for you to pay up."

"What... What do you want?" Charlie asked. "Do you want to make another deal?"

Joshua seemed to ponder that a moment. As if the option hadn't occurred to him. "What do you propose, Charlie?"

"I want my friends to get away safe." Charlie said. "Let us dispose of the lycan, and we'll leave?"

"What do you offer for this deal?" Joshua asked.

Charlie thought for a moment. What could he offer Joshua to seal this agreement, and get them away safely? "My memories." He said.

"Your memories?" Joshua sounded surprised.

"Yes. Take them away. The memories from before and more if you like. Only let me remain enough to know my friends, my brother got away safely."

Joshua thought about it a moment, then shook his head. "No, Charlie. That simply will not do. I'm here for my payment."

"What do you want?"

"Ifotia." Joshua said.

Charlie took a step back. "What the hell are you playing at?"

"You have a goddess, Charlie. She is a divine weapon, and I want her." Joshua said.

"She isn't mine to give." Charlie said.

"But she is." Joshua said. "She is bound to you, to your group. One way or another, she will leave with me tonight. You will not try to stop me."

"The fuck I won't!"

"You won't, Charlie. She is mine, and you're going to give her to me." Joshua said. "Come out, and introduce us, Charlie."

At that, the void was gone, and Charlie stood again within the barn. Just outside the circle of power, directly in front of him, stood Ifotia. "Holy shit! I thought you were outside," he said, and kicked the dirt to break his circle. He felt the power release, and watched color resaturate the scene around him.

"I was outside. Then you all entered here. I joined you," she said.

"How did you get in? We boarded the door. Is there another door?"

"I can be where I'm needed, Charlie. I am of the divine. As you know."

"You'll have to explain that better to me later. We need to finish our task." Charlie said. "Grey!" he called.

"Yeah, Charlie."

"Are you solid?"

"I'm better." Grey said. "What's up?"

"I think I know what we can do about our beady eyed friends outside."

"What d'ya got, Charlie?" Grant asked.

"Did a communing spell." Charlie explained. "Only rather than getting the spirits, I got Joshua."

"What did he say?"

"He's cocky. Thinks he has us whooped." Charlie said. "But he let something slip. Says his freaky lil' friends won't hurt us unless we hurt them."

"Yeah! That would explain how they reacted in the woods when we first saw 'em!" Grey said.

"Exactly." Charlie agreed. "Also means we need something to draw them away. Something that isn't us, to attack them, so we can take out the lycan." Charlie looked at Grey. "Was hoping you had something you could conjure up."

"Ah. I don't know, Charlie." Grey said, defeat in his tone. "I'm really spent. Got, maybe two, or maybe three, attack spells at best. Then I'm all guns."

"Ain't nothing wrong with guns." Grant said.

"No, there ain't. Only they don't do us much favor in drawing away the creatures." Charlie said.

"I may be able to draw them away." Ifotia said.

"No!" Charlie exclaimed. An embarrassingly strong reaction to her offer. No one else knew what Joshua was after, and Charlie wasn't ready to say. "Sorry. No, I need you with us."

"I may be able to help." Cahya said. "One moment." he reached into his bag. The bag slung over his shoulder hung at hip level. It looked like it wouldn't be large enough to fit a half-gallon of milk inside it. Yet they all watched as Cahya extended his entire arm deep into the bag. He held the bag tight to his shoulder as his hand searched within. He eventually pulled out a small stuffed animal. It was a gray mouse, with pink ears, and a long tail. "Ah! Here it is. Perfect." Cahya presented it for all to see. "Yes. This will do nicely."

"You're going to save us with a stuffed mouse?" Grant asked.

"Precisely." Cahya said, the warm, childlike excitement in his voice returned. "This little guy was gifted to me by the daughter, of the head, of our Sect the Open Eye. Today, he will be our salvation."

"What do you need from us?" Grant asked.

"Allow me a moment." Cahya said. They did so, and moved away so he could stand by the door. The impacts of the creatures outside hitting the barn increased. Like they knew he was near the door. In the increasing mayhem, Cahya focused. He softly said words, while he gently pet the mouse. He did this for a minute, or two. When he finally looked up at Charlie, and the others, his eyes glowed an amber hue. He smiled. Kicked the door open behind him. Then Cahya threw the stuffed mouse out the door, through the protective spell placed by Grey, and into the waiting hoard of small, black, cat-like creatures.

Charlie couldn't believe what they saw next. The stuffed animal tumbled in the dirt, bumping into a couple of the waiting red-eyed creatures. Dozens of pairs of eyes turned to observe the tiny gray mouse. No doubt motivated by it having bumped into them. A similar rich amber glow emanated from the little mouse. It was violent, and sudden, as the tiny stuffed animal exploded in size, and came to life.

With furious hunger the now living giant more rat-ish creature snapped at the little red eyed cat-like things. It captured one in its mouth, the mouse chomped down, and the cat-like creature poofed into dark, murky smoke, and released a screeching cry of protest as it expired. Like an avalanche of snow the remaining red-eyed kittens fell upon the giant rodent. The churning, violent ball of chaos tumbled away from the barn. The mouse, and all the red-eyed creatures together, were soon far from the barn.

"Jobs not done, boys." Grant said.

"Damn. That lil' guy really came in handy." Grey said to Cahya. "You'll need to show me that trick sometime."

"I would be most happy to share that with you." Cahya said.

They stepped out from the barn. The night was dark as pitch. Little fires lined the property from the remnants of the explosives. Most of the barbed wire fencing was down. No doubt trampled by the hordes of little demon kittens. In the center paddock, where the herd originally was, stood two figures. Joshua was easy enough to make out. He stood there smug, in his well-trimmed clothing. Next to him was the wolf.

Joshua's hand stroked the wolf's mane. Glimmers of magic came off the wolf's fur, and Charlie could see much of the wolf's wounds were healed. Movement came from his right, and Charlie looked to see Bob was out on the back porch.

"Mr. Grant! Do you need me to do anything?" Bob called.

"Stay with the Lowe's." Grant instructed. "Keep them safe. No matter what happens next. Do not come out."

"Right. Ok." Bob said. "Do not come out. Alright, Mr. Grant. We'll be here." he said, as he backed inside the home, and locked the door.

"What's our plan?" Grant said to Charlie.

"We kill the wolf." Charlie said.

"Simple as that."

"I like simple." Charlie said.

"What about your friend?" Grant asked.

"He's gonna watch." Charlie said. "Like the bitch he is."

Grant chuckled. "How are we doing this?"

Charlie looked to his left. "Grey, you stay back, work defense."

"Will do, Charlie."

"Nikolai," Charlie said. "You move between me and Grant.," he looked around. "Where is Cahya?"

"He said he would ensure the demon kittens stay occupied." Nikolai said.

"Is it time to fight?" Ifotia asked.

"It is." Charlie said.

Without another word, Ifotia raised her arms. Ash swirled around her, and she began to glow. Large, radiant wings unfurled from her back, and like an ember from a flame she lifted into the sky.

"Perfect." Charlie muttered to himself. He had hoped to keep her close. Charlie checked his weapon, his available ammo. "This is gonna hurt." he said partially to Nikolai, and mostly to himself.

"Shall the dance begin?" Joshua called out.

"Yeah." Grant lifted his rifle, and unloaded the weapon's complement towards Joshua.

Bullets hit home, but left no lasting effect on the demon. Instead Joshua brushed at the holes in his shirt like he cleared away dust. Playfully he poked a finger through one whole, and out another. His other hand continued to calmly pet the seething lycan. "Go." he said quietly.

Like water through a broken dam, the beast surged forward. It moved directly for Charlie. Charlie lifted his rifle. The wolf was gone. Nikolai had interceded, tackled the beast, and rolled it to the side.

The wolf was back on its feet. A claw lashed out at Nikolai. It missed his body, and tore his shirt from him. Nikolai moved with the attack. He came to his feet, two curved blades in hand. The Karambit knives shimmered in the light of the moon. Nikolai turned to the lycan, his lips pulled back into a fierce smile, his fangs clearly visible. His eyes had gone white. The vampire was set for battle.

A quick POP! POP! POP! Erupted as rifle rounds connected with the lycan's back. It roared in displeasure, and turned toward Grant. At that moment, Nikolai moved in. He sliced with both his blades. One connected with the front quadriceps above the lycan's left knee, while the other sliced deeply into the ligaments at the bottom of the right hamstring. The Beast howled, swiped for Nikolai, but the vampire was already gone. Blood streamed from the wounds.

The beast lowered itself to all fours. It seemed to assess the scene, then the wolf moved upon Charlie. This time, the lycan was intercepted by Ifotia. She swooped in from above, and unleashed a fireball to the beast's face. The lycan thrashed at the sky, but she was gone.

Nikolai moved in for another attack, but the creature was ready. The lycan's massive claw struck out, caught Nikolai in the stomach, tore into him, and threw him to the side. The beast turned, and once again zeroed in on Charlie. Muscles tensed within the beast, and claws dug into the ground for purchase.

Two gun blasts rang out as Grant came in from the side, and unloaded his shotgun at the creature. Not all the shots rang true, but one connected with the wolf's rear left knee, and blew out the joint.

The world took on a higher detail for Charlie. Sounds were more crisp, the details more vibrant. More than that, Charlie felt like he could see where the current of these actions were headed. This battle wouldn't last much longer. Meaning, Joshua was soon to make his move. He couldn't say how he knew but he knew it. Like all he needed to do was pay attention and he would see everything. Charlie focused on the lycan. He sought it out with his mind. The details unfolded within his mind. The beast's intentions, its fears, and what it would do next. The creature looked at Charlie. As if laughter were in its eyes. Grant was reloading. The wolf was ready. Grant was too close. "No!" Charlie yelled.

The lycan struck out at Grant. It swiped its claw back at him. Grant evaded. The claws of the beast caught Grant's vest and dug in. The force tossed him to the side, and he lost hold of his shotgun. Grant's body flung through the air, and landed hard upon the ground. He laid unmoving.

"Hey!" Charlie yelled. Fury raged within him. "You want me. I'm right here. I'm right here!" he yelled. "Come show daddy what you can do!" he punctuated that final statement by loading another magazine into his rifle.

The lycan turned, all eyes on Charlie. It moved toward him. Charlie stood, positioned the rifle against his shoulder, and took aim. But he hadn't aimed at the wolf precisely. Instead his eyes were beyond the wolf, seeing Ifotia. She had landed near Nikolai. Charlie knew their bond had grown. She seemed to assess Nikolai's wounds, and she looked angry.

Charlie rechecked his sight on the lycan. It was steady. He kept one eye on Ifotia, and one on the beast. Systematically he started unloading rounds into the wolf. Each one hit. The shoulders. The chest. The head. It didn't seem to matter. He felt the creature's exhaustion. It was injured. It was angry. It was hungry. The beast moved steadily toward Charlie. As he reloaded, Charlie watched Ifotia. She seemed... brighter. The lycan was now thirty yards away. Charlie repositioned his rifle. Twenty yards. He aimed. The lycan roared. Ten yards.

Fire burst upon the lycan, flaming wings opened, and taloned claws ripped at the wolf's face. The creature howled in pain, and anger. The werewolf struggled. It tried in vain to grab at its assailant. Charlie aimed, and waited. Not wanting to hit Ifotia. Only as he watched he saw that it was not Ifotia at all. The lycan was being attacked by a creature that Charlie could only describe as a phoenix. A giant bird of fire, and power. Charlie moved to his brother, and found him breathing. He retrieved Grant's shotgun, and loaded it full with six rounds.

The bird was outside of the lycan's reach, taunting it. The werewolf bled profusely, and was clearly injured. Charlie had no desire to wait for it to fall. He cocked the shotgun.

"Hey! You fuck!" he yelled, and stepped toward the wolf. They were maybe fifteen feet apart. He knew he had the werewolf's attention. Charlie fired. Blood flew from the creature's chest. "Not enough?" he asked, and released another shot. The blast ripped into the front left bicep of the beast. It fell forward to the ground, unable to stand on one good leg alone. Anger, rage, irrational vengeance all pulsed through Charlie's veins. "You done fucked up tonight, boy," he said as calmly as a man drinks water, and stepped up to the failing lycan. He cleared the round in the shotgun, aimed, and unloaded each remaining round into the neck of the beast. Its head barely hung to the body when he dropped the shotgun. He left the beast to lay there and bleed out.

Grey ran to help check on Nikolai, while Charlie saw to his brother. Everything seemed all right. Grant was conscious, and claimed he was ok.

"Charlie?" Grey called.

"Yeah, Grey."

"Something's not right."

"What's wrong?" Charlie said. "How bad is he?"

"Not with Nikolai. He'll be fine."

Charlie turned to Grey. "What's wrong?"

"Where's Joshua?" Grey said.

Charlie leaped to his feet. Grey was correct. Where was Joshua? Charlie couldn't see him. Grant was at his feet. Nikolai and Grey were to his right. He looked to the farmhouse, and saw Bob's ever pleasant face through the window, flanked by Mrs. Lowe. He turned, and could see Cahya in the distance, along with the giant dust storm Charlie couldn't only assume was the mouse versus a million mini cats battle royale. Charlie turned again and found Ifotia. But no Joshua.

"What is it Charlie?" Ifotia asked.

"I don't know. Something isn't right about this." Charlie said. "It doesn't feel finished."

"No truer words." Joshua said. Charlie looked towards the voice. There he stood, behind Ifotia. Joshua grabbed Ifotia by both arms, smiled, and said. "Thank you, Charlie." Then they were gone. Both Joshua, and Ifotia.

Charlie moved to where they had been. He knew it was pointless. They were gone. Still he stepped forward. As if he could follow them to wherever they were. Charlie screamed. He screamed a cry of pain, failure, and frustration. Screamed until his ears rang, and his stomach ached.

"What did he mean, Charlie?" Grey asked.

"What did who mean?"

"Joshua." Grey said, his tone sincere. "He thanked you before they vanished. What did he mean?"

Charlie looked at Grey. Shame, and regret were clear on his face. He could feel it as plainly as he knew Grey saw it. "He told me, Grey. That was my price to pay. I was supposed to let him take Ifotia." Charlie couldn't see Ifotia's bird. "He took her as my payment." Charlie's eyes searched for any sign, but there was nothing. They were gone.

"What's he gonna do with her?"

"I don't know, Grey. But we need to get her back."

CHAPTER 20
THE CHOSEN

"I know it wasn't my fault! That doesn't change a goddamn thing." Charlie said. "He told me what he wanted. He fucking told me!" he slapped the dashboard. "I should have tried harder to stop him. Shoulda kept her closer to me."

"What would that have solved?" Grant asked. "Tell me how it would have gone differently."

Charlie leaned his weight back into the front passenger seat of the van. He looked out the window. His fingers fiddled with the edge of the window. It was just he, and Grant in the van. The rest of the crew joined Bob in the purple Windstar. That was Grant's doing. "I don't know." Charlie said finally. "Things probably wouldn't have gone any different. Hell, he was likely just waiting to make his move."

"We'll get her back, Charlie. We will." Grant said. "For all we know, she may get herself back."

"True." Charlie conceded, his tone reluctant.

"Our best move now is to regroup, and determine how we defeat Joshua."

"It feels like no matter what we do we're only left with more questions than answers." Charlie said. "Why were we sent here to begin with? To deal with whatever was killing those cows? We've resolved that issue. Maybe it's best if we leave."

"You don't mean that."

"Don't I?" Charlie said, his tone sharp, and challenging.

Grant looked over from the driver's seat. Their eyes met. This was how it went for them, wasn't it. Charlie was the older brother. Everything was bigger with Charlie. He was taller, larger, and stronger. Charlie certainly got into more trouble, and sometimes Grant thought it seemed like Charlie had more fun. Beyond all that, Charlie cared more. He could empathize, and really feel what others felt. There was little that Grant felt that matched the passion he knew his brother felt in life. Unless it was punching Nazis, Grant had a deep seeded love for punching Nazis, along with any of those small-minded, race supremacy asshats.

Charlie shook his head, and looked away. "Grey, and Cahya have a plan."

"That's what they said."

"I swear if this is anything like the incident with the Tallahassee twins in Florida, I'm gonna smack the shit outta Grey."

"Tallahassee what?"

"They were a set of twins I was sharing time with, and... well, that doesn't matter. Just know, if Grey mentions Jolly Ranchers, oh... I'm gonna smack him." Charlie said.

"Noted." Grant took a breath, and paused as they turned a corner. "Kinda miss her. Ya know?"

"Ifotia?" Charlie asked. Grant nodded. "She does leave an impression."

"It's wild, considering she'd only been with us a short time." Grant said.

"Yeah. Feels more like she'd always been with us. At least for a longer time than now." Charlie paused. "You lost many people, Grant?" he asked.

"People come and go in life." Grant said. "The people who have mattered are still here. Except daddy."

"Yeah," Charlie agreed. "Except daddy."

"I guess the answer is no, Charlie. I haven't lost many people. Have you?"

"A couple. Enough to know it isn't a habit I'm keen on developing." Charlie said. "We need to get Ifotia back."

"Yeah, brother. We do. We will." Grant said.

They pulled into the parking lot of their motel. The purple Windstar was already there. Charlie was certain Bob had driven. Bob had a thing with other people driving the WIndstar. Charlie was sure he was one of the few people other than Bob to have driven it. That was simply due to circumstance. That and the fact that Charlie had a couple dozen copies of the keys made in case he ever needed to, ya know, borrow the vehicle. Still, with Bob's pension for maintaining the speed limit, and the fact that they left first, there was no way Bob would have beaten them to the motel. Charlie allowed himself a smile.

"You're being creepy again." Grant said.

"I suppose I am." Charlie said. "Did your people get things cleaned up?"

"Yes. I talked to Franklin, and a clean up crew is on site at the Lowe farm."

"Franklin?"

"He's one of my support assistants."

"Oh, fancy. Little Grant is moving up in the world. You have assistants." Charlie mocked.

"That isn't quite how it is."

"I'm just ribbin' ya, little brother."

"I have three assistants. Franklin, Analise, and Wally." Grant raised chin, and smiled.

"Three? You have three assistants." Charlie was intrigued.

"More like a dedicated support team. But, yeah."

"Why haven't they been offering us more support?"

"They have." Grant said. "Who do you think sends me my daily reports, and updates?"

Charlie let out an exasperated puff of air. "Three assistants. Look at you. I can't even get a date."

"You can have Wally if you want. He can be as helpful as a toaster with a broken dial." Grant said. They laughed together as they exited the van.

IFOTIA KNEW WHERE THEY WERE. SHE KNEW THE KIND OF PLACE THEY WERE. The hazy reality, and monochromatic tones. That all at once appeared like a fluffy fog you could drag your hand through. There was no sound, not like in the realm of men. No ambient sounds, no white noise, only the hush of nothing. They were between. On the edge of the celestial planes. Yet, as clearly as she knew where they were, and that he brought them there, Ifotia had no idea of how to return.

Time moved differently here. She could feel it. Having been with the humans for as long as she had, being out of the realm of men, she could feel the separation, the slowed nature of things.

He sat in a chair across the space from her. The chair was not there when they arrived. It appeared as he moved to sit. Would a chair appear for her if she sat? Ifotia was not inclined to find out. A smirk rested upon his face. He was smug, confident, and every facet of him was off putting to Ifotia. She watched Joshua extend his hand to the side of the chair. A glass appeared, filled with some kind of orange colored beverage. He took it in hand, sipped, and placed it upon the end table that presented next to his chair. Nothing else filled the oddly lit space.

"You are welcome to sit, my dear." Joshua said. "In this space you are welcome to do, or have most anything. Think of what you desire, and it will be here. Provided it doesn't exist to bring harm to anyone here. Namely me."

"Why am I here?"

"Ah, to the point. You have been spending too much time with Charles, I think." Joshua said, that smirk still hung from his lips. "No warm-up, or how do you do? No introductions? Are you now a creature free of manners, or decorum? Surely a lesser divine being such as yourself could afford more graciousness than this, yes?" he asked.

"No. I do not believe so." a familiarity stirred within her. Something known was close.

"You cannot leave." Joshua said plainly. "Perhaps that was not what you were thinking just now, but nonetheless, there it is. You are here, with me, for as long as I see fit."

"Why should I believe you?" Ifotia asked. "I know of your betrayal to Charlie. How easily you lie."

"Betrayal? No. No. I helped Charles."

"You misled him to his potential demise." Ifotia said.

"I set him free." Joshua contested, his voice one of satisfaction, and confidence. "The poor soul doesn't even know what he is. Doesn't know what he is capable of. No. I set Charles free so he could be ready for what is to come."

"Why am I here?"

"Right, the direct approach." Joshua took another sip of his drink. "Mmm... Well, you're here because I want you here." he said with a smirk. "Does that satisfy you?"

"No." Ifotia said plainly. The awareness within her grew. It was like feeling your body warm after being in the frigid midwestern winter air for too long. Like she was thawing. Was it because of where they were? Was it because they were close to the celestial planes? It wasn't limited to a physical sensation. Her mind felt open, awakened. Ifotia remembered things, reasons, and motivations behind what had happened. This realization thrummed within her, and she breathed deep. Ifotia looked upon Joshua. She saw him differently in that moment. A shadowy, blue-purple aura hung upon him. Their eyes met, and she felt the fire of knowledge brighten within her. "Who are you aligned with?"

Charlie looked at the supplies they had in the van. It appeared to be everything Grey had said they needed. Milk, candles, a large, long chain, and the tools needed to collect three liters of Charlie's blood. They also had a large plastic jug, latex hose, and a syringe. A massive syringe. "Grey! What the hell is this?" Charlie held up the syringe, and waved it at Grey.

Grey adjusted something on the GPS at the front of the van. He looked at Charlie as he waved the syringe in the air. "Oh, yeah man, that's a turkey baster."

Charlie stammered. "A... a what? Turkey baster?" he said. "Did I miss part of the plan?"

"We need something to collect your blood, Charlie."

"So you get a needle, a standard syringe. You do not get a turkey baster!"

"We tried. When we asked at the pharmacy they thought we were going to use it for drugs." Bob offered.

"Yeah, and when we left a squad was waiting outside." Grey said. "We had to drive around for a while before they left us alone."

"Who's idea was it to go for the turkey baster?" Charlie asked.

"That was my idea, Charlie." Cahya said generously. "Surely an item designed to pierce flesh, and inject liquid, could be used to pierce flesh and remove it."

"We weren't swimming in options, Charlie." Grey said.

"I can tell." Charlie said.

"We did get you this." Bob extended his hand to Charlie. In it was a bottle of whiskey. "Joker's Wild."

Charlie smiled. He couldn't help it. Charlie took the bottle from Bob. "Yeah, heh. Joker's Wild." he looked to Bob. "Thanks."

"Of course, Charlie." Bob said. "We are all in this together. We want to get Ifotia back as much as you."

Charlie nodded. "I appreciate that." he smiled, held back his chuckle. "Though I don't think anyone wants her back more than Nikolai."

"Charlie." Nikolai said in protest.

"Don't be bashful now. You're too old for that." Charlie said.

"Yeah man. No one can blame you. We all see how she is around you." Grey said.

Nikolai gave them each a look, unamused, but acknowledged. "She... She is someone who understands."

"You ain't gotta explain nothing, brother." Charlie said.

"I'd like an explanation." Grant interjected.

"Ignore him." Charlie said

"That isn't fair is all." Grant said. "We're all out here risking our lives, and the vampire starts a romance with a goddess. What is happening to the world? Next you're going to tell me that Bob started a romance with a pretty diner waitress, and is fixin' to get hitched."

They laughed, a relieved, welcome laugh from the stress at hand. Bob, pink in the cheeks, and unable to make eye contact with anyone, fiddled with his multitool. "Oh, well, Mr. Grant. I'm a happy bachelor. You know that." Bob said, and the group laughed more. They all needed it.

"You guys found a location?" Grant asked after they calmed.

"Yes, we surely did." Cahya said. "Enough room for the spell, and for some mayhem. Perfect spot for a date with a demon."

"Always so chipper." Charlie said.

"Life will be how it is." Cahya said. "You know this, Charlie. It is not for me to be upset about. Not for any of us."

"You're probably right." Charlie said.

"We should get moving, how far away is the location?" Grant asked.

"I've entered it into the GPS, Mr. Grant." Bob said.

"Excellent." Grant said. "We're burning daylight, boys. Let's go get our goddess."

The park was an easy drive to get to, and they found it vacant in the waning daylight. Bob led the way in the purple Windstar. They took a service road that brought them beyond the picnic area, and near to the river. Bob indicated for them to park near a utility out building. They did, and then they unloaded their gear.

The ground was soft, but not wet. This was good. Too much water would disrupt the spell. Charlie took the butt of his rifle, and began working with Grey to carve out the pattern of the binding circle into the ground. As they did this, Nikolai came walking up carrying a stone too large for a normal man to carry.

"Set it right there. Yeah. In the middle, but don't step on any of the lines, please." Grey said, and Nikolai did as directed. Grey observed his leonine footsteps were sure. Each one placed like those of a cat within its home territory. He reached the middle of the binding circle, and set down the large stone. "Perfect!" Grey said.

"Is that big enough?" Charlie asked.

"It's a part of a whole." Grey said. "The stone, with the chain, is for binding, and holding the demon down. This piece of stone was cut from a larger stone that rests in the water."

"In the river?" Charlie asked, and Grey nodded in confirmation. "That's brilliant. With it being in the water, he won't be able to cut the connection once established."

"Exactly, Charlie. The hard part will be tying the stones together." Grey said. "We solved that by using a portion of the larger stone. The stone's own connection to itself will aid in the binding spell."

"That is brilliant." Charlie repeated, and finished his portion of the circle. "What do we do next?" he asked.

"We need to make a circle for you, and for me." Grey said. "We'll position them to connect them at the northern and southern points of the binding circle. We just need to factor in your blood."

"How do you mean?"

"We didn't get any drawn in advance, and it is a key element to drawing the demon here since you are connected." Grey said.

"We'll be fine." Charlie said.

"Yeah?" Grey asked.

"We'll be fine." Charlie assured. "These are conductive circles, correct?"

"That's it, Charlie. Yes." Grey said.

As they dug out the symbols for their circles, the edge of their respective circles touched the binding circle at one point. Nikolai, and Grant placed the heavy chain across the binding circle from east to west. There was a centerline dug into the ground, and the chain was set into it. With the chain in place, Cahya approached with thirteen gallons of milk. One by one, he poured each gallon of milk into the small trench that held the chain.

"I don't understand the milk, Grey." Charlie said, as he stood from his work. "I understand the magic, the circles. I understand why we need my blood, and that the chain is for binding. Why milk?"

"It looks like milk." Ifotia decided out loud.

"What on earth do you mean?" Joshua asked. He followed her gaze. "Ah, yes. I can see how the space could look milky. Truth be told, I'm beyond noticing."

"You are of the kingdom of Heaven, yes? You are from His myriads of angels." Ifotia said. "But you are an angel no more."

"We're always angels, my dear. Call me any name you like. Call me a demon, like Charles does. You'll be as correct as you are wrong. We are always angels. I'm simply of the group no longer allowed home. It is of no consequence. The Master has been given this world into his hands, by the Father, that he may test the hearts of men. He grants me my providence."

"Why do you need me? Do you know what I am?"

"Do you?" Joshua asked.

She did know. Now more than ever it seemed. Pieces clicked into place, and she was growing ever sure. Though not sure she could beat Joshua alone, at least not here. Add that to not knowing how to get home, and it was an unwarranted risk to fight him now. She decided she needed to trust that Charlie, Grey, and Cahya would be able to use their combined magics to get her home.

Ifotia took an involuntary step back. Home. That was an interesting feeling. Is that what it was? To be with them, to be in the realm of man. Was it home? She must have looked shaken by it all.

"It is ok, dearest. We'll be together, and I will help you learn all you need to know." Joshua offered.

"I know what I am."

"Splendid! Then tell me this, my elemental goddess." he paused to watch Ifotia's reaction. There was none. She did know who she was. "Do you know about Charles, and his companions?" Joshua asked. "Surely it is not lost on you the perplexity of their group."

"What do you mean?"

"Come now. A vampire, a magical monk, a government special agent, a conspiratorial wizard, and the one who chooses, all just happen to connect with Charles in his Norse, gothic, goodness? You think that is a coincidence? Could that really all come to be simply because Grant Bowman's employer happened to assign him to this little case in Iowa? No."

"It was you?" Ifotia asked.

"Most certainly it was. Myself, and my companions have plans. We're playing a game, and we like the pieces on this board." Joshua stood, and stepped close to Ifotia. "Join me. Join us. Join the winning side."

Ifotia's eyes shimmered with confidence. "I am Ifotia," she proclaimed. "I am of the Archon, of Hephaestus and Hestia, the elemental gods, rulers of the materials of existence. I am the embodiment of fire, the divine." she paused, closed her eyes, and she saw the eyes of Charlie Blackwater. He was sitting in a circle of power, adjacent to a larger circle. Across from him sat Grey in a circle of his own. She watched as Charlie raised a plastic cylinder. It had a latex hose stretched over one end, and on the other was a glimmering, violent looking needle. Charlie pressed the needle into his forearm. Blood flowed freely out from him, through the cylinder, and through the hose. She watched the blood reach the milk. It mixed, the red and white swirling within each other like mist. She felt the magic stir, and heard Grey begin to say the words. Ifotia opened her eyes, grasped Joshua with both hands. "I am here to see the prophecy fulfilled. To stop the coming war. I am here to help Charlie destroy you."

CHAPTER 21
SET IN STONE

Dirt, water, and power churned through the air in a vortex. The wind howled in Charlie's ears. It pulled at his duster. Small particles of earth collided with his face. He had to squeeze his eyes tight to protect them while he still strived to see. All of those sensations paled in comparison to the sensation of the turkey baster needle stuck into his forearm. It hurt. Not just hurt, No. It was the kind of pain that only comes with the body being violated in a fully unwelcome way. His blood flowed from him. He had no idea how much he had spent. What he did know was he didn't have much more left to give. It was everything he could do to stay conscious, and repeat the words Grey told him to say.

Across from Charlie, Grey yelled the words to the spell. Sweat poured from him. The physical strain of holding the spell together grew ever more evident. Grey began the third round of the spell. Blue light began to emanate from the shallow trenches of blood and milk. As close as they were, Grey drew close to his limit.

"Cahya?" Nikolai called out through the chaotic scene. He, Bob, and Cahya were all within a few steps of the circle, and Grey. While Grant was on the other side, close to Charlie. "Is there something you can do to help?" The sound of his voice must not have come through clearly, as Cahya looked at Nikolai with a confused look on his face. Nikolai looked toward Cahya, and reiterated "The magic. Can you help with the magic?"

"Ah, yes. Yes, I most assuredly can." Cahya said. Cahya continued to look at Grey.

"Now would be a good time to do something." Nikolai yelled.

"I am." Cahya said. "I needed to first remember where my tools were." He opened the satchel he wore over his shoulder, and reached inside. "Pardon me," he said, as he stepped away from Nikolai.

Nikolai watched as Cahya reached the full length of his arm into the bag. He had heard stories of bags like this. Bags, buildings, even vehicles that were larger on the inside. He'd heard some were vast. He always relegated those stories to BBC programming, and circus sideshow clown antics. Seeing this with his own eyes was impressive. Nikolai thought of all the ways he could benefit from a bag like that. He'd need to ask Cahya where he could acquire one for himself. For now he watched as Cahya reached in, and looked to move his arm about inside the bag, while he never seemed to stress, or stretch the bag at its sides or bottom.

After a moment's search, Cahya pulled from his satchel a nine-foot long metal pole. It looked as much like a lightning rod, as it did a javelin. Cahya positioned himself. He faced the center of the main containment circle. Had straight lines been drawn in the dirt at 45 degrees to the left and right of Cahya's focus, the lines would have passed just behind Grey, and just at the adjacent outer edge of the main circle of power. He thrusted the metal pole into the dirt at his feet. He assessed his work, and looked pleased with himself. Cahya repeated this effort at the remaining three corners around the circle. Each time he reached a point he pulled another nine foot metal pole from his satchel. With all four in place, he reached into his bag again. This time he retrieved a shimmering silver sword.

Grey neared the end of the spell. His voice was hoarse, and blood ran from his nose.

"Go to a corner!" Cahya yelled. "Each of you, to a corner." The three listened. Grant, Nikolai, and Bob each took a corner. "Grab hold. Firm!" Cahya said, and watched as each man did as directed. He then took the sword, raised it above his head, and pointed it to the sky. At that moment lightning formed between the erect metal poles. Strands of cracking, twisting electricity, like those seen on Tesla coils, moved between polls. Occasional bursts of power were pulled from the sky, to the sword, and added to the web of growing power between the polls.

Grey's back straightened, as he completed the third and final series for the spell. With each final word his voice rang out with an uncommon power, and command. He emphasized each syllable. Grey said the words.

The world cracked. The reality of man, and the realm beyond were in a tug of war, and with a burst of power and light, the night split open. All at once the wind stopped. Sound stopped. The only light that remained was the natural light of the evening. Their collective eyes adjusted to the dark after seeing that brilliant explosion of light. They saw nothing. The only sounds were their strained breathing, the river not far off, and clapping. Someone was clapping.

Charlie pondered the paradox of how becoming accustomed to something wasn't the same as beginning to enjoy it. He strained, willed his eyes into focus. There was an amber glow. Like a soft flame. This one appeared to have wings. From the light of a hovering bird he saw the shadowed forms of two figures. They stood in the containment circle. The shorter, thinner figure was clapping. Joshua.

"Bravo. Bravo, indeed." Joshua said. "Fine show calling us back here. Was that you Charles? Are you finally coming round, as it were?" he breathed in a deep breath. "No, not Charles at all. This was you, Grey." Joshua turned to look at Grey. When he moved, a blue-white webbing of power clung to his lower calves, ankles, and feet. He turned at the waist, however his footing remained locked in place. "Mmmmm... Clever. Quite clever."

Ifotia, who still remained next to Joshua, attempted to back away, only to find her feet were bound in place as well. She looked at Charlie. His countenance was wavering, and she saw where a small trail of blood still dripped from his weakened body.

The night air cracked as two gunshots sent bullets into Joshua. One hit his upper chest, and the other hit his left shoulder. His body turned from the impact. He did not fall. Joshua turned to look at the approaching Grant, who held his handgun directed at Joshua.

"Grant!" Grey called out. "Do not cross the barrier of the circle."

Grant looked down, seeing then how close he had come to stepping into the containment circle. He positioned his feet, and repositioned his gun towards Joshua. He prepared to fire, and noticed Joshua was not bleeding. Grant sighted his weapon. "Let her go."

"Always the consummate agent." Joshua said. "Though were you a bit more observant you would see I do not possess her. More true to the point, I was in her clutches when we arrived."

"Fuck your semantics, smart-ass." Grant said. "We're done with you and your bullshit."

Joshua always looked like a casual businessman. This night was no different. He ran his fingers over the holes in his shirt. As if to silently punctuate the reality of things, Joshua inserted his index finger into one of the bullet holes. He made eye contact with Grant, moved his finger within the hole, and then removed it. "I'm only allowed one of these, if it wouldn't be too much trouble." Joshua said. "It is of very little interest for me to fight you."

"That's alright. I'm interested." Grant said. "Let's balance you out," he said, aimed the gun for Joshua's right shoulder, pulled the trigger, twice, controlled and clean. Nothing happened. Looking past the sight he could see Joshua smiling. Beyond Joshua, Grant saw Cahya fall to one knee. "Cahya?"

"It is ok, Grant Bowman. It is but a small bullet wound. I have suffered, and will suffer much worse." Cahya said. He tended the wounds. One bullet hit the meat of his thigh, the other his right shoulder. He retrieved a salve from his satchel, applied it to the wounds, then wrapped the wounds in gauze. The salve glowed a soft green hue as he wrapped his wounds.

Joshua tried to move again. Bright blue-white light shone from the strands of power that held him in place. He closed his eyes.

"Ifotia, can you move?" Grant asked.

"I cannot." she said. Ifotia looked to Grey. "This is a good spell."

"Hey, thanks." Grey said. "I will try to get you free. We must be careful not to break any of the lines of power."

"I will not move." Ifotia returned her eyes to Joshua. "I will perish with you if I must."

Joshua didn't open his eyes to reply. "You'll perish with me, but you won't join me. That is reasoning I simply do not understand."

"How many of you are here?"

"Of me? There is only one of me, divine one."

"You know of what I ask." Ifotia asserted. "Tell me how many lesser divine beings have made it through."

"Enough." Joshua said. "Perhaps more than enough, but enough. But one can never have too many friends."

As Joshua talked, Nikolai moved in his leonine way, and stalked his prey. Only his eyes were not on Joshua. He watched Ifotia. Slowly he stepped around Grey's back; careful to avoid the circle of power Grey still sat in. Grey observed him.

"What are you doing?" Grey whispered in a hiss.

"I am going to get her." Nikolai said.

"Uh, Nic, I'm not sure." Grey began, but before he could finish Nikolai moved. He watched his friend thrust himself forward. Nikolai's feet pressed the dirt down, and back, as he launched himself toward Ifotia.

Ifotia and Joshua looked at each other as Nikolai's feet left the ground. The air hummed in his ears as he took flight, and rushed directly toward Ifotia. His plan was simple. Grab her, and fly her out, before Joshua could react. His feet would not touch the ground, and since he planned to lift her up, the tension of the containment spell would not fight to keep her still. Especially at the speed he moved.

Now in the air, he was twenty feet from her. Ten feet. Then five. Nikolai extended his arms to grab Ifotia. Their bodies connected, he pressed her up, ripped her free of the containment spell. A thunderous pop filled his head, followed by a pain in his right ankle. He wasn't sure what had happened, but he couldn't feel Ifotia in his arms anymore. There was the taste of dirt, and grass in his mouth. The pressure on his ankle released.

"NO!" Joshua yelled so loudly the earth shook. "No. No. No. You will not separate her from me."

Nikolai then realized he was on the ground, in the circle, with Joshua. Who was now furious. Nikolai tried to move, but it was slow going. The containment spell pulled at him. Most of the tension focused upon his legs and feet.

"What have you done?" Joshua asked.

Nikolai thought nothing of the question until he felt hands grasp his collar, and throat. The hands gripped him tightly, pulled him back, and he saw the rage filled eyes of the demon that held him. They were wide, and had filled in fully with black. Joshua looked away from Nikolai, while he held him tight, and looked to the others.

"Where is she?" Joshua demanded. "Where is Ifotia?"

"Let him go." Charlie said, barely sitting up. "Let him go, Joshua. Your business is with me."

"Charles. You fool hardy human. I gave you such a gift, and you've squandered it." Joshua said. "I'm done with you. Our bargain is satisfied. I had what I wanted. Now give her back to me." the passion in his voice increased. "Give me Ifotia!"

"We're not giving you shit." Grant said. As he did, he watched as Nikolai twisted with the karambit in his hand, and plunged the knife deep into Joshua's chest.

Joshua released the grip he had on Nikolai, and dropped him to the ground. At that, Grant fired his weapon, two, three, six times. Each shot landed true, ripped into Joshua's body, but there was no blood.

Joshua staggered about as much as a man stuck standing in one place could stagger. Each bullet rocked him. His body responded to each impact. They waited, watched, wanting him to fall. He did not fall. Instead, Joshua reached up, pulled the karambit blade from his chest. He flipped it in his hand, and plunged it down into Nikolai's prone body. There was an audible sound of impact, both solid and wet together. Joshua ripped the blade free from Nikolai's body. Blood came with the blade. It flowed up, and out from the wound. Joshua stood, and pulled Nikolai up by his hair, to his knees. With thunderous impact he drove the curved blade into Nikolai's back, and let him fall to the ground.

"Nikolai!" Charlie cried.

"You son of a ..." Grant began, but then cried out as pain drug down his body like claws upon his skin.

"Yes." Joshua said, pleased. "That's it. Feel the pain. Embrace it." his hand held out towards Grant. "Savor it, for if there is pain, there is life." he lowered his hand, and as he did Grant collapsed to the ground. Joshua continued to speak, as if to an audience. "Some say love is life's great gift, they are wrong, it is pain. Pain is sweet, present, real. Pain is sure, and inclusive. In pain there is life, and there simply is no life without pain. Where you can have life without love. What kind of gift is that? No, life's great gift is pain. To suffer is to know true life. So, you're welcome, Grant. Have you ever felt more alive?"

"Leave Mr. Grant alone!" he yelled. No one expected his voice. No one expected him to stand next to the metal pole when he did. But he did. No one expected him to ever do anything, and time and time again he was there. Bob was always there. "Leave him alone."

"Ah, Bob Doe, the one who chooses. It is truly good to see you. Though we're a tad ahead of schedule. You lot are quite terrible with keeping to a schedule, aren't you?"

"I'm not sure what you mean by that. I am quite organized, and use two schedules to balance out my obligations."

"I'm sure you do." Joshua said. "As fitting as it is that you'd be concerned with balance."

"Yes, I certainly do. That is why I told Mr. Grant I could only help on this assignment for another week. Then I have to get up to Minnesota to check on a client's furnace. I do HVAC work, you see. Though I will have to stop by Mr. Lowe's farm, and see if Mrs. Lowe can spare some lemonade for the road."

"Are you quite finished?" Joshua asked.

"No." Bob said in an uncommonly calm tone. He pulled his hand from behind his back. Unscrewed the top of the flask he now carried, and took a sip of the whiskey inside. The liquid's warm bite moved down his throat, and he winced involuntarily. Bob closed the flask, tossed it to a watching Charlie, and then looked at Joshua.

"Liquid courage?" Joshua asked. "Understandable need." he said, raising his hand toward Bob.

"Joker's Wild." Bob said, smiling.

Fire filled the air above their heads. The rich, strong call of a raven filled the air, and Ifotia's bird of fire swooped and swirled. Joshua couldn't pull his eyes from the creature.

"Charlie." Bob called.

Charlie looked in time to see Bob toss him a shotgun. He caught it, checked, and confirmed it was loaded. Charlie looked toward Joshua. His aim would need to be sure. If he missed it could hit Grey. "Grey!" he called out.

"Yeah, Charlie." Grey called back.

"Remember Tallahassee?"

"The Twins?" Grey said. "You told me to never bring them up again."

The raven of fire swooped down at Joshua again. Its call rang out like a brass horn.

"Do you remember why?" Charlie asked.

"You said being with them was bad for your knees." Grey said, his voice trailed off at the end. "Charlie?" he asked, sounding worried.

"On two, go left!" Charlie said.

"Charlie!"

"On. Two." Charlie emphasized each word as its own statement. He took aim, as the raven came through for a third pass. "One!" he saw Grey ready himself to move. "Two!" he yelled, just as the raven passed over Joshua. Grey dove to his left. Charlie squeezed the trigger. The shotgun boomed that comfortable familiar roar, and Joshua's right knee exploded.

The power of the circles broke with Grey's action, and the binding spell began to dissipate into the air around them.

Joshua's hands hit the ground, as he fell to his good knee. He surged with anger toward Charlie. "You heathen fool." he cursed. "Let One Eye in all his acquired wisdom see this as a taste of what is to come. You vile, heathen, beast." Joshua spat.

The ground shook, and pain raced up Charlie's back. He dropped the shotgun, and writhed uncontrollably on the ground. Tension built, and he felt as if his muscles and tendons were going to rip clean from the bones.

"He is my heathen beast," she said.

Joshua released Charlie, turned to the voice, to find Ifotia at the edge of the circle. She had changed. She glowed a soft amber warmth. Large wings, twice her size, extended out behind her. They matched the wings of her raven. She wore a drapery of fire like a stola. It fell elegantly against her curves, both accenting, and covering her powerful body. There was no tunic, or shawl, and why should there be? She was divine after-all.

"They are all mine." Ifotia said in that matter of fact way which welcomed no dispute. "Your assault upon them is at its close."

"You returned to me." Joshua still knelt upon his one good knee. The previous gunshot wounds had filled in his body. All that remained were the holes in his shirt, and a healing wound where Nikolai had driven in his blade. "I will leave them be. I will." Joshua said. "Have them release me, and let us leave this place. Together."

"No." The single word answer hung like the bang of a gong between them.

"You will come with me!" Joshua yelled.

Ifotia entered the circle upon the strength of her wings, and floated toward Joshua. As she did her eyes took in the still bleeding form of Nikolai upon the ground. Hot, scorching anger filled her being, as she looked down at Joshua.

"Yes," he said. "Yes, come. Come, and join me." Joshua repeated to himself as she drew close. He pulled himself to his feet. The wounded knee looked scarred, but had mostly healed. He extended his hands to Ifotia.

The last of the blue-white light of Grey's spell drifted up from the blood and milk. Joshua was free. Once again, Ifotia stood before him. She took his hand. "Joshua." She said, ensuring she had his full attention. Her wings extended out fully. Her raven hung in the air effortlessly behind Joshua.

"Ifotia." Joshua said. "I will leave them be. Let us depart. Together. The others can take it from here."

"There is one final thing to do." she said. Her eyes focused upon his. The light of her warmth was hypnotic, and captivating. With one hand in his, she took her other and lightly touched his face almost tenderly. They were close. Ifotia closed her eyes, and kissed Joshua.

Charlie couldn't believe his eyes. All at once he wanted to cry out for her to stop, to vomit, or to run away. Instead he watched. Sickened, mesmerized, and enthralled, he watched. As he did he noticed that Joshua seemed to freeze, his hand upon Ifotia's arm, their lips pressed together, but he wasn't moving. Then his color started to change. Not just the color of his flesh, but his clothing too. The color drained from them, and a dry, stone like visage remained in Joshua's place.

Power began to flow out from Joshua like streams of smoke. A stream went to Charlie, Grant, Grey, Bob, Cahya, and Nikolai. It went into them. Through their nostrils, and skin. Charlie could see the smoke flow to Nikolai's wounds. It sealed them closed. He looked to Cahya, who breathed in the smoke. Charlie saw what looked like the same smoke coming out from under the gauze bandages he had over his own wounds. Charlie also felt it work within himself. It did more than heal him. Charlie found he felt like more. Like he was more.

Ifotia pulled away from Joshua. She looked at Charlie, and smiled. She came to him, helped him to his feet. "It is over," she said.

Charlie moved past her without a word. He needed to know his friend was all right. He sidestepped the stone statue of Joshua, and knelt down by Nikolai. He seemed like he had awoke from a hard nap. "You ok, buddy?"

"Hello, Charlie." Nikolai said. "Is it over?"

"Are you alright?"

"I am a bit... hungry." Nikolai admitted.

"Come on." Charlie helped Nikolai up to his feet. Charlie looked to Ifotia. "It's not over. I heard what he said to you."

"Yeah, um, I heard him too." Grey said. "He said he wasn't the only one."

"If more came through, there's only one place I can think of where." Charlie said. "We need to check it out."

"You thinkin' what I think you're thinkin', brother?" Grant asked as he walked up to join them.

"I reckon I am, but this time we go with catnip." Charlie said. He looked at Ifotia, eye to eye. "We need to revisit Hell's Gate."

CHAPTER 22
BROKEN GATES

"Sign here, please?" requested the young agent in the dark blue suit. They all seemed to have dark blue suits.

"How many of these do we need to sign, Mr. Grant?" Bob asked after the young agent walked away.

"Don't ask Grant. He has assistants to take care of pesky stuff like paperwork." Charlie said.

"You have assistants?" Bob said, surprised. "When I offered to be your assistant you said that you didn't do that sort of thing."

Grant looked caught off guard, but recovered. "Budgetary changes," he said. The reply seemed to satiate Bob's curiosity. "Thank you, Wally." Grant said to another young agent in a dark blue suit.

"Wally?" Charlie said. "Wally, as in your Wally?"

Grant looked at his brother, gave him a wink, and signed the document Wally had presented to him. He spoke to the young agent. "After you're done here, I need a follow up from Franklin regarding clean up at the Lowe farm."

"It's underway, sir." Wally said.

"I need a follow up. Understood?"

"Yes, sir. I will let Franklin know." Wally said, and excused himself.

"Man." Charlie kicked his feet back, and leaned against the side of the van they had him sitting in. "It's gotta be nice." He looked about at the three nondescript vans, and at the dozen agents that had come in to help them. They had shown up mere moments after Joshua was dealt with. "Why couldn't these clowns have shown up to help us out sooner?" Charlie asked Grant. It was only him, Bob, and Charlie in the van.

"These are mostly medical, and sanitation agents." Grant said it like he was reading a shopping receipt. "They don't do field work. Wouldn't have done us much good."

"Ah, so these are the same people who cleaned up at the Lowe farm?"

"Correct. They sweep in, clean up evidence, or remnant data that could help a shrewd investigator piece together what had taken place." Grant explained. "They do good work."

"Of course they do." Charlie said. His tone rode the line between sincerity and sarcasm.

"My personal favorite was how they handled crop circles." Grant said.

"Your team did that?" Bob asked.

"I think he means his team covered them up, Bob." Charlie said.

"Right." Grant agreed. "Some incidents are too exposed, or too large to easily write off as a gas leak, or weather balloon. The crop circles were definitely too exposed, both in known witnesses, and the size of them. They did a good job troubleshooting the situation."

"What will they do here?" Bob asked.

"Once we get this area cleaned up, it will likely be reported out as troublesome, out of town teenagers, causing a ruckus. Kids get a lot blamed on them that doesn't belong there." Grant tilted his head to the side, a contemplative look on his face. "Suppose that's the way the world works."

With almost comedic timing, Grant finished his statement, and a young man approached in a dark blue suit. That was where his similarities to Wally stopped. This young man moved with confidence. His skin was a rich, warm brown tone, and unlike Wally, he didn't look like he had just woken from a video game nap. "Pardon my delay, Special Agent Bowman," he said with a purposeful interest. He nodded at Bob, and Charlie in acknowledgement. "Hello, gentleman. You must be Bob and Charlie. Good to meet you. My name is Franklin."

"Hello, Agent Franklin." Bob said, and gave a slight wave. Whereas, Charlie only smiled, and nodded at the young agent.

"What do you got for me, Franklin?" Grant said.

"We are at seventy percent, sir. The Lowe farm has been cleaned, and the family compensated. Bob Lowe, the owner."

"We've met."

"Yes, of course, sir. Well, Mr. Lowe has agreed to amend his statement, and we will be running a piece in the local paper reporting wolf attacks. Tracking is in place to show the pack moved in from the north west in search of food."

"That's good, Franklin. Why are we only at seventy percent?"

"While cleaning the Lowe farm anomalies were found." Franklin paused. "They are better explained at the farm, sir."

"We can head that way when we are done here. Will you be there?"

"I will meet you there, sir."

"Anything else?"

"We cleared up the incident with the Sheriff's office. He was not the easiest to deal with, but his secretary was most helpful." Franklin said, and handed Grant a thin folder. "It is all documented inside, as you asked, sir."

"Very good." Grant took the folder and looked inside. A smile spread across his face. "Very good, indeed. Thank you, Franklin."

Loud voices could be heard a short ways away. Charlie got up to see who was arguing. He found Grey standing between the stone statue of Joshua, and some clean up agents.

"Now, listen, man." Grey said. "You gotta understand. Technically, I made this statue here, and I am keeping him."

"Sir, please step aside," one of the clean up agents said.

"I will not be stepping aside. You all can continue with your procedural truth hiding, but this belongs to me." Grey said, as he noticed Charlie approaching. "It belongs to us. To us!" he gestured toward Charlie. "Tell 'em man. I'm keeping stone Joshy boy here."

"Sir." one of the clean up agents began.

"Don't... call me Sir." Charlie snapped.

"This isn't an area of negotiation for us. We have to clean up everything."

"Grey, why do you want to keep him?" Charlie asked.

Another group of three agents began to move around to take the statue from the rear. "Hey. Hey! Trying to sneak will not work. No. I see you." Grey said. His anxiety, and stress were starkly clear. "Stop!" he yelled.

A loud clap of metal was heard as two rear doors of a nearby van flew open. A shirtless Nikolai stepped out, and moved toward the group. As he walked he removed the IV from his arm. His wounds were healed, and noticeable only if you were aware of where they were before. Nikolai strode through the initial agents unconcerned of how much of their body may have been in his path.

"Hey Nic." Charlie began, unable to capture his friend's attention. The agents had seemed to step out of Nikolai's way after he soundly collided with the first couple agents. "Nikolai. Calm down. Wait a moment."

Nikolai paused next to Charlie, looked at him without moving his head. "I am calm," he said, and without warning he kicked forward, sending the statue to topple over.

Startled, Grey jumped out of the way. The stone statue of their foe thumped heavy on the ground, and a deep cracking sound was heard. Grey knelt, and examined the statue. The statue had split through the waist, at about the level Nikolai had kicked it. He looked up to ask Nikolai why he did that, but Nikolai had already moved and was next to him. Grey watched Nikolai bend down, scoop up the upper half of the statue like he was collecting laundry, and turn to the agents.

"This is ours. You may collect the rest." Nikolai said, with a nod to the agents. He looked at Charlie. "We will be in the van."

Charlie watched Grey and Nikolai leave with their spoils, and then said to the agent who stood next to him. "What the hell are you doing? Clean this place up!"

Cahya joined Charlie as he headed toward the van. "Are you well, Charlie?" he asked.

"Not as well as I will be once we have beers in us later."

"Yes, that is undoubtedly so. Perhaps Grant will be able to use his expense account to sponsor our efforts tonight?"

"That sounds like a brilliant plan, my friend. Let's talk to him about it in the van."

"I'm going to ride with Bob in the Windstar. We're going to cash out at the motel, then meet you at the diner tonight for supper." Cahya said.

"Then I'll get him on board. We're headed out to the Lowe farm. Have you seen Ifotia?"

"I have not, nor have I seen her bird. I do hope she is well."

"I'm sure she's fine. She saved our ass, didn't she?" Charlie said.

"She did. She is a valiant warrior goddess. Thank the gods she is on our side."

"You said it, Cahya. You said it." Charlie said. They walked together towards the vehicles, not saying much more. Cahya went to the purple Windstar as promised, and Charlie to the van.

Ifotia waited by the van when Charlie arrived. Nikolai and Grey arrived a moment later, after having loaded their stone bust of Joshua into the purple Windstar. Grant reminded them they were burning daylight. They all got in the van, and headed out to the Lowe farm.

The last clean up van was preparing to leave as they arrived. Agent Franklin waited with Bob Lowe on the front porch.

"Hot damn, it's like nothing ever happened out here." Grey observed.

"Looks like the company replenished his stock as well." Nikolai said.

They parked the van and got out. Agent Franklin had waved down the clean up crew to wait before leaving, and had them come over to meet Grant.

"Everything looks in order, Franklin. What is the situation?" Grant asked.

"It's in the van, sir." Franklin said.

Opening the van released the unmistakable smell of blood, and death. In the back of the van, in a black bag was a body. Franklin gestured toward the bag.

"What? Who is it?" Grant asked.

"It's the wolf, sir."

"Bullshit." Charlie said. "I saw the beast up close, and there is no way he'd fit in the bag."

"Based on the evidence we found, I'd agree with you... Charlie." Franklin said. "The thing is, he changed." Franklin unzipped the top of the bag to reveal the face of an older man. His face was aged, and rugged. His hair and beard was a salt and pepper mix of dark and gray.

"Hey, yeah, I know who that is." Grey said.

"I do too." Grant said. "His name is Rick Offerman. He owns the farm down the road. We never made it over to meet him."

"That's right." Charlie agreed. "He only reported one cow ever being killed. We didn't think we would find much usable data there."

"We may have been right." Grant said, looking at the old man. "Or, we may have saved ourselves a lot of time. We'll never know." he looked at Franklin. "Was there anything else?"

"We found this, sir." Franklin said, handing Grant a small stuffed mouse.

"That's Cahya's mouse!" Grey said.

"Seems to be." Grant agreed. "Imagine he'll be thankful to have this back." Grant turned the small stuffed creature in his hand. It had small bits of stuffing showing where it had been bit through. "What did you find by it? Did you see any creatures out there?"

"This little guy was located about 25 yards into the woods, at the edge of the property. We detected no sign of the small black cat-like creatures you described." Franklin said.

"That's because they disappeared." Mr. Lowe said from behind Grant. "I already explained that to them, Agent Bowman." he said. Everyone turned to look at him, and waited for Mr. Lowe to continue. "We knew what to look for, after that night. We saw the eyes in the woods. Watching. They were there each night, until last night. Then they disappeared. Their glowing red eyes flicked out like someone turned out the lights."

"Last night you said?" Grant confirmed.

"That's right. Just disappeared."

"Thank you, Mr. Lowe." Grant said. "If there's nothing else, we need to go."

"That's all I have, sir." Franklin said.

Mr. Lowe stepped closer to Grant. "Here you are." he handed him a large glass jug full of yellow liquid. "If nothing else, it's for Bob. It's my wife's lemonade," he said with a smile. "A thank you for all you did for us."

"Looks like they restocked your herd." Charlie said.

"Came out to that this morning. It was like they had never left. We cannot thank you enough." Mr. Lowe said.

"Lemonade is more than satisfactory." Grant said with a smile, as he set the jug in the back of the van. "You take care." he said to Mr. Lowe, and gave a wave to Franklin.

"The fucking neighbor?" Charlie asked rhetorically after they had left the farm. "Can you imagine? Finding out you were living next to a werewolf?"

"Yeah. Mr. Lowe seemed to take it well." Grey said.

"Makes me wonder if they told him." Charlie said. "What do you think, Grant? Did they tell Mr. Lowe?" Grant didn't respond. His eyes remained firmly forward. "Hey. Grant." Charlie said, slapping his brother on the shoulder. "You with us?"

"They didn't tell him."

"What?"

"Mr. Lowe. The team would not have told him what they found. That isn't their purview. They are there to clean up."

"That makes sense. Good we didn't tell him then I suppose." Charlie said. "Not like he won't put two and two together soon enough on his own."

"Yeah, man. He'll definitely notice his neighbor is gone, or dead. Stories get around." Grey said. "They always try to keep their secrets, but they get around."

"Standard protocol dictates they will release a story that the neighbor moved, and put his home up for sale. We have to do these things all the time." Grant said.

"That story works fine in the city, Grant." Grey said. "Out here, stories circle and spread. He'll learn the truth. I'm not saying he'll learn it from me. Just saying, farmers don't commonly up and move like that. People talk."

"Speaking of talking. Where is your head at, brother?" Charlie asked.

"We're not done."

"What else do we need to do? Everyone is dead."

Grant didn't say anything right away. He drove on, and followed the curved road. The familiar scenery emphasized their destination with each passing tree. "We're not done," he said again.

The tall ornate metal gates to Hell's Gate loomed warm and threatening in the afternoon sun. They all exited the vehicle. Charlie couldn't speak for anyone else, but he wasn't going in unarmed. Grey, Nikolai, and Grant seemed to share his sentiment as they also collected weapons for themselves.

Charlie noticed as they geared up that Ifotia didn't look the same as when he last took note of her. Gone was the flowing, luminescent gown, and back was her dark leather pants, and black top. "You look good." Charlie said to her. "I'm happy you are alright."

"Thank you, Charlie. I am happy to be alright." Ifotia said.

"Watch my six in there, would ya? Last time we were here a shadow kitty tried to eat my face." Charlie said.

Ifotia raised her arms, and seemed to breathe in with her whole self. Out of her stirred light and form, and the fire raven called out as it flew up from Ifotia's body. She lowered her hands. The bird flew higher and higher. Ifotia took a breath, and looked at Charlie. "We will be watching over you."

"We? As in you and that thing?"

"Torchlight." Ifotia said. "His name is Torchlight."

"Alright. Well, hello Torchlight." Charlie said, and mimed a hat tip toward the soaring bird. "Nice to meet you."

"That thing is awesome!" Grey said. "So are your wings, even though you're not sporting them now."

"I call them when they are needed."

"Yeah, nice! I need something like that... someday." Grey said with a chuckle.

They left the van unlocked just in case a quick retreat was needed, and headed into Hell's Gate in a tiered formation. Grant took the lead, followed by Grey and Nikolai side by side, with Ifotia and Charlie at the rear. Light flickered in through the canopy above. Every cracking branch was a potential creature. Each rustle of the leaves, an oncoming attack. The shadows of the leaves, and branches teased their eyes with unfounded threats. A short time passed, and Charlie realized they had now gone further down the path then they had their first time. He thought of saying something to his brother. When he looked toward Grant, he saw it just ahead.

The wood accented peek of a Tudor style cottage home rose above a thick hedge. Though Tudor in style it was not of plaster and plank. This building was as much a cottage as it was a small-scale estate home of stone, hard woods, and quality materials.

They spread out to search the interior, and exterior of the home. It was empty of life, but not the signs that life was once there. Evidence was found of bound people being kept in the home. As well as bones scattered about, and blood stains on the floor, and walls.

"Grant!" Charlie called out. "I'm out back. You need to see this," he yelled.

The others all came out to meet Charlie on the back deck. Beyond them in the backyard was a stone altar, a carved summoning circle of stone and cement, and four pillars with runes carved into them. The group went down to examine the area. Grey looked at the pillars. Charlie studied the summoning circle. Grant took photos of everything. While Ifotia walked the perimeter of the yard.

"Someone took a hammer, or pickaxe to these pillars." Grey said. "Looks like they were purposefully damaged to keep them from doing whatever they did."

"It is a gate." Ifotia said.

"A gate to what?" Grant asked, while he continued to take photos.

"I cannot say for certain. When Joshua took me, we were in a part of the celestial realm, and some of my deeper memories returned to me. I do not recognize all of these symbols on the pillars." Ifotia explained. "I do recognize this symbol here," she said, pointing to one at the upper area of the summoning circle.

"Wait, so this is more than a summoning circle, this is a gate to another dimension?" Charlie asked.

"Correct, Charlie. A gate to another dimension, or another world. Some can be used to reach another time." Ifotia said. "This gate will never work again."

"We need to know what was brought through." Grant said.

"Yeah, I agree. How do we do that?" Grey said.

"This circle is mostly intact." Charlie observed. "I can use it. Not to summon anything. I can use it, and ask the spirits what happened."

There was a quiet moment, like a collective thoughtful breath, and then Grant spoke. "Give it a try."

Charlie knelt in the center of the circle, while Grey and Nikolai cleared away any leaves and debris. He focused, pushed his will out from him, and said the words. The remnants of dense power hung in the air around the cottage. The spirits came to Charlie. They felt relieved to connect with him. They too were free of Joshua's interference. There was a comfort in that for Charlie. He asked the spirits what happened here.

Images of the backyard, undamaged, and active came to Charlie. He saw a hooded figure as it stood over the body of a young man. The young man wasn't fighting. He wasn't protesting at all. Like he wanted to be a part of what was to come. The figure pulled back his hood. Josual stood over the young man. Around him stood four other hooded figures. Joshua was decisive in his action as he took the young man's life. His blood flowed over the stones of the altar, and light spanned between the four pillars. The young man's body arched, and was consumed with fire.

Beyond Joshua, and the other four hooded figures, a fifth figure stepped from the gate of fire between the pillars. This was the largest of the six. Once free of the gate the figure looked to stand over eight feet tall. Charlie could see a smile form upon Joshua's face, and he heard him say "Excellent. Now we are all here."

The vision flickered in clarity, and Charlie found himself kneeling in the circle upon the stone. Ifotia looked at Charlie. Their eyes met.

"That is what he meant, when he said the others." Ifotia said.

"Who said that?" Charlie asked.

"Joshua, before I kissed him. He was begging to be with me. He said the others could take it from here. They are who he was referring to."

"There were five of them." Charlie stopped, like a final thought came to him. "There are five other gates. Like this one. I can feel them."

"Do you know where they are?" Grant asked.

"Yeah, um... Washington, Minnesota, Texas, Toronto, and... Fuck."

"You ok, Charlie?" Grey asked. "That isn't a place," he said snarkily.

"What is it brother?" Grant ignored Grey.

"Florida." Charlie finally said. "The fifth gate is in Florida."

EPILOGUE - DINERS AND DECISIONS

Epilogue - Diners and Decisions

The Midwest suburbia homes varied little in appearance as they drove through the neighborhood. Charlie figured that meant they were all built around the same time, or at least by the same builder. None of these homes looked more than twenty years old. Each was set back with deep front yards, and more mature trees than not. The kind of neighborhood a person could raise a family in. Charlie hated it.

"You know they're waiting for us at the diner." Grant said.

Charlie flipped through the folder Grant had received from his assistants. "This is brilliant, and you know it."

"I wouldn't call it brilliant."

"Whatever you say, brother." Charlie tossed the open folder down between them in the purple Windstar. "You are the one who thought to get his address."

Grant killed the headlights as they came around the corner. "What was the house number again?"

"879." Charlie said. "Why did we take Bob's Windstar for this?

Wouldn't your van have been the smarter choice? Ya know. In case things go sideways."

"The sheriff knows what my van looks like. Hell, he likely has the plates recorded." Grant pulled the Windstar to the side of the road. "Let's be quick about this. I've been holding it all day for this special moment."

"We're burning daylight, brother." Charlie said with a laugh as they slid out into the night.

The sheriff's home was a quaint rambler with a single car garage. A lamp's light shone from what was no doubt the living room area. In the front yard was a mature maple tree. Grant positioned himself on one side of the tree, balancing himself with his left hand against the tree. Charlie took the other side, using his right hand to balance himself.

"Did you grab the toilet paper?" Charlie asked.

"Yea, it's in the Windstar."

"Why is it in there?"

"Are you thinking of taking your time out here? Just squeeze it out and we can get out of here, and clean up at the diner." Grant said.

"Shit man."

"That is why we are here, brother." Grant said sarcastically.

"Oh shut it."

They dropped their trousers and began the work they came to do. Grant wasn't joking. His body was ready to unload, and it did so expeditiously. Charlie was still squeezing it out when Grant stood to head back to the Windstar.

"Hurry up." Grant said.

Charlie was about to retort when there was a clank, and the sound of an old shaky, aluminum screen door opened. The kindly tone of a female voice was heard, followed quickly by the unmistakable jingling of metal tags on a dog collar.

"Charlie, pinch it up, let's go!" Grant said, as he headed toward the van.

The jingling came closer. No doubt a dog looking for its own place to unload the day's work. Charlie could see the small shadowy form. He smiled to himself, relieved that this shadow didn't have glowing red eyes. That tiny bit of brevity loosened up his reluctant body, and he emitted a loud, flatulent, release from his bowels.

The dog started, and began barking. There was another sound of the woman's voice, only this time panic and concern were present. No doubt concerned over the noise Charlie made, and how that impacts the safety of her dog.

Charlie moved to his feet. He prayed his body didn't have an unplanned encore in store, and saw a second light come on as the worried wife ran inside calling loudly for her husband. Charlie turned, and ran. He barely got his pants fastened when he dove into the opened side door of the purple Windstar. He could see the clearly confused sheriff silhouetted on the front porch as Grant drove them away. It was brilliant.

They suffered their uncleanliness all the way to the diner, where they cleaned themselves, and joined the others for dinner.

Cahya surprised Nikolai when he pulled blood pudding from his magical bag of everything. Grey, and Charlie, ordered steaks. Which went well with the copious amounts of beer Cahya, and Charlie, consumed together. Bob had a sensible dinner, with milk, and played the group every Steely Dan, Phil Collins, and Simon and Garfunkel song the jukebox had available. Ifotia treated the table to perfectly cooked bacon, and they all enjoyed some pie. Grant had ordered the pork chop, but his meal was interrupted by a phone call.

"Agent Bowman?"

"Who's this?"

"Is this Agent Bowman?"

"You know it is. Who is this?"

"Hello, Agent Bowman. My name is Major Sebastian Cox. I'm calling on behalf of General Ranbash. You are needed in Colorado."

"As nice as it is to be needed, that doesn't work for me."

"Make it work, Agent Bowman. Your companions are needed as well. This relates to what you found at Hell's Gate."

The call disconnected, and Grant, annoyed, tossed his phone on to the table.

"What's wrong, Mr. Grant." Bob asked.

"Who's up for a drive? That call just said we, all of us, are needed in Colorado." They looked at each other, not one of them too certain they wanted to go to Colorado for unknown reasons. Grant continued. "They say it's related to what we found at Hell's Gate."

There was a pause as they chewed over that information, as well as their dinner.

"Guess we're headed to Colorado." Charlie said.

"Yeah. Let me update my people." Grey said, and excused himself to step outside.

"Yes. I should do the same. The Sect of the Open Eye encourages free travel, but it is good to keep in contact. Excuse me." Cahya said, and followed Grey outside.

"You got this?" Charlie asked Grant, motioning towards the evidence of their feast.

"I got this. I'll meet you all outside." Grant said, and headed to the register counter to pay for their meal.

Nikolai stood and headed outside, while Charlie headed toward the little boys room, as he called it, to see a man about a horse. None of that made any sense to Ifotia, and she chose to follow Bob to the vending machine. He wanted to get a couple Dr. Peppers for the road.

"Would you like anything, Ifotia?" Bob asked. "I would be happy to get you something."

"What are you going to enjoy?" she asked.

"Oh, my favorite is Dr. Pepper. Have you had one of those before?"

"I have not." Ifotia said. "I would greatly enjoy trying one of them, thank you."

Bob handed Ifotia her soda. He opened his own, and she followed his example. They both drank.

"What do you think?" Bob asked.

"That is delightful. Certainly a good choice."

Her words struck a chord within Bob, and he stopped to look at Ifotia. "May I ask you a question, Ifotia?"

"Of course, Bob. Always."

"Did you hear Joshua, when he referred to me as the one who chooses?" Bob asked. "I'm sorry. It's just you saying I made a good choice, reminded me. I heard him say that, but I am not sure what he meant." Bob took a quick sip of his soda, as if grasping for reprieve. "Did you hear him say that?" he asked.

"I did."

"Oh, good. So it wasn't just me."

"No. I heard him."

"Do you, umm... Do you know what he meant by that?" Bob asked.

Ifotia was silent for a moment, as if she considered something. "I do." she took another drink of her soda.

They stood there a moment, comfortable together, in their uncomfortable silence. Bob finished his soda, and purchased another, but didn't open it.

"Ifotia. Would you share with me what Joshua meant when he called me the one who chooses?" Bob asked.

She seemed to consider again, only not as long. "It is two fold, Bob." Ifotia explained. "You are the one who chooses, because there is a time coming where you will need to make an important choice."

"Oh, well. I can make choices. That isn't so bad."

"There is more."

"Oh. Okay." he waited for Ifotia to continue.

"You are able to be the one who chooses, because of who you are. Because of who you come from. You are destined for this purpose, Bob. It will be inescapable." Ifotiae said.

Bob took it in. Nodded, and walked with Ifotia to the vehicles, and to their waiting friends outside. Grant was already in his van, and looked no more amused than any other time. Charlie and Grey joined him, with Charlie in the shotgun position.

"I'm going to ride with Grant." Ifotia said.

"Ok. Yeah." Bob said.

"Thank you for the Dr. Pepper." she said, as she fell into step with a waiting Nikolai. They joined Grant, Grey, and Charlie in the van.

Bob got into the purple Windstar. Cahya waited in the front passenger seat. "Hi-ya, Cahya." Bob said, as started the Windstar. "Ha, that rhymes." They shared a laugh at that, while Bob followed Grant's van to the road. As they pulled out onto the interstate Bob thought more about Ifotia's words, and hadn't noticed that Cahya had tried to tell him something. "I am sorry, Cahya. What did you say?"

"No need to be sorry, my friend. I was only saying I entered in the GPS coordinates that Grant gave us. Says it will lead us to a quiet, out of the way hotel, overlooking a ravine. We'll rest there before going to Colorado."

"Oh, well, that sounds very nice. Thank you."

"It is my pleasure." Cahya said. "What captured your mind?"

"My mind? Captured?"

"A moment ago. You were lost in thought."

"Oh, I was thinking about what Ifotia said to me. Working it out. I think I understand now."

"That is very good." Cahya said. "Understanding is key to growth, and happiness. What did she say to you?"

Bob continued to look forward, out the front window of the purple Windstar. He was sure he understood. Ifotia was not one to mix words. And the thought of her words warmed him, and gave him a healthy fear. When he answered Cahya, he did so confidently. "Ifotia said I'm the chosen one."

End of Book One

DERT CONCEPT ART BY ANTHONY HARY

POLICE -IOWA
013666953

About the Author

Anthony Hary is a Minnesota based author and illustrator. He loves stories of all kinds. Thankfully, his amazing family supports his love for stories, and his passion to tell them.

He started in comic books with writing and illustrating the graphic novel FIFTEEN MINUTES. Adding novels to his repertoire he became the creator of the Lore of Man universe with the first novel DECEMBER REIGN: Book One of the Lore of Man, and the sequel, AUGUST RITES is releasing soon.

THINGS ONCE LOST: Dedicated Ethereal Response Team book 1 is a dynamic story that takes place within the Lore of Man universe with a whole different set of characters from the main story. DERT book 2 is titled: LESSER DIVINE BEINGS.

Follow 9Ravens on social media or at 9Ravensllc.com for updates around Anthony's future projects, and releases.

ALSO BY ANTHONY HARY

www.ingramcontent.com/pod-product-compliance
Lightning Source LLC
Chambersburg PA
CBHW061155210726
48294CB00006B/1685